ELKWOOD KIDS

a novel by Vincent C. Russo

For more information, email vcrwrite@gmail.com.

ISBN (paperback): 979-8-9915086-0-5
ISBN (ebook): 979-8-9915086-1-2

vincentcrusso.com

Foreword

"Come back. Even as a shadow, even as a dream."

Call out to them. The lost ones, somewhere out there, wandering the hills and trees. Tell them, now, "Come home. Come back to me." Perhaps they will answer. Perhaps, even, they will be at your doorstep, knocking. Calling back to you.

What answers when you call may not be that face you remember. A favorite teacher, a grandparent, a childhood friend. Who knows where they go? Are they lost, forevermore, in the haze between night and moonlight, or are they out there waiting to be brought back?

If they aren't out there, what is it that creeps up to our door, asking to be let in? Nails tapping on the window, anxious hands jiggling the doorknob. What's out there, asking us why we aren't opening the door?

Do you dare to find out? In the hours after midnight, where all is still but the doorframe giving to the curious fumblings of the visitor, you may step up to the glass and see them. There is fog, and you cannot tell whether or not the face beyond is the face you sought for. Their eyes flick from the doorknob to meet yours, and still do not confirm whether they are alien or familiar.

What's out there? What are we hiding from in our grief?

Is it the dream, or is it the shadow?

Table of Contents

Chapter One 1

Chapter Two 16

Chapter Three 27

Chapter Four..44

Chapter Five...55

Chapter Six 72

Chapter Seven 82

Chapter Eight.. 101

Chapter Nine.. 116

Chapter Ten... 129

Chapter Eleven.. 152

Chapter Twelve.. 165

Chapter Thirteen... 172

Chapter Fourteen.. 181

Chapter Fifteen 195

Chapter Sixteen... 212

Chapter Seventeen 225

Chapter Eighteen.. 231

Chapter Nineteen.. 237

Chapter Twenty 242

Chapter Twenty-One 251

Chapter One
Learning to Lose

Across the Midwestern United States, there are towns that seem to exist in a different timestream. They're slower, simpler. Elkwood, Missouri was one of those places, not quite caught up with the times. While other towns learned their lesson, Elkwood stubbornly held onto the past. Even after the fresh scares of the late 20th century— the new threat known only as "strangers" —Elkwood kids were still able to roam our little town freely. Explore the woods. Play after dark.

Any kid will tell you. There's only one game to play after the sun goes down.

"Six... Seven... Eight..."

Lucy Huntz and I had been together practically our whole lives. Without measure, she was my best friend in the world. She was also great at hiding, and even as I was counting up to twenty, I was mapping out where she might be. Mr. Trellis up the street had lost his dog a few weeks prior, so his backyard was a safe and open place to slip into and vanish, especially behind the tall oak the dog used to be tied to at night. That wasn't Lucy's style, though. She liked to get under things— really make you duck down to find her.

There had been others playing with us. Nate Potts, another close friend of ours from school, Tommy Barnes, Emma Ritter. They'd all gone home by now, though, so it was just Lucy and me. That was the best time there was, just the two of us. That was when the game was the most fun.

"Eighteen… Nineteen… Twenty!"

I whirled around the moment my hands left my eyes, thinking I may spot her, still trying to find a decent spot. I don't know why I thought that would work. Like I said, Lucy was a damn good hider.

"Ready or not, here I come!"

We were ten years old, nearing the last breath of fifth grade. It was the beginning of March, when winter still hadn't quite seen itself out, but spring was hovering impatiently in the doorway. A cool breeze licked the back of my neck. I shivered.

Some kids hated seeking. There was a bit of unease to it all, searching blindly near the woods alone. Every once in a while, someone would hear you approaching their hiding place and jump out with a shriek to scare you. I loved it. The excitement made the game more fun. The unease brought stakes to it. It was a hunt, but who was really hunting who, if the stakes were "don't get scared?"

There's no feeling in the world quite like it.

I crept around, scanning the treeline for her. Sometimes she slipped up and peeked out from the trees, giggling as she watched you. This time she didn't. I kept on.

Mr. Trellis's yard was empty, but I felt like she might've come here. Something in the air was making me tense. Despite the cold weather, someone must have been barbecuing, because there was a wafting aroma of sour smoke tickling my nose. I walked around to the front of the pale blue house, and stared for a while at the old, rusty pickup he drove. Surely not. The car was gross.

I looked under anyway.

"Boo!"

Frightened, I fell back onto my ass as Lucy laughed at me. After the initial shock, I was laughing, too.

We sat there until the giggling subsided, and then looked up at the sky. "The stars look nice tonight," Lucy said.

"Yeah," I said dumbly. I took in the night's canvas, the type of sky you can only see in a rural area, where Earth's light hasn't destroyed the brilliance above you. Back then, the beauty was normal to me, and I took it for granted. All I knew then was that there was no trace of sunset, and the moon was high and bright. Time to go home.

Our routine went as follows: meet by the woods, count to three, sprint home. Count while you run. Compare numbers at school the next day. Whoever was fastest wins.

"Are you ready?" she said.

I nodded. We counted together.

"One, two, three!"

And we ran off into the dark.

***

Lucy didn't come to school the morning after hide and seek. I waited for her at the bus stop, but her mom didn't walk her up like she did most days. I assumed Lucy was sick. Sometimes, she got what my parents would call "allergy attacks" after long nights of playing in the woods. I got on the bus and rode in placated silence.

I was called to the principal's office near the end of the day. I tried to recall exactly when my dad had made the dentist appointment, but I was sure it was next week, and closer to lunch time. I dragged my feet a bit, thinking, despite it being impossible, that they'd seen me take a quarter off the playground three weeks prior. Maybe they just had to be sure it wasn't mine. I considered confessing as I walked into the office.

If my parents alone had been sitting there across from the principal, maybe I'd have gone through with my confession, and today I'd be a quarter poorer. Seeing the police officer next to the desk, standing and nodding away, speaking those hushed adult words that so quickly freeze a child's lungs, I forgot there was ever a quarter to begin with.

Mom hadn't been crying, but Dad's eyes were a bit puffy. Instantly my lunch punched at my throat. Seeing my father upset was decidedly abnormal. "Hey bud, can you sit down for us?" the officer said. "You're not in trouble, we just wanna talk."

I sat between my parents and immediately relaxed under my father's grip on my shoulder. I wasn't in trouble, so it must not be all that bad. Still, something was wrong. The air in the room was practically visible— thick with something sickly and awful. Maybe it was the cafeteria pizza in the back of my throat playing tricks on me.

"Son, you're Lucille Huntz's friend, right?" the officer asked. His stubble was suddenly off-putting in a way it had been comforting a moment before.

"She doesn't like being called that," I said instantly, intending to spite his question, but in retrospect answering it even more affirmatively than a "yes" could have.

The officer nodded. "My bad. Lucy Huntz." I accepted this with an polite stare. "I'm sorry to say, but Lucy didn't come home last night."

Before the words garnered any meaning in my head, my father's grip had tightened. Then, my eyes began to water. And then the sentence made sense. "What do you mean?" My voice didn't crack, but it was small in a way that surprised me.

"After you came back home," my mother's voice came, "Lucy went somewhere and we're not sure where."

I shook my head, but was still looking at the officer, vaguely aware of my principal in my peripheral vision, pulling a tissue from the box on her desk. "I watched her go back toward her house."

The officer wrote this on a notepad. "You saw Lucy walking toward her house."

"She was running. We were racing." The officer wrote more.

"Did you see Lucy get to her house?"

"No. Her house is too far."

A bit more writing, and the officer considered me for a moment. At the time it felt like he thought I was lying, but I know now he was trying to ask the right questions without giving away his— and my parents' — worst suspicions.

"When... where did you last see Lucy?"

I waited for a second. I was being overly literal in my head. I had sort of seen Lucy several times running home, glancing over my shoulder, giggling as I went. "Close to the woods. I got to the street before her."

The officer turned his attention to my mother now, who'd let out a small, whispery noise when the word "woods" left my mouth.

"How far are the woods from the street?" he asked, a bit too quickly.

Mom let the silence after the question sit for a second. "Not at all. They couldn't have been running long before they were back near the lights."

"We weren't," I said. "I counted how fast I got home so I could see if I beat her. I got to the street at fourteen." I'd gotten to the street somewhere between nineteen and twenty, actually, but I'd made up the decision to lie to Lucy when I got home, and didn't remember the truth at the time. Even though Lucy lived further away from the edge of the woods, she always beat me home. Just like hiding, she was a good runner, too.

The officer nodded. "Did you see how long it took for Lucy to get to the street, son?"

I shook my head. "She takes a shortcut and gets to her back door. She never goes to the street."

This seemed significant by the way his eyes moved, but I thought it was obvious. Lucy was fast, and she had a shortcut. She *should* have gotten home before I did.

My principal spoke for the first time. I realized the tissue had been for her. She was wiping her eyes. "Do you know Lucy's shortcut? Which way would she have taken?"

I shook my head again, this time more slowly. "I tried to get her to tell me because she always wins, but she said it was a secret."

***

I spent every day of the first month without Lucy convinced that she'd be home tomorrow. She was hiding in a tree or a cave out in the woods, and had just gone too far and wasn't sure how to find her way home. The search parties would bring her back. They had dogs, and flashlights, and every adult in my neighborhood and half the teachers at my school were out until midnight each night, calling for her to come home.

Everybody's hope did little to prepare me for the worst. I don't blame them for hoping, but sometimes looking back, I wish they'd told me the truth. My parents, the officer (Sergeant Dunn), my principal. All of them promised through their tears that they were going to find Lucy. They had to lie to me, but they also had to lie to themselves.

In the second month, I knew what the adults had known for weeks by that point: Lucy was never coming home, not tomorrow, not next week, not before summer break. Being ten at the time, I didn't know how to tell myself what I knew without it throwing me into hysterics, so I never said it out loud. In my heart, though, I knew, and I could even feel— staring tear-veiled out at the treeline each sunset —that my friend Lucy was dead.

There had been assemblies at school when Lucy first disappeared. Friday, the day after Sergeant Dunn questioned me, school was called off so that a long weekend could be given to the search. On Monday my class shuffled into the gym with all the others.

No one knew what the circumstances were. That Monday was simply a solemn gathering where we were told that Lucille Huntz (I glared at the principal, she knew better) was missing and they were doing everything they could to find her. Then Wednesday, the principal brought in police, Dunn included, to warn everyone about strangers, not to go with them, to avoid being alone at night. That Friday, when the gloom of defeat began to show on the faces of teachers, the faces of my parents, the assembly was led by a park ranger who gave us warnings about every dangerous animal that lived in and around our hometown, and some that might find their way here from neighboring ones.

Once I'd finally accepted she wasn't coming home, I dodged the thought of the assemblies as much as possible. The idea of a stranger, watching us play from the woods, waiting until it was just her and I alone, waiting on her shortcut, the one he knew and I never got to, shook me. A stranger grabbing her up in the dark and killing her was horrifying. The idea of a wolf or pack of coyotes doing it was worse. I'm sure if I were older, I'd have imagined things worse than dying, like the adults were pretending they weren't imagining.

Lucy's parents took longer than I did to accept the reality of the situation. When all the search parties were gone, when people at school stopped whispering about Lucy, when my mom and dad stopped asking me if I was okay because my eyes were no longer swollen from sobbing, the Huntzes were still out there calling Lucy's name, begging her to come home. My dad would sometimes put on his boots and go walking out, and Mom would insist he shouldn't, but he would anyway.

Katie Huntz and my father had been friends since they were my age. They went to the same school Lucy and I had, and they'd roomed together throughout college. Katie was my godmother, and Dad was Lucy's godfather. I understood even then why he needed to help her, but I had also begun to understand that there wasn't really anything he could do to help. When I watched him go out so many nights through the window, his flashlight beam swaying off toward the trees, I always thought about what they might be saying.

Sometimes, I thought Katie and Derek, Lucy's dad, would blame me.

Every once in a while I would remember that I'd lied to Sergeant Dunn about how fast I'd been running. I thought maybe that they'd figured it out— that they were mad at me for lying, that they were right to be, because they would have found Lucy if not for me.

They gave me looks here and there, when I was walking to the bus stop with my mom. I attributed those looks to blame, as spring began to turn thick and warm with the onset of May. Every time I caught their eyes, it made my stomach jump. Sometimes I thought they might tell the police, and that I'd go to jail for lying and making Lucy disappear.

Katie came by to talk to my dad one week before summer break. I've gone back and done the math. May 17th, seventy-two days since the game of hide and seek. I knew my dad would talk to Katie a few times a week, usually on the walking trail in the forest as Derek continued to yell for his daughter in the background. This was the first I'd physically seen them together since New Year's Eve, when the Huntzes had come to our house with Lucy.

"Grant, I'm sorry I haven't been listening," she said from the other room. It was after she had gathered enough composure to quit crying.

"You don't need to apologize," Dad said. "If anything ever happened to Ben..." he was quiet for a bit. "I'd probably lose my mind."

"I'm losing mine, but I'm trying to get it back. We've been talking a lot." Katie's voice was trembling, the way it does when you want so badly to just say a thing your body needs you not to. Eventually, she said it anyway. "As much as we want to find her and even though we're going to keep in touch with the police, we think it would help to have a funeral so we aren't so... stuck."

I'd been to a funeral for my grandfather. I remember it not affecting me much at the time, but then crying a lot the night after. I was crying as hard as I did then hearing the mere suggestion Lucy should have one of those things. She didn't deserve to be dead. Even if she was, even if I knew she'd been dead the moment she left my sight? It didn't matter. I wouldn't go. I'd stay in my room. And if Lucy turned up one day, I'd get to tell her, "Everyone went to your funeral but I knew you'd come back."

When Katie had finished talking to my dad, she came to where I was sitting, on the stairs that led up to my bedroom. She knelt down in front of me. "Hey, kiddo."

"Hi, Aunt Katie," I said, trying to hide my eyes from her.

Her hands clasped around mine and she sighed. "I'm sorry you have to be going through this, Ben. I wish none of us had to. And, I know you might think…" She waited a while, long enough I thought she might have decided against continuing, but finally the rest came. "You might think this is your fault." Ice in my lungs. "It isn't. It's not your fault or anyone's."

Katie's voice caught on "anyone's." I instinctively looked up. Tears were rolling down her cheeks, and now, her eyes were hidden from me. I shook her hands off mine, startling her for a moment, but then wrapped my arms around her.

"It's not your fault," I repeated back to her.

***

Maybe I had gotten distracted, or maybe Katie's consolation turned my mind away from rebellion, but as fate would have it, I went to Lucy's funeral. The picture they chose to mount on the easel next to the (*empty*) casket was a good one. It was one her parents had professionally taken, of her in a blue and white dress, with a big, matching blue bow tied around her blonde hair. She was lit only by the sun, sitting in a field of summer flowers. Her grin was the same she had when someone made her laugh so hard she nearly cried, and looking back I think maybe she wasn't playing along with the picture taking, and Derek or Katie had to work for that smile.

Looking at the picture, I was hit with a flood of emotions. For the first time in my life, the thought of how pretty a girl could be struck my mind. The thought that followed was less benign. *Guess she'll be that pretty forever.* I began to cry harder than I had already been.

There's not much else to say about the funeral. It was the typical, somber, relentlessly Catholic affair that all funerals tend to be. God's plan was mentioned, mysterious ways, one day His children will rise again. Most of it's a blur, and one I don't care to dwell on and decode. Nothing to be found there but pain.

That day of mourning opened the final week of school, a burning, hellish crawl into the arms of summer. When the doors finally opened to the crest of June, I felt the first sip of relief I'd had since March.

In the months following Lucy's disappearance, there hadn't been any other child disappearances in our town, so the police lightened up on the "no minors out after dark" rule they'd put in play. After all, Elkwood was different. Kids get to play at night here.

I'm sure many people took advantage of the lack of curfew that summer. I didn't, however. I would play with other kids in the daytime, when the sun was high and scorching. When the sun began to set, I'd go straight home. I don't know if I realized how scared I was at the time. Regardless, I'd go home and start drawing in my room the moment I'd scarfed down whatever dinner my parents had made. This was a new ritual, a fervent desire to pour my heart onto a page rather than a mound of tissue. It helped to ease my mind. I would mostly draw Lucy, frustrated that I could never quite capture the way she looked. Truthfully, it was far from "not quite." If I still had those drawings, I'd be embarrassed to even glance at them, I'm sure.

Drawing Lucy became too hard to bear sometime in the late weeks of July, and I started to draw other things. It's another big blur, no specifics I could remember, but it was something to do. Nate tried to get me to stay out later in the evening, but he never managed it, not that summer, or ever again.

Summer turned back to fall eventually, and school began again, a fresh start I'd desperately needed. The pain had compartmentalized: it still hurt sometimes, but not quite as powerfully or frequently. I tried to separate myself from it as much as possible. Sixth grade was the big leagues, middle school. No time to dwell on the past.

So, sixth grade became seventh. And seventh became eighth. I enrolled at Elkwood High School toward the end of that year, and eighth grade rolled into ninth on that last, lustrous middle school summer, one where Nate and I parted ways when his family moved for his dad's job. Tommy and Emma were around, but it was never the same as having Nate, and didn't even scratch having Lucy. They faded away when freshman year was on the cusp of beginning.

The last time I saw Katie and Derek was my fourteenth birthday, the June before freshman year. They'd been trying to sell their house for the last several months and were finally moved out by that day. Katie told me she loved me, and I said it back, though it had been so long since I'd seen her before that, I'm fairly certain I didn't mean it. They bought me a pack of sketchbooks and pencils as a gift, though, and that was nice. I was getting decent at drawing by that point.

When they left, I went to Lucy's house alone. The new owners hadn't moved in yet, so it was empty. I knew that there was a loose bolt on the window to the basement, and I jimmied it open and climbed in.

In the dark, I felt afraid. But like playing hide and seek at night, something I hadn't done in over four years by then, it was a thrilling fear. I knew I shouldn't be here, and that if I got caught, I'd be in trouble, but I stilled my breath and stepped forward anyway, turning on the flashlight I'd swiped from my dad's shed.

Everything was so barren. Cement floor, wooden ceiling, no furniture, no boxes, no washer or dryer. Just a void of a basement, with some minor water damage at its edges. I sighed. I didn't know what made me come here, but I went to the rickety staircase anyway. I should have left, but I needed to see.

Up the stairs I went, through the fridgeless kitchen, and down the first floor hallway. The white door to Lucy's room was familiar, the green paint on the walls around it was not. It used to be blue. Lucy loved blue. I was standing still now, breathing slowly, knowing I should turn back.

I stepped forward and closed my free hand around the doorknob. As I turned it slowly, the afternoon sun from the window across the room struck my face and made me squint.

As I entered and regained my vision, my eyes stung at the sight of how empty it was. There was no bed with the blue floral blanket. No little TV in the corner. The white wardrobe that had too many stuffed animals sitting atop it was gone. Every trace of Lucy had been scrubbed clean from the room.

With nowhere else to sit, I chose the floor. I exhaled and took in the emptiness once again. It was all coming back, that hurt I'd been stifling over the years. I let it come, and let my eyes water.

"Hey, Lucy," I said. "I'm uh… I'm sorry I came over without asking. I just wanted to, um," I was shaking, struggling to choke the words out, "I wanted to see you one more time before the new owners moved in. I know you're not... I know you're not here, but I feel like you are, sometimes. When I pass your house, sometimes I think I see you in the window, like you're trying to get me to come find you again."

I sobbed, then sucked in a breath. There was still a lot I needed to say.

"I wish I'd thought to go home sooner. Or that I'd made you play one more time. Maybe then, you'd still be here or... or maybe it would have been me." It was cold here. I shivered and shifted into the sunlight. "I'm starting high school soon and Nate's moving and I just wish you were going to be here with me. You deserve to be here with me. I can't— I can't even think about what it's going to be like without you there. And your parents are gone too, and they took all of you with them."

More sobbing. I furiously wiped at my eyes and nose.

"When the new people come, you're really gonna be gone for good. So, I just needed to come and see you and tell you that... wherever you went, I miss you. I'm so sorry that I wasn't there to help you. I should have—" I stopped myself and took a deep breath. It was a long time before I could speak again. My body was trembling, and I felt like someone could walk in on me at any moment, like someone was staring at me from around the corner.

I finally found my voice again. "I just love you so much, Lucy. But I know I have to keep going, so... I'm going to. I'm going to."

Chapter Two
Freshman Year

School years always open in a neurotic, disjointed haze. The first few weeks are plagued by the bustle of everyone just trying to adjust to their new situation. Chaos is the only certainty, and freshman year began no differently.

When I'd finally settled into the flow of my classes and the significant increase in homework load, freshman year was much the same as middle school. I was quiet the first month. Having none of my old friends around made that easy. I brought one of the sketchbooks I got from the Huntzes to school and scribbled away at any bit of downtime I had. Lunch period was the best. I picked a corner and ate my food and drew without any interruptions. Until there was one.

"Cool if I sit here?"

I didn't look up at first because I didn't think they were talking to me. Then, I slowly turned my gaze. I recognized him. I had English and Algebra with him. His name was Nick Lauer. He wasn't from town. Like most of the unfamiliar kids who went to Elkwood High, he commuted here from Fairweather, or at least I assumed so, as he wore a Fairweather Bobcats (the mascot of their middle school) hoodie.

"Yeah, sure," I said quickly, and turned my attention back to my drawing.

Nick spent a few minutes eating his lunch quickly, and a bit too loudly. It was distracting for a moment, but quickly blended in with the cafeteria chorus around us. Once he'd thrown back the last of his carton of milk, he exhaled loudly, tapped the table a couple times, and then leaned forward.

"Whatcha drawing?" I stopped. Nobody ever asked, so I never had to explain it. I looked at the page. I didn't know what it was. There were shapes and lines sprawling and interconnecting, an abstract mess of pencil scratches. When trying to capture Lucy had become too difficult, both in skill and emotion, I'd taken to a less concrete form of drawing.

"I, uh, don't know." I leaned back so he could see.

Nick looked at the page for a long time. His small, heavily freckled nose was scrunched up tight. It made my stomach a little upset, watching him scrutinize this like it was anything serious. I was half expecting him to just start laughing at—

"That's badass, dude." Oh.

"Ah, thanks, I'm just kinda doodling. It…"

"Helps you chill out?"

I never thought of it like that. "Yeah. I guess so."

"You're Ben, right?"

"Yeah, uh, Ben Mitchell."

Nick nodded matter-of-factly. "Nick Lauer. You live close by?"

I nodded now. "Not far. I used to take the bus to middle school, but I'm so close to here I could walk."

"Must be nice, it's like twenty minutes from my house on a good day. I'm waking up at like six, I'm so fucking tired—"

***

Nick and I were attached at the hip from that day on. He was a bit distracted in his own way, never sticking to one subject for very long. Sometimes I felt like I couldn't keep up with how fast he was thinking all the time. He had a lot to say about cars and comics and movies. I knew my movies okay, but there were a lot I hadn't seen that sent him into hysterics. He insisted that I needed to watch *Pulp Fiction* several times a week.

We picked up others throughout that year. Justin Cross was a quiet one like me, though he never opened up with the group as much as I did. He was a watcher: he would smile agreeably and nod when someone said something he liked, frown and raise one of his thick eyebrows when they said something he didn't. Bette Hurley was freckled like Nick, but she had a thick head of brown hair where he had a ginger buzz cut. Bette liked to draw like I did, but she was better at drawing real things. She had notebooks full of pictures of people, characters she'd imagined and neatly written traits and little stories about in the margins and on the backs of drawings. I could've spent hours flipping through that book, but she'd often get embarrassed and snatch it back before I'd had it very long. Then there was Nancy Kisner, just about the only person who could keep up with Nick in the world.

She knew everything about something, a little something about everything, and she loved to explain it all out. She was a great storyteller. Even when it was something I'd never care to hear about otherwise, I never found it hard to listen to Nancy. She lived on my street, so once we'd gotten comfortable around each other, we walked home together most days. She easily rivaled Nick as my favorite friend. Something about her energy brightened me up.

Freddy Thatcher was the odd one of the group. He joined sometime just before the Christmas break, just by sitting down with us at lunch. I was half-paying attention to my drawing, half-listening to Nancy talk about a show her mom watched that she "haaated" when he sat down beside Nick.

"Yo, Thatcher," Nick said (high school boys seem to love calling each other by their last name, except when their last name is a first name— Nick was usually "Lauer," but I was never "Mitchell").

Freddy had a thick nose and hair so blonde I'd have believed he bleached it. His eyes were the kind you see all the time around teenagers. Pink at the edges, semi-vacant in the pupils; the kind of eyes where you can't tell if someone's sleep-deprived or stoned. He and Nick were in History together, and Nick had mentioned hanging out with him a few times, since they were both from Fairweather.

Freddy just gave Nick the signature "sup, bro" head bob and settled into the chair. From that point on, he hung around with us.

I didn't take to Freddy like I had the others. He wasn't completely quiet once he'd gotten used to us, but he wasn't universally talkative, either. He talked about hunting and joining the Marine Corps one day, which was all fine. He was passionate about guns, though, a topic he'd prattle about relentlessly, and had scars on his hands from cutting himself cleaning his dad's rifle. Nancy told me his backstory in great detail one afternoon as we were walking home from school, about how his mom had died of cancer when he was only four, and his dad was a strict, mean, military sort. Freddy was a Boy Scout in middle school but now had been signed up for ROTC, and Nick had been up too late one night and saw Freddy out jogging at 4 AM. I felt sorry for Freddy, but I also got a feeling he wasn't here because he particularly liked anyone other than Nick. It seemed like Freddy wound up with us because no one else would have him.

I was never a social butterfly myself. If Nick wasn't so good at charming his way into social groups (ours was only his favorite— he weaved through all the others, too), I probably wouldn't have friends myself. As much as I didn't connect with Freddy, I understood how hard it was to find people, so I accepted him from a comfortable distance.

Nick and I hung out at my house once every couple weekends, usually spending an entire evening well into the early hours of the morning watching DVDs he'd brought over. I wound up liking *Pulp Fiction* a lot when he showed it to me that winter, an admission that Nick met with an outpour of, "See, Ben, I told you, I fucking told you, man!"

Nick liked to take walks at night. He told me in Fairweather he'd sneak out at one in the morning and go prowling around, maybe stop at a gas station and get a soda. Every time he tried to get me to come, I feverishly refused. One night in January he kept pushing.

"So, we gonna go check out the forest? I heard the owls are really creepy."

I shook my head. "It's *all* creepy here at night. Not worth going." He was giving me a look that twisted my insides. It wasn't that he was judging me, Nick was by default a passive judger. It was that he was disappointed. I hated that I was bringing down his good time, but I couldn't help it. The mere idea of being out there was quickening my heart, and an involuntary twinge of anger slipped into my mind.

"Come on, Ben, it's so nice. I bet you can see even more stars out here by the woods than I can in Fairweather, dude."

"Nick, I'm serious. I don't like going out at night."

"Have you ever been out at night before, or are you just too much of a pussy to—"

"Drop it, Nick. Fucking drop it."

He nodded. "Alright, I'm sorry. I wasn't trying to like, force you, I just think you'd like it." I didn't say anything else about it. We moved on to another movie, and Nick never brought it up again.

***

The second semester of freshman year dragged along, any snappiness of the first discarded with the new year. Still, it was a comfortable sluggish, the kind where you're not too concerned if it ever passes. The kind you can settle into like a big, soft recliner, rocking away the hours. When May finally came back around, though, we all were buzzing with excitement at the advent of summer break.

"Guess you and Freddy aren't going to be around at all," Nancy said to Nick the Monday before break.

Nick shrugged. "There's a bus that runs here once a day. I might catch it here and there."

"You ever taken a bus before?" I asked.

"No, but I could probably figure it out. It's what, like two bucks to ride?"

"Five," Bette said.

"Jesus Christ, who can afford to pay that everyday?" Nick sucked air through his teeth. "Doesn't matter anyway, I'm sure my dad would bring me out once in a while. He brings me to Ben's every couple weeks or so." A silver car honked. Nick's dad. "Guess I'll ask him right now. See you tomorrow." Nick hopped in the car, dramatically swinging his backpack in with him, and was gone.

I tightened the strap on my own backpack and yawned. Late weekends with Nick were doing a number on my sleep. "What's Nick's dad like?" Nancy asked me.

I considered the question for a minute. "I don't know. I only met him like, twice. He usually just drops Nick off at my place and leaves. I don't usually go out there."

"So no idea if he'll actually be around this summer?"

"He'll probably say yes. He seems cool enough. It is a decent drive, though."

On my fifteenth birthday, Nick came with Freddy, who didn't have much to say but had brought me a gift card, which was unexpected. Nick had given me a DVD of Pulp Fiction with "Told you so" written in permanent marker on the cover. Justin hadn't given me the gift when he showed up, but I found a bundle of sketchbooks not unlike the ones Katie and Derek had given me by the door later that night.

Freddy's dad picked him up in a big, black jeep. He gave me a solemn nod and left, which I took as a "Happy birthday."

I looked at Nick as they drove away. "You're not going home?"

"Uh, yeah, if that's alright. I can call my dad if—" I knew the look on his face. Early in the school year, he was always quick to head home when it was time. As of late, he'd gotten less excited about being back in Fairweather. I couldn't be certain, but I was almost positive it had something to do with his dad.

"Nah, don't worry about it, my parents won't care if you stay."

"Okay, I mean if you're sure."

I didn't say anything else. We returned to the living room, where Nancy was talking to a raised-eyebrow Justin. She turned her attention when we entered. "Freddy's gone?"

I nodded. "Yeah, Nick's staying, I guess Thatcher wanted to get back before it got too dark."

Bette nodded. "I should probably head home soon."

Nick shook his head. "Come on, you can stay. You live what, two blocks away?" He looked to Nancy and Justin.

"I live a few blocks over, but I don't mind going home late," Justin said.

"Yeah, I live right up the street," Nancy said. "I can go whenever." She looked at me.

"You all can stay as long as you want," I said, stretching and settling onto the couch. "Just be careful getting home."

Nick shook his head. "Y'all are so scared of the dark, huh?"

"Stop it, man," I said instantly.

"I'm sorry, I forgot." He changed the subject. "So, I did talk to my dad, and he said he'd bring me up every week or so. But he doesn't wanna make the trip twice in a day like during the school year so, he told me I need to stay with someone if I do come."

"You know that's fine with us," I said.

"Well, I just wanted to make sure, because… I think I'm gonna come up a lot."

Nancy said, "We were all worried it'd be like once a month at the most."

Nick was rubbing his hands together. "I'd much rather be here than at home."

It was quiet for a bit, but then we started talking about other things. Eventually Nick perked up and was going a mile a minute.

Sunset sunk into nightfall, and Bette started cursing in whispers. "I really should have left sooner, I've gotta go."

"I can walk you home," Justin said, and immediately stood up. "Happy birthday, Ben."

The goodbye was short, and they were gone. Nancy stayed, less talkative than usual. Nick was filling the gaps, talking about his new TV show obsessions, a slew of popular dramas that sounded way better the way he described them than they were in practice (I wouldn't catch up on them until years later). Eventually, I excused myself to the restroom.

When I came back out, Nancy was there.

"Are you worried about Nick?" she asked. Of course she'd be the one to notice.

"Yeah," I said, "I don't know what's up with him. He usually stays the night, but then he's in a huge hurry to get home the next day." Instinctively, I followed it up with, "Have you heard anything about his dad or..."

She shook her head. "No. He doesn't like talking about it. He always changes the subject but—"

"Lauer changes the subject a lot."

"Yes." She glanced over her shoulder, back toward the living room. "Do you think his dad might be, you know?"

I thought about it. The idea made my stomach turn. "Maybe, but he doesn't seem like that. Nick said that his parents were getting divorced when we first met."

Nancy nodded enthusiastically. This was new information to her. She liked learning new things, happy knowledge or not.

"I should probably get home, but I want to make sure he's okay."

"I'll make sure. We'll probably wind up staying up all night watching movies anyway." She smiled at that.

"Sorry I didn't bring a gift."

I shrugged. "I told you not to."

"Well. Happy birthday." She hugged me. Nancy had hugged me before, she was a serial hugger, but this time she squeezed me tightly, pressing up against my chest. I hugged her back. We lingered for a bit. Her hair smelled nice.

She let go, and we headed back to the living room. Nick was throwing the Pulp Fiction DVD up and catching it like a baseball. "It's too quiet out here."

"I'm probably gonna head home, actually," Nancy said. Nick looked a little disappointed, but nodded. "Are you going to be here tomorrow?"

"Most of the day, probably. Might stay another day if Ben wants, but we'll see."

"Okay," she said. "I might come over again, let me know when you guys are awake."

I saw Nancy to the door and watched her head off into the night. The hairs on my neck stood up. A familiar feeling.

"So, birthday boy, we gonna watch this movie or what?" Nick said from right behind me, startling me.

"We already watched it," I said.

Nick let out a dramatic sigh. "How many times have I told you you can not watch this movie too many times. Come on."

Chapter Three
The First Leaf of Autumn

That summer I saw as much of Nick as, if not more than, the entire school year. He came to my house at least once a week, and sometimes stayed for two nights instead of just one. My parents were pretty easy going about it all. I know they worried about me after fifth grade, worried I wasn't going out enough, worried I wasn't making enough friends, worried I'd never recover from all that had happened. Having Nick, and the rest of the group to boot, made it easy for them to quit worrying so much.

Nick was the type of friend you think you could never be tired of when you're with them. The energy, the enthusiasm, the humor they bring to the table, it elates you just being near them. In early July, I began to notice just how tired I was when he left. It was like my bones were made of metal, too heavy to really move. I'd sleep early after he left, and at a decent time the rest of the week, and then he'd return, the herald of near-all-nighters.

I'd never trade any of those experiences for the world. I needed them. That didn't mean I wasn't starting to get a bit slow because of it. Drawing became hard; I'd lose focus easily. I started parking myself in front of a TV more often than I had ever before. It was hard to motivate myself to do much else but recharge when Nick left.

Spending time with Bette helped that along. Nancy lived closest, but Bette was second closest, and she liked to be home by dark like I did, so I never felt like I might cut it close seeing her. There were days where I'd be silently begging Nick's dad to pick him up sooner so I could run off to Bette's to fit in a drawing session. She liked to sit in the park near the elementary school and sketch the way the trees caught the light, or write more pages of notes on a new character in her book. She was finally giving me more chances to read it before she'd become flushed and asked for it back. I understood, but I was always eager for more.

Justin was a bit of a recluse. We didn't see much of him all that summer, but when we did, it was the usual affair. Sit, nod, occasional scowl. He'd started punctuating his scowls with a dissatisfied, "Hm." I never saw him alone, and practically never with less than the full group (sans Freddy).

There'd been some dead air with Nancy after the day after my birthday. She'd come by to spend the day with Nick and I, but hadn't stayed very long. At the time, I thought maybe her parents had been upset she'd been out as late as she had, and I couldn't blame them. After that it was a few weeks before she came by again. We went to the park with Bette, and she was the soundtrack to Bette and I's work. She would pause every so often, and I'd glance at her, and she'd look away and continue on.

Nancy never seemed to want to be alone with me that month, though in July, she started meeting me to take walks down to the creek behind the old hardware store, one that had shut down before I was born. Kids liked to go to the creek to try and find snakes. I just liked how the water sounded, rolling over the rocks.

I was listening to her talk about her mom's friend Sandra, a stylist at a salon who'd met Jon Hamm when she worked in St. Louis. I had been trying to learn to skip rocks across the creek, but I'd never quite gotten the motion of it all right. One more and I was finished, I would continually tell myself, but I could never quite stop myself from picking up another.

"You suck at that," Nancy said.

I laughed. "Wow!"

"Well," she said, gesturing to the pile of rocks just visible below the water's surface.

I nodded. "Yeah. Yeah, I do." We were laughing, and then I was sitting on the ground next to her. "Maybe I'll figure it out eventually. Or maybe I'll wind up stopping the creek." She giggled a bit again.

Nancy's shoulder was touching mine, and I was aware of her fingers brushing mine as well. I didn't try to move away, but I also tried not to acknowledge it either. Something about it was terrifying, but not in the bad way. In the good way, the seeking in the dark way.

"You always listen to me," she said. Her voice was low and whispery. I'd never heard it do that before. "You never tell me I should shut up or that you don't care."

"I like how you talk." I shrugged. "I don't really know most of what you're talking about but... I like how it sounds. You make it interesting."

Her fingers slipped over my hand, and she leaned her head over against mine. "My mom thinks I'm annoying. I'm pretty sure Justin thinks I'm annoying."

I mimicked Justin's "Hm," which got a little chuckle from her.

"Sometimes I think Bette's listening to me, but I don't know how much Bette listens to much of anything. And Nick, he just... he's a talker like me, and I don't blame him, considering..."

There was something strange about talking to her like this. There had been that one, serious moment at my birthday, one that we were coming back to now. "Considering?" I asked, playing dumb.

"Considering everything with his parents. I don't know if he's okay, but I can tell he's trying to talk over it." She was right. Nick was in even rarer form. "Mile a minute" would be an understatement; he was traveling lightyears. Maybe that was what was exhausting me so much.

"I think he will be okay. I don't think he is right now though." I considered my words carefully, though I wasn't sure why. Suddenly, I was so aware that everything I was saying sounded wrong, like anything that came out would be stupid. My heart was beating fast. "I'm trying to do everything I can to help. It's... a lot though."

"Yeah..." she said. We were totally silent for several minutes, only hearing the trickle of the creek, the chirping of crickets as the sun began its afternoon descent.

Shockingly, I was the one who spoke first. "This was the first year in a while I've ever felt good, you know? I had a rough time in middle school."

"Me too." I believed her. I wouldn't tell her that it wasn't the same.

"If Nick hadn't talked to me at school I never would have met you. Or any of the others. I mean, I would have, but it wouldn't have been the same."

Nancy's hand closed around mine now. Her fingers were cold, but it felt nice in the summer sun. "I'm glad I met you, too." I turned my head toward her, and met her eyes. They were that warm kind of brown that can be a burning, golden color in the sun. I couldn't look away from them. She made no move to away either.

Nick had sat me through enough movies to know what I was supposed to do there. It played in my head a hundred times in the fraction of a second. Every fiber of my being was screaming, "Kiss her, stupid, now's the time!" but I didn't. Not that day.

***

The kiss came in early August, as sophomore year peered through the curtain, waiting for its call. It was one of those rare occasions Nick wanted to walk when the sun was out, an event I was fully prepared to take advantage of. We made our way up my street, passing Mr. Trellis's house, where a new dog, a bloodhound of two years, was chained to the tree. It greeted us with a honking bark, which I had learned by now to ignore.

What was once the Huntz home had changed. The chain link fences had been replaced by a tall, wooden fence that obstructed any view of the back yard. I'd heard the new owners had begun building a pool, and that they may have plans to throw parties for the neighborhood the following summer. I hadn't cared to learn their names or faces. They were standard, clean cut, white collar folks who'd just hated their decent home in the city and scalped a cheap property in what some might call "the country." The tall tree in their front yard had begun to brown in some places. Walking past it all made my head feel hot, my teeth clamp down. I tried to make it quick.

Nick didn't have Nancy's penchant for social cues, body language. Nancy could read somebody easily, Nick barely knew how to read at all. He didn't see me staring at the blasphemous fences, or checking the windows to see if... Maybe he did see it, maybe I had just mastered hiding it.

We had planned to meet Justin at a deli near the town hall, the last place where a jobless high schooler could afford to buy a respectable sandwich. He'd called the night before, which was abnormal for him, especially to make plans of all things. He had also asked if Nick was there, and when I told him he was, he seemed happy with it. It felt odd, but I tried not to overthink it. I tried telling myself Justin was finally opening up.

Nick was going on about a show he'd been trying to get me to watch (we'd started to run out of movies, and it turns out you *can* watch Pulp Fiction too many times, because even Nick was getting sick of it). I told him, "I mean you can try and rent a DVD, but honestly, I don't know if we're gonna have time."

Nick's mouth was open, he was about to argue, but we were both startled by Justin, coming around the corner quickly, wide-eyed. "Hey guys," he said. He was tapping his foot quickly where he stood, a nervous tick that I'd only seen once, right before a big test in a class he was struggling with (he aced the test, good for him).

"Hey, dude, I thought we were meeting you at Marelli's," I said.

"You look freaked, are you sick?" Nick added.

Justin tilted his head back and forth, considering. I'd never seen him moving so quickly. "Yeah, I know, but uh, my house is right here and I'm kinda strapped, can we eat here." It was not a question. I swallowed, suddenly concerned.

"I can buy your sandwich, dude," Nick said.

"Guys. Seriously." Justin's pupils were massive. I looked hard at Nick.

"Come on," I said to him, purposefully slow.

Inside Justin's house, we found Bette and Nancy sitting at his kitchen table. Bette was drawing, and Nancy was talking, until she saw Nick and I. She smiled at me.

Since the day at the creek, I'd been making more plans with Nancy. Pushing the sunset just a bit further with each excursion, going to the park twice a day if I'd already seen Bette. A week prior, I'd even told Nick I was busy the coming weekend so I could see her again. We'd held hands a lot in that time, at places where we were certain we wouldn't run into Bette or Justin or anyone from school, and especially not any of the group's parents. Of course, my parents and hers knew, and her mom had seen us once, thinking half a block from her house was far enough to dodge prying eyes, but they'd spared us the embarrassment. A bit of the edge Justin's out-of-character behavior had brought on subsided.

Nick took a seat, and I sat between him and Nancy. Justin sat down by Bette.

Everyone was silent, looking at Justin. Waiting for, "So I guess you're wondering why I brought you all here." Instead, all we heard was his foot tapping against the tile floor.

"Okay, so like, what's the fucking deal, man?" Nick broke the silence.

Justin clenched his left hand into a fist. He tried to do the same with his right, but I noticed he was struggling to. "Justin?" I asked.

"I, uh—" Justin, when he had something to say, would cock his head to the side, let his mouth hang open, and raise a hand, pointing all his fingers rigidly forward. His hands did not come up from the fist-and-a-half, but he did position his head just-so. The words didn't come at first. Nobody tried to talk over him, he'd find it.

Justin was shaking. Nick leaned in to whisper (what Nick called a whisper) in my ear, "He's freaking me out, man."

Nancy spoke up, "Justin, are you okay, do you need us to get anything?"

Justin found the strength to spit out a few words. "No, I'm okay, I— I'm fucking scared."

"Hey, we're all cool," Nick said.

"You can talk to us," Bette said in a small, cautious voice.

I felt uneasy. The hairs on my neck were standing up again. I started to tap my foot in time with Justin's. Why was his fucking hand doing that? What was that? Was that...

"Justin, your fucking hand is bleeding," I said. Everyone looked down. Justin didn't seem shocked.

"I cut it pretty bad last night," he said plainly.

"Like… on purpose, or—"

"No, not on fucking purpose, Ben."

"Okay, dude. I'm sorry."

"It's fine, I'm sorry, too."

"It's bleeding a lot, Justin," Bette said. "You need to wrap that up."

Justin nodded enthusiastically. The pain must have shocked him back into focus. He and Bette left the room, leaving a small pool of blood on the table where his half-fist had been.

Once they were out of earshot, Nick turned to me, nervously giggling while he spoke. "Yo, what the fuck is happening right now?"

I shook my head. "I don't know… I don't know."

Nancy was shivering. "I have *never* seen him like that." Nancy had been in Justin's eighth grade homeroom. She'd known him longer than even social-butterfly-Nick had. I put my hand on her knee.

"It's okay. I'm gonna see if they need help."

"Can you stay here?" she said quickly. Her eyes were pleading.

"Okay. Yeah, yeah I can stay here. Nick can you—"

"Way ahead of you, man, someone's gotta tell him he needs fucking stitches." Nick shot up from the table in his typical fashion and rushed off.

Nancy put her head on my shoulder. I felt my shirt go warm and wet. "Hey, hey," I said, wrapping an arm around her. "He just got hurt, he's fine."

Nancy looked up at me and wiped her eyes. "You're right, I'm just freaked out. He's always so..."

"Chill."

"Yeah. I mean he didn't yell at you, but it felt like he did, because like, that's the loudest I've ever heard him talk." I nodded. "What do you think happened?"

Justin and Bette entered the room, followed close behind by Nick. Justin's hand was wrapped with gauze. "I guess we're about to find out."

Once Justin had cleaned the blood off the table, he sat back down. I kept a hand on Nancy's leg, unconcerned with being noticed now. Comforting her was more important than anything else, though I was plenty spooked myself. This time, Justin's signature, stiff-handed speaking pose came out.

"Last night," he said flatly, "I was walking home from Bette's. I stayed there 'til like, ten, maybe eleven, I don't remember. And I decided to go walk over by the woods. Sometimes I just like to listen to how it sounds. You know, bugs and owls and whatever."

"Sure," Nick said glibly. I kicked his foot.

"So I'm over there, and I see something in the trees. I don't know, like, it looked like there was a kid between the trees, peeking out at me." I stopped breathing. "So you know, I'm like, 'there's a fucking kid in the woods at eleven, they need to go home,' and I start walking toward them and telling them it's late and the sun is down and whatever." I wanted to start bouncing my foot, but my whole body was frozen. I would have run out of that room if I could even move my eyes away from Justin's bloody fucking hand.

"Kid takes off running into the trees, like the dark part of the trees," Justin continued. "I could just like kinda see them as they went, but it was so fucking dark. I don't know, I couldn't tell who it was, so I couldn't tell their parents or anything so..."

"You chased the kid?" Nick asked.

"Yeah," Justin said, nodding. His eyes were gargantuan. I felt every hair on my arms and legs: needles standing straight and sharp. "I chased the kid for a bit, I was telling them they need to come back, that kids have gone missing out there before. But they weren't listening, so I just had to run for a bit and then I was like, 'okay, dumbass kid wants to die in a fucking forest who am I to tell them no?' I figured I'd go call the cops or something so they can try and find 'em. But then..." Justin's wounded hand twitched.

Nick was shifting in his chair. "Come on man, not again, just fucking tell us."

"I heard this noise, like... like a cat or like a dog when it gets hurt, but big, fucking big, man, and I take off. I mean, I've never heard something like that. I think I was crying, so I could hear that, and that was fucking making it hard to see, but I ran in a straight line, so I knew I'd get out. I just had to fucking go. All the bushes and branches and shit were snapping and breaking and I could hear it breathing, but like it couldn't actually breathe, like it was choking and then it just— it fucking grabbed me."

I was heaving. I found my voice, strained and nearly silent. "What do you mean it grabbed you? What grabbed you?"

"Ben, I don't know what it was, if it was a bear, or like a fucked up wolf or something, but I could hear it right behind me and then I felt it whip my leg out from under me. It fucking crawled up behind me and tried to bite my hand, but I shoved it off and I was kicking, and I guess I kicked it somewhere good because it made that noise again and jumped off and then I got up and ran again."

"What do you mean, you fought off a bear?" Nick said. "Just like that?"

"No, I didn't just fight it off, it fucking bit me! I could have rabies or something, I don't know, but I didn't see it. It was there, and it bit me, but I couldn't get a good look at it, and it fucking bit me!"

Bette asked, "Did you tell your parents? You should go to a doctor."

"You know how my parents are, Bette, they'd think I was doing something stupid and got myself hurt."

"Well you fucking were," Nick said.

"Nick!" Nancy hissed at him.

"I know," Justin said. "I shouldn't have gone anywhere near the woods that late, but I saw that kid and thought, 'they need help,' and I just didn't think."

"I have to go," I said.

I was already standing up when everyone began protesting. "Dude, come on, what's up?" Nick asked.

"Just let me go outside for a fucking second. I need to breathe." I stormed off toward Justin's front door, clenching my hair as I went.

The summer air hit me, and I remembered, all at once, the funeral, the bedroom after Katie and Derek left, all the feelings of loss. It tore at my ribs from the inside, and my breath came out in shuddering, sobbing waves. This couldn't be happening, he had to have had some kind of nightmare, because if this was happening… If this was happening, then I knew, and I did not fucking want to know. I just wanted a fucking sandwich, not to go back there, not where I left this all the first time.

I was fully weeping when Nancy came outside. She immediately swept me into a hug. "Hey, what's the matter?" she asked. I could tell by her voice she was plenty shaken up, too.

We stood there, stupidly, with me hunched over crying on her, until she tugged my shirt and led me down to sit on Justin's steps. I let out several more pitiful sobs before I finally started to find my lungs again.

"Do you… Do you remember like, five years ago, a kid that went missing in the woods?"

"Of course, yeah. Lucille Huntz."

I sighed. "Lucy. She didn't like being called Lucille, she said it sounded like a grandma. Fuck. I— Lucy was my best friend."

"Oh… Ben…"

"Her mom was my godmother, and my dad was her godfather, and we grew up together until she— until she was just gone."

Nancy's hand gripped my shoulder, and she twirled off the step to kneel in front of me. "Ben, I'm so sorry. I didn't know you… I mean I knew kids who knew her but not like that."

I stammered a bit before I could get out the next bit. "She was the only person I ever cared about for the longest time. Even after she was gone, she was still all I thought about until…" I shook my head. "When I met all of you, you made it easier to move on. I had made the choice to move on, but I didn't have anybody. All my other friends, they weren't... I don't know."

"Ben..."

"If the same thing had happened to Justin, if whatever the fuck happened to Justin happened to her, I couldn't... It's just so fucking scary." I was crying again. Nancy hugged me, putting her forehead against mine.

"We don't know what happened. We don't. Justin barely knows what happened. It's okay. It's okay."

Nancy knew just how to say things to get me to listen. This was no exception. I never believed, from that point on, that anything else could have happened, but Nancy brought me back to a safer place. I could breathe, hearing her tell me it was going to be alright. Soon enough, I stopped crying, though I was still shaking.

"Thank you," I said.

"Don't thank me, I just want you to be okay."

"I will be. I'm sorry for storming out... I'm just—"

"You've got absolutely nothing to be sorry for, that's not your fault."

I took Nancy's hand and squeezed it. The sun caught her eyes, like the day at the creek. "I like you a lot," I said.

Nancy laughed silently. "Shut up."

"I'm going to be okay. Are you okay?"

"Compared to you right now, there's not a single thing wrong with me." I laughed this time.

"Yeah, fair." I glanced down, then looked back up at her eyes. "We should probably go back inside soon."

"Yeah."

"Yeah."

The silence hung there, as I leaned forward and pulled her face to mine. Her lips were soft, but I became quickly distracted and embarrassed by the tears that were staining her face from my cheeks. I pulled away. Her eyes were shut. I could hear footsteps coming toward the front door.

Nancy opened her eyes, and blinked a few times. We stood up and turned back to go inside.

***

Back in Justin's house, Nick was claiming he'd figured everything out. He ushered Nancy and I to Justin's family computer, where he had pulled up a video. "It makes perfect sense, okay? This is nothing man. Well, it's something, you still fucking need stitches, but that's beside the point." Nick looked hard at Justin. "So. Have you ever seen a coyote?"

Justin shook his head. "Maybe."

"You would know. They're all the fuck over Missouri, but, they hunt in packs, so you never see them alone."

"Hm," Justin said.

"Are you positive, like a thousand percent, that you saw one big something, or did you see a lot of somethings?"

Justin thought about it. "I guess I'm not totally sure."

Nick clapped his hands. "Great. So fucking check this out." He played the video. It was what looked to be a trail cam that hunters leave out at night. The forest in frame was that pixely, milky color of night vision. A few pairs of bright eyes pierced the treeline. There was only the sound of buzzing flies and crickets.

And then, the shrieking started. A horrible, shrill chorus of barking and howling. It was so grating my shoulders immediately tucked together, tensing in protest at the assault on my ears. "Nick, turn it down," I said.

He obliged, but then paused the video anyway. He turned back to Justin. "Is there any chance that that's what you heard?"

Justin did not look convinced at first, but then, with some nodding, the look of stress in his eyes melted into smooth relief. The edges of his eyes were shiny with the precipice of tears. "Yeah, that sounds like it."

Nick threw his hands up. "See, we're all worked up for nothing! Not nothing. You got bit by a coyote, you need fucking stitches, and probably a rabies vaccine or you'll be dead in like two weeks, but— Everything's good, right?"

Bette looked placated by Nick's theory. Nancy and Justin were both nodding. I was... torn. I mean, it made perfect sense that Justin was in the dark, heard that noise, and worked himself into a fit because he didn't know what coyotes sounded like, but...

"What about the kid?" I asked.

Nick shrugged. "Prefer not to think about it."

"Okay, but why did the kid run into a pack of coyotes like that? Like, ran into them and didn't get immediately mobbed by them?"

Justin spoke. "You know, I'm still not fully sure that I even saw a kid. Like I couldn't tell if it was a boy or a girl, what they were wearing. Maybe it was another coyote."

Nick snapped his fingers. "Yeah, yeah, Thatcher told me about that. Sometimes when they're trying to lure out people's dogs or whatever, they'll have one coyote go and lead them closer to where the pack is hiding. They were baiting you."

This got a nod from Justin. He was still shaken up, but clearly this had soothed his nerves. I thought about it, weighed it all out, but soon enough, it all clicked together. It made perfect sense It also didn't change anything. Coyote, wolf, bear? No option was particularly good. And, no option made me feel better about... before.

Bette spoke up. "We should go to the doctor. We need to call your parents and tell them."

A bit of fear returned to Justin's face, but he nodded anyway. "Yeah. Okay."

I left with Nick and Nancy and began walking back the direction we had been coming just over an hour prior. I had been hungry when I left my house with Nick but now my appetite was gone. Nick had a look of pride on his face, being the detective who'd cracked the case. He was uncharacteristically silent, basking in the victory.

My fingers were interwoven with Nancy's. It seemed silly to care if people noticed now. Nick had glanced down at them, and nodded the way someone does when you tell them something they so obviously already knew, and continued on, walking just a bit faster than we were.

Chapter Four
Homecoming

And, in a blink, we were sophomores, and the school year bustle reclaimed our lives. The first few weeks were a culture shock to the night owl I'd become. I hadn't woken up sooner than eleven the entirety of summer break, and now I was attempting to force my eyes open at 6:30 (failing, rushing to school at 7:15). The adjustment period was brutal, and I started the year just behind everyone else.

Justin was different. He'd always been the guy to meander until everyone else had left school, but he was hurrying home now, even though the sun didn't set until past 8:00 in the early fall. I didn't blame him for it. People probably looked at me in a similar way. Nick sure did.

Bette had gotten glasses just before school started, huge bifocals that made her eyes look massive. We'd all taken a lunch period to try them on and see how our eyes reacted. Nick was dismayed. "You're telling me right now I need fucking glasses?"

Bette laughed. "That's what I said."

Nick put the glasses up on his forehead. "I'd have to get contacts, I'd just have to. Can you imagine how dumb I'd look in glasses?" Justin nodded at him, Nick gave him the finger.

I had always enjoyed walking home with Nancy. On the rare occasions she was picked up early to see the dentist or to visit her grandparents in St. Louis, the walk from school to my house (seven blocks, max, but it felt like miles) was agonizing. Now the walk was all I looked forward to all day. Her voice was sweeter now. I found that any exhaustion, any frustration from the school day stripped away as she talked about the new drama in the halls, the bullshit homework she had, how worried she was about Justin because he seemed so—

"Scared."

"Yeah. He's not like, stroking out like he was that day. He just seems off."

"The stitches look really uncomfortable. He can't even write since it's on his right hand."

"Yeah that really sucks, I can't even imagine it."

I shrugged. "You know why I hate going out at night. I don't blame him for wanting to be home sooner after all that. I think once his hand heals up, he'll start to get over it a bit, but fuck, it'd be hard for me to." I waited a couple seconds. "Or maybe Nick's right, and he's rabid."

Nancy giggled. "Nick's probably right."

"Justin could turn into a werewolf."

"Werecoyote."

"Ew."

Every kiss after the first was better than the last. We were both firsts in that regard, inexperienced, innocent, just content to have our person. Nancy and I made plans to do homework, study, anything remotely academic, but we never seemed to be very productive. It didn't help much in closing the gap my sleep schedule had caused in my schoolwork, but I eventually caught up. Once that was done, I was able to have my cake and eat it.

Nancy's parents seemed to like me. I'd started drawing again, with more persistence, and they were pretty impressed with the abstract creations I was filling the sketchbooks from Justin with. Nancy's dad was protective, but never in an aggressive way. We had to leave the door to her room open, and I had to sit in a chair and not on her bed, but otherwise it was a lax situation. I had no complaints.

My mom and dad were working a lot, so they weren't home as much as they used to be. I found I liked the silence in the house without them. It gave me room to think, to draw wherever I wanted without worrying about them peeking at my works in progress (dashing them against the wall in their infancy, not by intention, but simply by looking at them before they were fully formed).

The year found its flow in late September. I was catching up in school with everyone, my sleep was back in order, and as the stitches were taken from Justin's hand, he seemed to perk up a bit, though he still would rush home everyday.

I'd only seen Freddy once that summer, on my birthday. I hardly recognized him when school started.

The unfortunate pseudo-bowlcut he'd once sported was shaved away into a high-and-tight military cut, which made him look much older than he had freshman year.

The acne he'd had had cleared up, and he often had stubble on his cheeks by the end of the day. He'd been working out a lot, clearly, and wore fatigues and boots to school everyday, even with how hot it was.

Freddy was bigger than most of the football players, and easily dwarfed everyone in the group, other than Justin, who was taller, but far thinner than Freddy. He was also more enthusiastic and loudmouthed than he had been freshman year. He talked with a booming voice that had deepened quickly over the summer. It didn't seem to bother Nick, but the two of them managed to control just about every conversation they were a part of.

When the group was hanging out together, Freddy seemed to tag along far more often. His birthday was in October, and Nick told everyone that Freddy's dad had been fixing up an old truck for him, so Freddy would be able to come see us more, and would probably be Nick's ride. Yay.

Still, it wasn't so bad. Freddy seemed to genuinely like everyone in the group now, even me. He'd ask Bette and I about drawing, Nick about movies. He tried to make conversation with Justin, but Justin never had much to really bite into. The one thing was, Freddy seemed to get tired of Nancy talking, and would frequently turn his attention away or exit the conversation early to move on. I could tell it bothered her, but I usually stepped in and gave her an ear.

Some of the more wealthy kids at school had latched onto Justin as a potential target to pick on. Isaac Anderson and... Tommy Barnes. Funny, how things go in small towns. Justin was tall and lanky and didn't really know how to speak up for himself. Tommy had always been a bit overbearing. The type of kid that maliciously teased because it made him laugh, claiming it was just a joke and everyone should understand that. Isaac and Tommy had started to become friends in eighth grade, and their closeness is part of what caused Tommy and I to drift apart, not that I missed him much.

The insults that were hurled Justin's way weren't all that significant, but in high school, the least creative, most bargain-bin slights seem truly, unfathomably crushing. It was mostly "faggot" and "bitch" but they occasionally called him "unibrow," despite the fact that his eyebrows were very separate. Justin tried not to let it bother him, but it did eventually grate on him enough that we could see it on his face. His "Hm"s were less pointed, he didn't smile when he nodded. It bothered Bette and Nancy especially.

One day, about a week before homecoming, Freddy had had enough. He was shaking his head looking at Justin at the lunch table. "Cross, this shit's stopping," he said, and pushed himself up.

The rich kids' table was across the cafeteria from ours, and Freddy was beelining straight for it. I looked at Nick. "The fuck is he doing?"

"I don't know, but it's probably gonna be funny, come on."

Nick and I followed Freddy, with Nancy not far behind. Freddy marched, and the movements looked slow, but he was damn hard to keep up with. I would have tried to stop him, I think, if I was fast enough, but he was already to their table by the time Nick and I were halfway across the cafeteria. Still, we could hear him. The room had started to quiet down when everyone noticed.

"Get the fuck up, Barnes," Freddy said.

"Huh?" Tommy's mouth was full.

"You and Anderson, get the fuck up, let's take a walk."

"What's your problem?" Isaac said.

"Problem is," Freddy said in a cold, seething voice, "that you keep fucking with Cross, and I'm gonna beat the zits off your fucking face if you don't stop."

Tommy swallowed and scoffed. "Fuck off, man."

Did I mention Freddy was fucking tall? He reached over two girls he was standing behind (who looked absolutely terrified, by the way) and snatched Tommy up by his shirt. Tommy didn't get all the way across the table. Freddy jerked his arm and threw Tommy to the side, sending him onto the floor.

Mr. Morris, the freshman English teacher, was the staff supervisor for that lunch period. He was a short man with small glasses and a widow's peak. He looked tiny next to Freddy as he ran up. "Mr. Thatcher, principal's office."

Freddy looked at him. "They're coming too."

"They were just sitting there, Freddy."

"They've been calling my friend a faggot for the last three weeks and I'm done, so either they come with us, or you wait two minutes until I'm finished here."

Mr. Morris looked Freddy up and down, trying to hold his ground, but then relaxed his shoulders. "Thomas, Isaac, come with us."

Freddy got detention for the outburst, but since he didn't actually hurt Tommy, he didn't get as severe of a punishment as he would have otherwise. Tommy and Isaac didn't mess with Justin anymore after that.

I started to warm up to Freddy from that point on.

***

All of us had skipped out on freshman homecoming. It had seemed stupid to even consider going back then. This year, everyone was talking about going. Justin had asked Bette, which everyone had expected, though the nature of their situation was still pretty hazy. Nancy and I weren't hiding the fact that we were together from anyone. Nick and Freddy both said they were going, but neither were making an effort to get a date.

"I mean really, when you think about it," Nick was passionately explaining, "if you've got a fifth wheel and a sixth wheel then it's an even number of wheels anyway and it doesn't even really matter."

Justin nodded.

"Okay," I said, "but you're gonna be bored as hell if you're riding alone with your dad there and back."

"Pops can probably pick us up later that night," Freddy said. "We can ride together, no big deal."

Nancy shrugged. "We're probably going to walk, if you want to meet us at Ben's and walk with us."

Justin scowled. "You're going to walk in your suit?"

"Yeah?" I said.

"It's gonna be hot," he said. "And it'll be dark, you know, by the time homecoming's over." He gave me a knowing look. I reciprocated it.

"Yeah, I guess I didn't think about that."

"It'll be fine," Nancy said, gripping my hand under the lunch table. "We can ask my parents if they'll pick us up."

ELKWOOD KIDS

The week was grinding along slowly as the dance approached. Anticipation is a ball and chain. When Saturday finally came along, I was wracked with nerves. It all felt like such a big deal. Everything's a bit like that in high school, each event the series finale, the cap to the trilogy, everything leading up to that point. I didn't want to look stupid, but pulling on my suit, I felt a bit stupid. You don't go to a tailor for a high school homecoming, right? The jacket was a little too big for my shoulders; my hands looked tiny coming out of the sleeves. I shook my head in the mirror and ruffled my hair, trying to get it to something that resembled presentable (as if anyone, myself included, had really cared how I looked before).

My mom was picking at me like a vulture. It was the most she'd paid attention to me in nearly a year, prodding and poking and trying to get everything just right. The ruffling of my hair was undone by the comb, a course I'd correct the moment she was out of sight. She pulled at the black tie, trying to get the knot into that perfect, presentable triangle, a pipe dream that would never see fruition.

Nancy and I had settled on pink as the color we'd try to match. I was wearing mostly black— the suit and tie both were —but the buttoned shirt I wore under my jacket and the boutonniere on my lapel were both a light shade of pink. As critical as I was of my reflection, I did wind up enjoying how the colors matched up well.

When Nancy's parents brought her to my house, I was floored. Her hair was curled and pinned up in an intricate style (a job done by her mom's friend Sandra, the stylist who'd met Jon Hamm). The dress she was wearing was modest, flowing down to her ankles, but left a lot of her shoulders and collarbone visible, and scooped fairly low between her shoulder blades. The makeup her mom had done was a shade somewhere between pink and purple around the eyes, not quite the color of her dress, but a hue that brought out that burning gold that I was so enamored with.

"Hi," she said, shyly.

"Uh... hi," I said, just as shyly.

The parents (the mothers in particular) herded us into a corner of my living room to take pictures. Both our moms had actual film cameras to take the pictures with, and were insistent upon filling up at least a roll of film.

"I feel kinda stupid," Nancy said.

"Me too," I whispered between camera flashes. "But you look gorgeous."

Nick wasn't wearing a suit when he arrived with Freddy. He just had on a black shirt and pants with a tie that shimmered with several shades of green swirling around each other. His sleeves were rolled up to his elbows. Freddy was dressed in his ROTC uniform, complete with a beret. Seeing him more "cleaned up," I almost forgot how scary he looked half the time.

"Are Justin and Bette coming?" my mom asked.

"Nah," Nick said. "Justin didn't wanna sweat in his suit."

We met Justin and Bette outside the school. Justin was wearing a similar suit to mine, though he also had a black vest, and the shirt underneath was a deep red. Bette was wearing a red, shockingly short, strapless dress that exposed the freckles dancing up her back and shoulders. She didn't look uncomfortable in it, though I'd never even seen her wear a skirt instead of pants before. Even with her huge glasses, she was very easily pulling the look off.

More pictures were taken, before finally we got to go inside (and I got to ruffle my hair back into an acceptable mess).

Does anybody remember homecoming? I mean, everybody remembers the pictures, and some of the dancing, but the little details in the middle, to me, only come in a wild blur of adrenaline. I know we danced a bit, talked a bit, drank some of the fruit punch which Isaac Anderson was offering to spike with a flask of vodka he'd swiped from his dad's cabinet. I remember nobody took him up on that.

I remember the last song mostly. It was a repetitive, slow dance song, which I recognized later in life as the instrumental of Boyz II Men's End of the Road (I'm still not quite sure what kept them from using the version with the lyrics). Nancy and I were swaying slowly in the crowd of other couples, Justin and Bette not far away. Bette was looking up at Justin, her eyes wet with that shine of "I love you so much if you talk I'll start bawling" kind of contentment. Nancy had her head against my shoulder, breathing softly against me.

I brushed her bare back with my fingers as we danced, sighing as I let the rhythm guide us, slowly, toward the end of the night. One of the DJ's lights swept across my line of sight and through my hair. Nick was sitting on the bleachers drinking from a plastic cup. I knew he'd found Isaac later on after the initial offer, and I'd wanted to say something to him, but the last call for the slow dance had pulled me away. Freddy was sitting near him, not looking at him, no cup in either of his own hands. Catching my eye, Freddy gave me a small smile, before turning and saying something to Nick. Nick looked down at his cup, up at us, and nodded, before waving to me, mouthing something that ended with the word, "tomorrow," and following Freddy out of the gym.

The music played on, and I said, just loud enough for Nancy to hear, "Nick went home, I think."

She breathed out against me and looked up. "That's okay. My mom is gonna pick us up."

Nancy's eyes burned golden at me again. I felt the words I love you, but chose not to say them. I leaned in and kissed her, as the song swelled and then faded into silence.

That song's in my bones, a part of me I'll never forget as long as I live. I remember it like my name, and I remember how in those moments, I knew how everything in the whole world was really, truly, okay.

Chapter Five
Loss, Reviewed

Justin hadn't had a reason to tell the police about the coyotes. We all agreed that, with the whole situation so easily written off, that there was no reason to even create a scare that a child might be missing in the woods with wild animals roaming around. And, if anyone was missing their kid, surely they'd go to the police themselves. It was all squared away. Handled. Done with.

Still, I wasn't so sure. I kept my mouth shut, for Justin's sake, but I had developed a new wariness of the woods, giving them an even wider berth, even in broad daylight.

After the end of the run-ins with Tommy and Isaac, and the passing of homecoming, Justin was back in his full stride, subdued and silent as that stride may have been. The scars on his hand were ever-present, but healed, and Justin was the same. Like Nancy and I, he and Bette weren't hiding that they were an item anymore. They both seemed happy, fresh into a dreamy honeymoon phase.

Nick and I weren't as attached sophomore year. We still hung out, but not nearly as much as we had in the thick of freshman year, the weekend after weekend of nonstop late nights in front of the TV. That didn't mean we weren't close. Nick's dad had just become more jaded about driving him into Elkwood, and Freddy's weekends were often beholden to his dad's regiment. I did make a few trips over to Fairweather, a town that was a bit less rural, but also less spacious. Everything was packed tight into one short stretch of suburb, surrounded by tall trees.

I had started hanging out with Freddy and Nick as a group though, and I understood how Nick must have felt from the opposite direction with Nancy and I. Nick was always the conversationalist, finding a way to involve himself with Freddy's rants about the military or hunting, even when he clearly had zero clue what he was even saying. Freddy called him on not knowing what he was talking about. Nick never backed down. I, meanwhile, was completely in over my head as Freddy explained his beliefs on the wars America was in, and how he was confident things would be better by the time he joined, while Nick was constantly joking that they could easily solve everything if we'd start flexing our nukes more. It was all nonsense, and I wasn't able to even keep in time with Nick's humor.

Regardless, they invited me along when they went to a movie at the theater in Fairweather, or if they were going to drive up to St. Louis to visit the zoo. I'd go when I could, but I'd started to see the weekend less as a time to share with all my friends, and more as the time to have Nancy totally uninterrupted.

November reared itself with a cold gust, following a four day weekend we'd been blessed with for Halloween. At school on Tuesday, all the classes were called into the gym for a surprise assembly.

The gym was humming with hundreds of voices speaking. Nick, in the center of our group on the bleachers, had the whole thing figured out. "No shot it's anything for real, man. Anderson probably got caught selling weed to sixth graders and now we all gotta sit through another DARE seminar."

"Never done DARE," Justin said.

Nick shot him a look. "No fucking way."

"Yeah, they never came to our school," Nancy said.

Nick lolled his head back. "You all are the luckiest fucking people alive, you know that?"

"It can't be that bad," Nancy said.

"It is," Freddy said. "Just about the most boring thing you can sit through."

"I got one of the shirts, though," Nick said, eyes shut.

"I've still got all three," Freddy said back.

Nick waved a hand at him dismissively. "There's no way in hell any of those fits you anymore."

"I can still wear the one from eighth grade, I think."

"No wayyy man, you're fucking huge."

Freddy shook his head. "I'm only like twenty pounds bigger than eighth grade."

"You could eat the you from eighth grade in like two bites max."

Microphone feedback screeched through the gymnasium, not totally silencing the rumble of voices, but cutting it in half. The deep voice of our principal, Mr. Weaver, an older, bald, bearded man sliced through the last of the chatter. "Good morning everybody, can we please bring our attention up here for a moment?" He waited before continuing. He cleared his throat as he spoke back up.

"As you all know, it was Halloween Sunday. We had a lot of students out late, which is normal, and expected, for the holiday." This felt odd. I didn't know why, but I could tell he was stalling. I scanned the room, and caught a familiar face standing near a few of the teachers, though I couldn't place him right away.

"There is no comforting, easy way to put what I'm about to say," Mr. Warner said. "But early yesterday morning, a junior at our school, Margaret Diermann, was found in the woods outside town. Dead." The chatter returned in the form of a small splash of whispers through the crowd, which quickly died down, stifled by the cold hand of shock.

I had known Margaret in passing, as I knew most people in my age group in town. She had been in the same homeroom as me, just a year ahead. She had told most of our sixth grade class that Ms. Prescott, the teacher, was awful, but I thought she was fine. I had never gone out of my way to speak to her, but I could picture her thin, mousy face. I could picture her eyes vacant. I looked over at Nick.

He mouthed to me, "Holy shit."

"Lieutenant Dunn from our police department has come to say some words, and then, we've notified all your parents that we'll be sending you home after this assembly."

I looked at the officer, dressed in a white uniform, the man I'd recognized from before. It made perfect sense. The stubble was gone, replaced with a thick, graying mustache, but Sergeant Dunn had moved up in the world. I wondered if anyone knew he'd been doing all the questioning the last time something like this happened, if they put him up to it as some kind of joke. *"Well last time you fucked it up, pal, but how about you give it another shot?"*

Dunn walked to the microphone. "Thank you, Mr. Warner," he said solemnly. "I understand that hearing that one of your fellow students, a friend, has passed away is scary, and overwhelming. We're doing everything we can to help Margaret's family through this." He wet his lips with his tongue and bobbed his head. "I can't share many of the details with you here today. This is still an open case, but right now we think an animal of some kind attacked Margaret when she was out alone, walking home on Halloween."

This time I found Justin's face. He was porcelain. I looked down. His left hand was clenched tightly around one of Bette's hands, his right, the scarred one, was slowly flexing in and out of a fist.

"That's not to say," Dunn continued, "that if anyone has any information of any kind, about whether someone would want to harm Margaret, for any reason, that we don't want to hear it. There are officers at the door handing out the number for our local precinct, and you can also come down and see me there if you know anything. It's on Main Street, right next to town hall." He looked around the room, gauging the field, the small shimmer of whispers that had begun. "I am deeply sorry for this loss. We ask that all of you keep your thoughts and prayers with Margaret's family."

Mr. Warner returned to the microphone, straightening his shirt. "Everyone, when it's time to leave, you all may return to your lockers and collect any belongings you need to take home and then dismiss as usual. We will be back at school tomorrow, but all homework you were given last week has been canceled, so please just take the evening to mourn. You may all leave in an orderly fashion, and make sure to get a number from the officers at the door if you know something that could help with their investigation."

The voice bustle continued, though its tone was notably more somber, tense. People pulled themselves from the bleachers, some (mostly juniors) were crying, others were just shaking their heads in disbelief. I stared down at Justin, then down at my hands. My ears started to ring.

"This is so fucked," I heard Nick say. I looked at him. He was looking back at me. "Dude, are you good? You look like you're going to puke."

"Babe," Nancy said. "Ben, are you okay?"

***

I woke up on the floor of the gym, on one of the mats used for sit-ups in P.E. I blinked, and saw Lieutenant Dunn kneeling next to me. "Hey kid," he said. "You passed out over there."

"I... I'm fine," I said. I was sweating, and my forehead felt cold. "Where's Justin?"

Mr. Warner was there, kneeling by Dunn. "Mr. Cross's parents picked him up, Ben. How are you feeling?"

I shook my head. "I'm fine, I just got a little..." I couldn't find the word. My head was still a little fuzzy.

Dunn squinted at me. "Jesus," he said softly, as recognition waxed over his face. "No wonder you got so worked up over there."

"I didn't get worked up." I decided I didn't like the mustache. I couldn't see his top lip, it was weird. "I don't like thinking about this anymore."

Lieutenant Dunn nodded. "I don't either. I was hoping we'd never have anything like this in my career again, kid, let me tell you. I'm glad we *know* what happened this time, though. Still not a time I want to be having."

Mr. Warner interrupted. "This time?"

Dunn nodded again. "Yeah, you remember five years ago, there was that girl that went missing out in the woods one night?"

Mr. Warner's eyes widened. "Oh yeah... what was her name?"

"Lucy Huntz," Dunn said. My body relaxed, but my head was still swimming. "We never found anything about her, it was... it was really awful." I started to roll myself off the mat. "Whoa, kid, you gotta rest here for a minute, okay? You fully passed out. You need to get your legs before you go anywhere."

"I just want to go home, I don't want to talk about Lucy." I started to push myself up. Dunn put a firm hand out in front of my chest, blockading me.

"We don't need to talk about her anymore. But you have gotta stay right there, okay?"

"Miss Kisner went outside to get your parents, Ben," Mr. Warner added. "They're going to bring you some water and then they'll help you out to the car."

I was annoyed on top of nauseous now. I leaned back onto my elbows and looked away from them. "They aren't here, we walk."

"I called them," Mr. Warner said. "They said they were worried about you and they would pick you up when we sent out the call last night, Ben." That made me angry.

"So what, they knew you were going to bring this up today, and they let me come into school anyway? What the fuck?"

Mr. Warner was usually quick to stamp out swearing when he heard it (Nick was caught several times a day, frequently slamming a fist down on the table, hissing, "He's not human man, how does he always know?"). He let me have that one anyway. Dunn was the one who butted in instead.

"I get it, Ben. You're messed up about a lot, but you need to chill, okay? Cool it, because if you faint again, we might have to take you to the hospital, and then you're gonna spend this whole day off there, and that would suck a whole lot right?"

I turned my head away again and shook it. "Whatever," I conceded.

Eventually, Nancy entered, followed by her mother and mine. They had a bottle of water from one of the vending machines, and what looked to be a bag of generic cheese balls, which weren't my favorite, but the vending machines were always pretty full of them, so I wasn't too frustrated with their choice.

"Ben, honey, are you okay?" Mom asked as she handed me the water.

"I'll be fine," I said. I'd mellowed on being frustrated with her, but that didn't mean I wasn't going to say anything. "I wish you had told me that this was going to happen, though. I don't think I would have passed out if I was at least ready for it."

Mom put her hand on my shoulder. "I know. We should have told you. We thought being with your friends would make it easier to digest."

Nancy took my hand. "Is Justin alright?" I asked her.

"He's okay. He was scared, obviously, after everything, but I think he's dealing with it as well as he can be."

Dunn, now standing, looked at her. "I'm sorry. What do you mean 'after everything?'" He looked at me now. "Was Justin a friend of you and Lucy?"

Mrs. Kisner spoke up. "No, Officer. Justin was out one night and ran into coyotes in the woods." I looked over to Nancy. *You told her?* I mouthed. *I tell her everything,* she mouthed back. Yeah, that sounded right. "They bit him, so I think he's a little shaken up, too."

Dunn pulled out a notepad, not unlike the one he'd had the first day I met him, though it was clearly fresher, and from a more expensive shelf than he'd been buying from at a lower pay grade. He scribbled something into it with a nice pen that was printed with a police badge, then looked to Mr. Warner. "What did you say Justin's last name was, Cross?" he asked.

Mr. Warner nodded. "Cross, how you think it's spelled." Dunn wrote it down.

"Ben, you think you're going to be alright?" he asked me.

I was contemplating his notepad, which was being slipped back into his shirt pocket. "Yeah, I'll be okay."

"Good. I am… I'm sorry. Take it easy tonight. Don't go out late. We'll be putting a curfew into effect tonight, I expect." I hadn't planned on it, but I nodded agreement anyway. He gave a satisfied half-smile, and marched for the exit.

"Take all the time you need to get your feet, Ben," Mr. Warner said, following Dunn's exit shortly after.

I rolled my head around, feeling the haze of unconsciousness starting to slip away. The discomfort of remembering, of wondering was left over, but I shoved them back, looking to the moms. "I want to walk home, I think. If Nancy is going to walk with me." Nancy turned to them quizzically.

Mrs. Kisner said, "If you think you can make it, and your mom is okay with that, Nancy can go."

Mom's mouth hung open for a moment, but then she sighed and said, "I would rather you ride home with me, but if you're okay, that's fine."

"Thank you," I said, shoving off onto my feet. I'd brought my backpack to the gym with me, so I was ready to go. Mr. Warner had left it at my feet on the mat.

As Nancy and I parted ways with our mothers to head home, Mrs. Kisner yelled after Nancy, "Nance, be home before dark, do you understand?"

"Yes, Mom," Nancy called back.

***

Nancy was clearly frazzled by the assembly. She didn't talk much on the walk, which left me to my thoughts more than I cared to be. I could see Margaret, drunk (she was a known partier) seeing what she thought was a kid in the trees, just like Justin had, and stumbling off after them, telling them it wasn't safe. I could see the kid turning around, and Margaret realizing, suddenly, she'd seen it wrong. It was a coyote. Before Margaret could turn and run for it, the others in the bushes fanned out. They leapt forward, pouncing. She'd scream and kick as they bit down, and as she fought, she managed to get just to the treeline, before one finally brought her to the ground, and closed its mangy jaws around her throat.

I could see Lucy never putting up a fight. She didn't see a child in the woods. She saw a doggy, and she loved doggies. I could see her going down in less than a second, dragged off into the darkness, too young to realize she was dying, too hurt to yell out for help. And there I was, telling myself if I lied, just by a few seconds, not a lot, that I could say I finally beat her home.

Tears were streaming down my cheeks, but I was noiseless. I made no attempt to wipe the tears away. Nancy noticed them, though. "Ben, come here."

She reached up and held my face in her hands, wiping tears away with her thumbs. "It's just hard," I said. "I don't want that to have happened to her."

Nancy's mouth twitched. She looked like she was just barely keeping it together. "I know. It's terrible."

"They were just… talking about it. I don't know, like it was some show. Like it wasn't hurting me just to think about what happened to her. I mean, he was the guy who asked me about Lucy the day she disappeared. He was the guy." My voice was small. I didn't like how it sounded. Weak, strained.

Nancy wiped another tear from my cheek, and pulled me into a hug. "They don't know what it was like for you. I don't think anyone gets over something like that easily." She rubbed my back. "I wish I could help you."

"You are helping," I said into her hair. "Just... can you tell me about something else? Anything? I just need you to talk to me for a while."

She rubbed my back more before pulling away. Her eyes were red like mine surely were. "Okay..." she said, tapping her foot. It didn't take her long to find something. "So, last week, one of the seniors got caught breaking into Marelli's."

"Wait, really?" I said, immediately invested. I used that to push it all away, but it wasn't totally working this time. I saw Margaret's face, Lucy's face, Justin's face. I heard the shrill barking of the pack, just beyond the brush.

I focused harder on Nancy's voice. "Really. He was there at like two in the morning, and I guess he didn't know Mr. Marelli lives above the deli—"

I zeroed in on her voice now, let her story carry me away from that unpleasant island of images in my mind. Still, even as the dread and defeat started to slink back into the dark they'd crawled out of, I could feel something else, just out of view. All the hairs on my body were standing up again. I felt like everywhere, all around, something was watching us.

***

I'd been paranoid for so long. Cowering at the night, dreaming of the people I loved being whisked away into the forest by something shadowy and unfeeling. Sleep was no escape from the constant fear that this all was going to keep happening— and not to me, but to everyone around me, until I was alone, isolated, surrounded by a ghost town and trees and the hunter in the darkness.

The feeling of being watched loved to rear its head, a shark fin on the wake, humming a string orchestra as it chanted to itself, "Capsize… capsize… capsize…" Every sunset Nancy tempted by pulling me back onto the couch, every suggestion Nick made of walking through town at night, every glance at the ragged scars left on Justin's hand were chum in the water for that feeling to come back. Something, Ben, is chasing you, looking you up and down, reading you, begging you to come out, come out and play.

Lieutenant Dunn had gone to the Cross home to get the details straight, put a pin in the whole Margaret situation. Bette had been there when he arrived to question Justin. She told us Justin had given a different version of the story, where the bits of uncertainty— the child at the beginning, what he'd thought was one big animal —had been swapped out with the coyote version of things. He said he thought he saw someone's dog and tried to follow it, and he started running because the coyotes were barking.

This all seemed to satisfy the police department, who issued a statement about the curfew they'd be enforcing. Minors were not to be out past 7 PM, unless they had a vehicle that they were driving, and the woods were off limits entirely. They said that they would be lifting the restrictions in December, as the activity of coyotes in the area was supposed to go down in the winter, but that in spring, they would revisit and consider putting the restrictions back in place.

Something about it changed the fear of it all. Like maybe now that the adults understood, things would be different. Nobody was going to be out late enough that they were in danger, at least through November.

Justin wasn't quite as frazzled as I expected him to be. He took the same comfort I did, I supposed, in the fact that the police and all our parents were informed enough to handle the coyote problem; A problem that was inspiring a solution more final than the shifting curfews.

Some of the neighborhood parents got together one night. My parents, Nancy's, Justin's, and a handful of kids from school's were all there. I was with Nancy at home, wondering what they were meeting about. I'd never seen that many of them gathered together like that.

"I heard my mom talking to Sandra on the phone," Nancy said. "She was trying to keep quiet so I wouldn't hear, but I still picked up a little bit. I think they're going to hire a hunter.

"A hunter?" I asked. "Like one dude with a rifle is gonna go out and kill all the coyotes because they got one person?"

Nancy shrugged. "One guy, or a few guys. I'm not totally sure. They said 'bow,' too, so I don't know that they'd actually want to use someone with a gun."

"He'd probably be safer with a gun."

"Yeah, but a lot of the seniors are still breaking curfew to go drinking near the woods. I think Nick and Freddy were with them last weekend. Maybe they're worried a stray bullet could hit one of them."

I sighed. "I don't know what's up with Nick." None of us were so innocent that we'd never drank. It gave a little flavor to the slow drone that sometimes weighed down small town adolescence. Nick was drunk frequently by mid-November, however. I was sure his grades were falling back, because he was constantly getting in trouble for ignoring his homework.

"Freddy doesn't like it either," Nancy said. "He was telling me and Justin about it. He tags along even though he doesn't like the seniors much."

"He's protective of everyone," I said, putting my hands behind my head. I looked down at the drawing in my lap, a mess of swirling, thick lines that broke off into zigzags. A storm, I thought. "He needs to tell Nick to calm down though."

"You're the only one who's ever been able to get Nick to do anything he didn't want to," Nancy said. She was also looking at the storm. I turned to her.

"I can't get Lauer to do shit."

She shook her head. "Sure you can. You can at least convince him not to do things. Nobody else has been able to get him to stay home after curfew but you."

"And yet he's getting fucked up at midnight with Phil Hunter and the twins when he thinks we won't know."

Nancy shrugged and shook her head. "Maybe you just need to be the one to do it. You're his favorite."

I felt myself blush a bit. Once I'd thought Nick was my best friend in the world, a brother in all but name. Now? I wasn't sure. The distance had started to feel like something more than my relationship eating at the edges of my time. Attributing it to another wave of my various paranoias, I ignored the part of me that said the distance was growing out of spite. I pushed back. "No shot I'm his favorite. I made him OD on half of his favorite movies. Unforgivable, honestly."

Nancy giggled. "You should try anyway," she said, in a low voice. "For me? Please?"

I looked at her. She was smiling, eyebrows raised, her eyes fiery gold. "Okay. For you." My hand closed around hers. I had dropped the ballpoint pen I'd been doodling with. It rolled under the couch, not to be found for years after the fact. "How long do you think that meeting's going to be?"

Nancy thought about it. "At least an hour. If they decide they're going to do it, then they're going to have to talk about prices and stuff. It'll probably be a while."

"It might get dark by the time they get back. The sun's already setting." Nancy shifted closer to me.

"Yeah, but I'm sure my parents will drive me home. I'm not quite ready to go back yet."

"I'm not ready for you to go either."

I was taking inventory on myself, running diagnostics on my heartbeat. Rapid. I looked for just a moment at the sketchbook, which I'd absentmindedly flipped over while setting it on the coffee table. It was on the page just before the stormy scribbling, a drawing of a circle, filled with thin, curved lines, a simple drawing I'd done earlier that day. The way the sway of the lines snaked and winded, but stayed parallel, slowed my heart a little. Like the flow of the creek: smooth, constant, contained.

When I looked up, Nancy was still looking at me. I tensed my arm a bit, and she came with it, into my lap in one fast, ungraceful motion, but one that at the time, was the most alluring thing I'd ever seen. She looked down at me, burning eyes posing a question.

"I love you," I answered.

"I love you," she echoed.

While Nancy and I filled those two hours alone with our first, and second, time, the adults were plotting a war. They'd decided that guns would do just fine, actually, if the police department would truly be aggressive with the curfew. It so happened there was a man in the neighboring town of Fairweather that had a sizable gun collection, and was willing to deal with the coyote problem for a very cheap price. Seemed he was bored, and had missed the last hunting season, itching to get his finger back on the trigger.

The hunter was experienced, and the father of one of the students at the high school. One First Sergeant Frederick Thatcher Senior was the man for the job, and on the phone with the war party, he promised Elkwood would never have a coyote problem again when he was finished.

Chapter Six
A Slew of Victims

The purge of the forest was a methodical, thorough process that took several weeks for Freddy's dad to even begin. Stakeouts, cameras, scents left to lure the pack further, further, right into the exact spot where he'd carry out the deed. And it wouldn't be able to be a one-off, either. He needed to spread out the massacre so that the pack wouldn't run away. That'd be a temporary solution, but Elkwood's community was demanding permanence. No more dead kids, not today, not tomorrow, and not next year either.

When he came into town, he was far different from how any of us had expected him. In the times I'd gone out to Fairweather, the Thatcher home was never considered as a hangout spot. Even on my birthday, when First Sergeant Thatcher had picked up Freddy, the windows of his jeep were tinted. I'd never gotten a look at him.

He was small. A head and a half shorter than Freddy (just an inch or two taller than Nick), and slight of build, all lean muscle, seemingly not a bit of fat on him, except a bit around his stomach, which I supposed was from drinking and not from laziness. He was not unlike Freddy in the hair: a blonde, neat military cut, though the short hair atop his head was losing luster, starting to become white. He had a thick, graying mustache, beneath which he often held a Marlboro between his coffee-stained teeth.

Thatcher hopped out of his jeep in a thick, army green coat and weathered jeans, heavy black boots, dust-laden, hitting the pavement with a clunk. We (Nancy, Nick, Justin, and I) watched him from up the block from town hall. He had on sunglasses, which he removed and folded into his jacket pocket, as he took a deep drag from his cigarette before flicking the butt out into the road. Then, he marched, in the same rigid, steady rhythm as Freddy, up the steps into town hall.

"He's intense, huh?" Nick said. "Stone cold killer, I guarantee it."

I shrugged and turned away. "What do they expect him to do, kill every coyote in the forest?"

"Probably," Nick said. "I don't think they're thinking like that, they're probably calling it 'population control' or something. But, I think most of them have it in their head he's gonna wipe the whole pack out and then some."

"Hm," Justin said, rubbing his scarred palm against his leg. "I'd rather they just put up a fence or something."

Nick looked at him. "A fence? You know coyotes climb right? All a fence would have done for you is made it so you couldn't run away."

"They just don't know any better," Nancy said. "They're animals, it's not like they killed Margaret for fun."

"Doesn't matter," Nick said. "This is how it always goes. If a dog accidentally eats a person, they put it down."

"How does a dog accidentally eat a person?" I asked.

"I don't know, like, you lose a finger or something and it comes and picks it up?"

"How do you even know that?"

"Same way I know everything."

"Did you consider whatever show you were watching might've made that up?" Nancy asked.

"Nah, nah, no way. Why would you even come up with something like that? It's absolutely true, and Sarge is all the proof I need. You should have seen all the guns he was getting ready with Fred. He's a one man army."

"If he does that, won't other things fill the spot?" Justin asked, still rubbing at his palm.

"Like what?"

"Don't deer and stuff overpopulate if there are no coyotes? Or won't the wolves come and live in the area the coyotes were?"

"I'm not convinced wolves even exist," Nick said. Any semblance of sincerity in the conversation was severed at that moment, and as we walked away from Main Street, everyone was asking Nick a thousand questions to try and get him to explain what he meant, but he continued in the way he always did, saying whatever he could to keep the ball rolling.

ELKWOOD KIDS

Freddy was staying alone in the Thatcher home while his father was camping the woods around town. We rarely saw the veteran leave the woods even when it was light and the predators were all asleep and hidden away. A few times he came back into town to buy beer or food, but otherwise, Thatcher's boots were planted firmly in the forest.

Three weeks later, the shots began. Every few hours, the raucous sound of a rifle firing would ring out into the dark of night. The following morning, Thatcher delivered three dead coyotes to town hall, proof of his kills. Nancy heard they'd told him not to bring the bodies there again. The shots started again that night.

It went on for just over a week before Thatcher was convinced he'd done all he needed to do. Freddy told us his dad killed sixteen adult coyotes and four pups in his mission, a number that made my gut turn to picture. I honestly couldn't even imagine that there had been so many coyotes close enough to town for him to hunt.

While it all made me feel a little dirty— like Nancy said, they were animals, they didn't know any better —it also had a strong effect on me. I looked out at the woods, thinking about how they looked in the dark, and that nagging feeling of dread that always came in nipping and biting. It didn't seem so real anymore. The things that had been chasing me since I was ten were all dead. There was peace in the thought that whichever one out there that had taken her could have been among the sixteen bodies at First Sergeant Thatcher's feet. I told myself that it was finally done, and for once, I really did believe it.

***

It was in the intermittent phase between First Sergeant Thatcher's arrival and completion of the job that

I did what Nancy had asked and tried to get through to Nick. She had brought it up again a few days prior, mentioning that when we had seen Nick at school that Monday, he was paler than usual and had deep circles under his eyes. It had definitely been worrying, but I just kept putting it off. Nick was not the type who could be smoothly confronted about anything. That's true of most high schoolers, honestly. Every single one, even if they're certain that they're at their breaking point, wants everyone around them to just let them do what they're doing, because at the same time they're at their wit's end, they know best.

I invited Nick over to watch movies like we had all freshman year and summer, a prospect he jumped on almost instantly. His dad was easily convinced to drive him out, being as Freddy had been doing nearly all the driving for the last month and a half. That Saturday I was rummaging through DVDs, trying to pick one Nick had left behind that we hadn't watched, or one that we hadn't replayed into intolerability. At some point I gave up and decided to let him pick, figuring that if the talk put him in a bad mood, getting to watch precisely what he wanted might cheer him up.

Nick arrived at around four o'clock Saturday afternoon, as the late November sun began its slow crawl into the west. He seemed full of nervous energy, bouncing and fidgeting with his jacket zipper, so before we lost the sunlight, we decided to go for a walk through the town.

We made our way down the hill where the edge of my neighborhood sloped into Main Street. Nick was talking about Freddy's friend Gates (I never got a first name) who was also planning on enlisting at some point. Gates and Freddy did shooting practice with Freddy's dad, and Gates was even more passionate about firearms than Freddy had ever been. Nick had been over one day when Gates arrived and had tried to get Freddy to use the really powerful stuff while Sergeant Thatcher was out and wouldn't notice.

"With all the stuff his dad brought here, I don't even want to think what the big ones are," I said.

"They're cool as shit, but Gates may be one of the dumbest people I've ever met. Glad Thatcher told him to fuck off, he'd have wound up shooting one of us."

A rare natural lull in the conversation took, and I pushed myself to find my courage. How the hell does anybody ever comfortably say, *"I wanted to talk to you about something"*? It's always such a choking statement to spit out. I didn't really want to talk about it, and I was beyond terrified that if I said that, he'd start lashing out, like he did when anyone made him feel cornered.

With an exhale that puffed my cheeks I finally said something. "Are you okay?"

Nick's pace slowed for a shuffle of a second. "What do you mean?" His tone had faded, his voice was just a hair quieter.

"I... Everyone's a little worried about you."

"I don't know, I'm fine," he said quickly.

I tried to find a way back somewhere less tense, but there really wasn't a way back. "You've been going out a lot, getting pretty wasted, and you just look tired. At school you're like a zombie."

"Did you call me just so you could get on my ass for hanging out with people? Did Freddy tell you I needed to stop?"

I let that sit for a moment as we wound past town hall. I sat down on a bench. "I'm not judging you or anything like that. Everything's been fucking hard. I'm not... I'm pretty fucked up about this whole Margaret thing. Justin could've died a month ago, and I—" I stopped myself. I didn't want to go there right now. "Nobody wants to lose anybody, and we're worried we're going to lose you."

Nick looked me up and down. I saw a crack in his wall break, and his shoulders relaxed. He sat down beside me on the bench.

"I don't know," Nick said, leaning his head back. "I'm just fucking bored, like... my bones are fucking trembling bored. Like I need anything to get out of my own body for a little bit."

"Like you're stuck," I said.

"Exactly like I'm stuck. And it's just—" he caught himself, deciding if he wanted to say what he was about to say. "I miss my mom." I nodded. Nick's dad had won full custody of him in the divorce. I don't think Nick had seen his mom since that day in court. I didn't think he'd even spoken to her on the phone since then.

I put my hand on Nick's shoulder. It was just like he said— his bones were trembling. He was shaking all the way up his spine. "I, uh... I don't know what that's like, and I'm sorry. I mean, my parents aren't home all that much, but I know that's still different."

"Eh, it's not your fault. My parents just happen to be pretty fucked up, that's all." He cleared his throat, and sleepily dragged his hand down his face. "I'm not good at thinking about what's bothering me, it's just... you know, you don't wanna go back to where you feel so bad."

"Yeah, I understand that." I thought about it, and decided. Of anyone, who I would want to know other than Nancy was Nick. I looked over at him. "When I was ten, I had this friend, and she went missing in the woods one night. She never came home, and I still don't know what happened to her. I think I know now, but they never found a body. She's just gone."

"Fuck," Nick said.

"It's... it's still not easy, but I lean on you guys to make it better. Nancy and Justin and Bette, and even Freddy sometimes, and... I wouldn't be able to do any of that if you hadn't come and talked to me. I probably would've been alone with that in my heart all freshman year. I don't know who I'd be right now if I'd had to go through that that way."

"Shit, man."

"No, like, thank you. My point is, I think you like to ignore things. And I don't blame you, because when I think about Lucy it almost always makes me feel like I'm losing my fucking mind. But if you try to ignore it all alone, and just drown it down without letting anyone help you... I think it's going to kill you, because it probably would kill me, too."

Nick thought about this. He looked down between his bouncing knees, fidgeting his fingers together for a while. "I haven't really told anyone about my dad, I guess."

"What about him?"

Nick sighed. "Ah, well... I don't know if I want to tell anyone, still. But you told me your friend might've gotten eaten," I let him have that, but my hand clenched a bit at it, "so maybe I should just, you know, get it out there." He looked up at a tall tree planted along the sidewalk. A few faded leaves drifted downward from the branches.

"You don't have to," I said.

"I think I should." He sighed again, and started bobbing his shoulders, trying to coax the words out of himself. "It was like right when my mom filed for divorce, it was just the one time, but he was uh, real pissed off. And I don't know, I talk too fucking much, and I was just mouthing off, and he let me have it pretty bad. I mean, I heard him fight with my mom, but I never heard him scream like that. I think he was drunk, maybe, or maybe I'm just particularly frustrating.

"He whacked me pretty good, it was more of a shove than he was hitting me, but even that kinda hurt, and I just like, hit the wall, man. It was like right before your birthday, when I was trying not to go home or whatever, cuz I just got it in my head that if he saw me again he was gonna really beat the fuck out of me."

"Did he try to?" I couldn't think of anything else to say.

"No, I mean I got up and I ran straight to Thatcher's house. And then the day after your birthday I called him from your house and he apologized and all this shit so I was like, I guess he's sorry. Fuck."

"You didn't tell the court about it."

"No. Why would I, right? It didn't bruise or anything and, I mean I miss my mom, man, but she's kinda nuts too. She was always so... I don't know. It seemed like lesser of two fucked situations to just roll with the shit, right? He went off on me once, I'd just avoid the motherfucker as much as I could."

"Shit," I said, rubbing my arm. "I'm sorry that I haven't been… here as much."

"Look, you and Nancy are… whatever and I don't care about that. You don't need to babysit me or anything, I'm alright."

"I don't think you are."

Nick laughed. "No, I'm fucked, but who cares? I'll… I'll try to chill out. With all the other shit. I just need something to keep my mind off of the bad stuff." I squeezed his shoulder again. "Ben, I'm gonna be good, okay?" he said.

"Okay," I replied. "Maybe we can start doing stuff more often then. Have Freddy hang around here. Have you gotten him on Pulp Fiction?"

Nick's ears perked up. "Fuck no, I haven't. He won't sit down and watch the fucking thing with me. I mean, God I hate that movie now, but he still needs to see it."

"He needs to," I confirmed. "Maybe he'll watch it if we both try to convince him."

I wasn't sure I'd broken through to Nick then, but I felt better just knowing what was tearing him up. It's always the not knowing that really kills you when people you care about are going through things. How can you help them if you don't have a single idea what's messing with their heads so much?

Chapter Seven
Comfort and Joy

December rolled in with a battlecry, sending a snowstorm over Elkwood that closed school for three days. A week after Sergeant Thatcher had slain the last of the coyotes, Nick had come over again, and was snowed in at my house for the weekend.

All my paranoia had seeped away, it seemed, with the grizzly justice exacted on the woods. My energy was now focused on my worry for Nick. Still, he seemed markedly happier than he had the last few weeks, possibly because the whole group was latching onto him and spending time with him more frequently, keeping him from people who didn't care if he was drinking all night or staying up until the sun rose.

Freddy had privately thanked me for talking with Nick. Apparently, Nick had told him about what I'd said, minus the parts about Lucy, and he said he'd never quite found a way to get it into Nick's head that he cared about him enough for Nick to quit.

In the midst of the snowstorm one night, I began to scribble at the edges of my sketchbook, letting the pen go wherever it wanted, as a chill seeped through the chip at the edge of my living room window. Nick was drinking hot chocolate my mother gave him, holding it a bit close to my face as he watched over my shoulder from behind the couch.

"How come you never draw real things?" he asked.

I scratched in a few circles in one corner, then rotated the book and did it in the next. "I don't think I'm very good at it. Bette's the one who can draw people." I thought about it for a moment. "It's jumbled and chaotic, but it's still something real. I just haven't figured out what it is yet."

The lines were scratchy and confused. I considered them, as the ink drew closer to the center of the page. The winding paths of the drawing didn't tell me what they were, yet. I shook my head and kept sketching away.

"So... you just go until it's something? What if it's nothing?"

"Sometimes it's nothing. I think it's usually nothing. Every once in a while, I can find the pattern. I've drawn a storm, or a river. It's not like, a portrait or anything."

The cold blew in through the window, and the hairs on my arms stood up. Nick took a long drink and asked again, "So have you tried drawing anything on purpose?"

"Not in a long time. Probably not since I was eleven or twelve."

He accepted this answer, though I could tell by the slight pout he wasn't happy with it. He plopped down on the couch next to me.

A week after the snowstorm, as piles of white snow turned to gray slush, I picked up the sketch on that page again, not quite finished yet. There was still a lot of negative space where I hadn't inked yet. I thought about what Nick said as I looked at it, finding the lines at the edges, winding branches of thick darkness, didn't evoke anything specific in my mind.

Yet... there was something about them that spoke to me. Abstract whispers in the little flicks of the pen. I started sketching again, winding the roots of the drawing from the week prior further and further toward the white at the center of the page.

Why don't I try to do something specific again? I thought, taking a wide crescent curve down the left side of the page, then mirroring it on the right. It could be anything if I just work on it enough. It doesn't have to be... I waved the thought away, literally shooing with the pen before returning to the page with it. It doesn't have to be perfect.

Once the tendrils of ink had finally settled, and I felt no more space needed to be covered, I tossed the pen aside, flexing my fingers and palm, sore from the constant motion. I watched silently as the ink went from that fresh sheen to matte dryness, looking in the ink for what this could be.

All the black was drawn thorny, a bit like barbed wire. There was so much overlap in it all that I found it looked like I'd just scribbled it in in some places. I shook my head. Not perfect. I slid the drawing onto the table in front of me and stood up. It didn't matter. It was done at least. Though, from a distance, I did notice something I hadn't seen before.

ELKWOOD KIDS

The ink was as random as could be— all purposeless shaped that resembled nothing more than millions of overlapping twigs, but in the middle, the shape, though skewed and pocked with thorns from where the ink ducked in, almost looked like something. I didn't give it much stock, thinking it was just the result of me not cutting into the negative space any deeper. Still, the white left on the page had the makings of a person's silhouette against the dark.

***

The holidays brought a close to that year, with a lighter, less oppressive shower of snow. It was the kind of scene movies and sitcoms prime you for: where snow falls from Christmas Eve to the moment your final present has been opened, and the smells of cookies and peppermint and hot chocolate roll throughout every home on your street.

We'd all gathered up at my house on the 24th, having few extended family members to even consider visiting. The parents of Elkwood were close enough that we weren't forcing them to sit idly in the corner, as most class-party gatherings did. My parents in particular had become good friends with Nancy's throughout the semester, and Justin's parents had known Nancy's from middle school.

My parents, against my light protests, had invited Nick's dad to join the party. Since hearing about their situation, I found myself tasting sour spite in the back of my throat at the mere mention of Mr. Lauer. Thankfully, he didn't seem all that interested, though he'd been completely willing to bring Nick and Freddy by. Sergeant Thatcher was busy that night, still skinning coyotes and packaging pelts and meats to be sold and donated, but he gave Freddy a night off from assisting in the duties to enjoy the holidays.

All of us were getting to the point where we were starting to think about getting jobs (key word: starting) and were too low on money to afford many gifts. Nick had organized an impromptu Secret Santa two weeks prior, throwing all our names scrawled on scraps of looseleaf into the pom beanie he wore in the winter time. He'd been allowing his hair to grow out, and as he passed the hat around for us to draw names, the short mess of it was totally flat on the top, and sticking out on the sides. Freddy shoved his hand through the top so it would stick up everywhere, getting a half-hearted slap from Nick.

I drew Bette's name, and sighed contently. She was an easy one. Anyone who draws knows there's only one common gift they get more than socks (and it's one that always has a use): sketchbooks, notebooks, any stack of paper you can find. Bette had been filling them up in piles lately, at one point commenting that she'd gone through an entire book just over the week of the snowstorm.

I had found one better, walking through the notebook aisle of the hobby store in town. I peered around the shelves and over my shoulder to make sure no one else had come in looking for their own gifts, and picked up a thick book with a pastel blue cover; a label on the front had "Composition" written in a typewriter font, and three lines below, common enough to see in books all throughout school, but something about this one spoke to me.

Inside, the book seemed to be more than a simple composition notebook. There was a totally blank page, followed by a page with a dot grid, followed by two pages of lined paper, repeating until the book reached eighty pages total. I guessed it was intended more for architecture-type projects, but given the dots on the gridded pages were so faint, it was like having two sketches followed by notes. Instantly, I thought of Bette's books, filled with drawings that she followed with extensive notes. An easy gift, if there ever was one.

First in our gift circle was Nick, being the impromptu organizer of the whole event. The box with his name on it was small, which got an immediate, exaggerated eyebrow raise from him. "Someone think this was funny?" he asked. "Justin's box is bigger than me."

"Just open it," Freddy said. Nick rolled his eyes and started pulling off the wrapping paper (a simple base-green-red-striped plaid). There was a small cardboard box inside, the kind that's folded to hinge and fold back into itself to be resealed. Nick was about to tear into the cardboard. "The flap, Nick," Freddy said.

Nick looked at him. "Guess I know who got my name, then. Thanks for ruining the surprise, kind of the point of the whole thing."

"Just shut up and open it, Nick," Nancy said.

With another roll of his eyes, Nick pulled the flap out of the box and opened it. He squinted at it, then turned to Freddy. "Where the hell did you get this?"

Freddy shrugged. "You know my dad's got those leather burning tools, I just bought one from the clothing store back home and did the letters myself."

"Dude, you made this?"

"Not really, I just put the letters."

Nick hooked an arm around Freddy's neck and hugged him. "This is so fucking cool," he said. He pulled away from Freddy, who was a bit flushed, and pulled the contents of the box out, immediately flipping the letters on the object toward me. "Ben, look at this shit, man."

He was holding a brown wallet that had the words "BAD MOTHER FUCKER" burned into it, just like Samuel L. Jackson had in Pulp Fiction. I scoffed, "No way."

Nick handed the wallet around to everyone. The lettering wasn't exactly like it was in the movie, the letters were more solid, but it was close enough that Nancy and I (I'd made her watch the movie with me too, on the DVD Nick had bought me) were very impressed. "Isn't that the fucking coolest thing ever?" Nick said.

"Language, Nick," my mom called from where the adults were sharing a bottle of wine in the kitchen.

"Sorry!" Nick called back. "Yeah, I guess I can't bring this to school, huh?"

"Warner would take it immediately," Bette said, handing Nick the wallet back.

"Still, this is awesome, I can't believe you came in here trying to show everyone up, Thatcher," Nick said. He gave Freddy another squeeze around the neck, which Freddy reciprocated this time.

Freddy was next in the circle. His box was of a similar size to the one Nick received, though slightly longer and not as wide, and cheekily wrapped in camouflage paper. He opened it and pulled a lid off the black box inside, finding a folding hunting knife with a deep-brown, wood-grain handle. He opened the blade and inspected it, marveling that it wasn't a cheap one.

Justin, the buyer of the gift, corrected him. "I got it from the pawn shop on West Brook, it wasn't too expensive. Dad helped me fix it up a little in the shop."

Freddy nodded, taking a piece of the wrapping paper and testing how sharp the knife was by running the blade downward through it. Very sharp, it looked like. He thanked Justin and went to Mr. Cross and shook his hand, ever formal, ever regimented, before returning to his seat and sliding the knife's clip into his belt.

Bette was next in the circle, and studied my box carefully. I think she was trying to see who wrapped it by how neat the bell-dotted red paper was folded, as she glanced at Nancy before opening it (joke's on you, Bette, I had my mom wrap it because I'm hopeless). Beneath the paper, I'd put the notebook in a shoebox along with a pack of pens that I knew Bette liked, a variety I always borrowed from her when we went to the park together, but never felt passionately enough to shirk cheap ballpoints for.

Bette pulled back the lid of the box and pulled out the book, flipping it over a couple times and remarking on the pretty color, before looking inside. It was a simple gift but her eyes lit up, her pupils massive beneath her glasses, as she looked at how the pages were set up. She looked up at Nancy, who pointed a finger at me.

"Thanks Ben," Bette said, rising from her seat and coming to me. She gave me a quick hug, awkwardly as I was sitting and facing her. "Where did you get this?"

"The hobby store, in the sketchbook section. It was pretty much the first thing I saw, but it was perfect."

Bette sat back down and neatly tucked the book and pens into the backpack she'd brought with her.

Justin was next, and while the box wasn't as big as Nick said, it was pretty damn big. He laid it neatly across his lap and studied it, quietly deciding which side to open it from. Once the paper (a silvery, sleek sheet with green

Christmas trees spattered across) was off, he found the thin sort of box that clothes are packaged within.

Inside was a thick, gray, winter coat, which Nancy had picked out with me at a secondhand store in town. Justin stood up and bashfully tried it on. It was a good fit.

"You were talking about how cold it was in the fall, and how you outgrew your other coat, so I thought this would be good," Nancy said.

An enthusiastic nod from Justin confirmed it. He sat down, still in the coat.

Bette's gift to Nancy was a voice recorder, the kind you simply hold a button to speak into, which I guessed was, as well, from the pawn shop in town. Nancy had recently mentioned she was consistently forgetting things she wanted to tell people, but she didn't have any interest in writing them down either. I wondered if she'd actually use the little machine or not, but she seemed incredibly pleased as she turned it over in her hands.

"I guess the surprise is ruined, then," Nick said, looking at me.

"You draw my name on purpose?" I asked.

"No, but I did spend a week or two panicking about what I'd even get you. Didn't even think of the notebook thing."

"How?" Freddy asked.

"Shut up," Nick said back, pushing Freddy. Freddy caught his hand and slid it back toward him slowly before pushing the side of his head.

The box Nick had wrapped was messy, to say the least. The wrapping paper was a simple red that he'd accidentally torn in some places, patched with tape. The places where the wrapping paper was folded were crumpled, scrunched, but, looking at it, it was honestly much better than I expected Nick to tolerate getting right. "Hate to ruin something so pretty," I said.

"I'm a vessel for my craft," Nick said, "Just open the damn package." The wrapping paper came off easily, as I revealed a shoebox not dissimilar to the one I used for Bette's gift. I opened the box, and inside, I saw two books, both of them paperback, with well-worn covers.

Each book was an art book, one of which was a book of abstract art, thicker than the other in the box. I did a quick flip through, finding interesting and wild sweeps of paint done by artists from decades prior. A lot of it reminded me of my own drawings, albeit more sophisticated, done with more... purpose. The other book was full of instructions on basic anatomy. As Nick would put it, it was how to draw real things.

"I know you like what you do, which is what the bigger one is for, but I think you'd be pretty good at all the other shit if you practiced, so, I grabbed the other one, too. The library back home was selling off a lot of books."

I stood up and went to Nick, stepping over Justin's massive box as I came. Not before noticing Nick's hand was still resting on Freddy's knee, I put a hand out and pulled him to his feet, wrapping him in a hug. "Thank you," I said, squeezing him tighter. He felt thin, but he was still strong, and seemed pretty determined to outdo me, popping my back with his arms.

"Ah, whatever, they were cheap," he said as he pulled away. He stretched and cracked his neck as he and I looked over the pile of wrapping paper surrounding the group. "Think your mom and dad will do it for us?"

"Absolutely not," I said, immediately kneeling and collecting my trash.

The others helped us, gathering up the discarded paper, as the snowfall just crawled along, drifting past my windows softly, stealthily. When a trash bag had been stuffed with paper, I started to take it out to the trash can in the driveway, but then stopped. I don't know what the prospect of the cold, just-wet night was doing to draw me in, but as I glanced at the moon, but a few days shy of full in the sky, I made a decision.

"Hey, do you guys want to come with me?" I asked. "I kinda wanna take a walk."

Five pairs of eyes locked on me in the foreground, and two pairs (Nancy and I's mothers) in the background. They were quiet now, though the fathers were talking about something with beers in hand— the wine had been long-drained —and did not notice.

"Are you for real right now?" Nick asked. "You like drunk or something?"

"No," I said, a little nervous now. "I think I just... want a little fresh air."

"Well, shit. I'm down." Nick turned to the group, not asking so much as telling with the gesturing of his hands. "We gonna take a walk or not?"

Nancy spoke up. "I mean, sure, if you're sure, Ben. We don't have to walk, we can just hang out outside. And I don't know if your mom would want us to, you know..." Nancy looked back at my mom.

"If you all just stay near the streetlights, it's okay," Mom said. "The woods should be safe now, but I still don't want you all going into them tonight. Not while it's snowing."

"We won't," I said. "I just need to stretch my legs."

Justin dumbly stood up, pulling Bette, hanging on his arm, up with him. He was still wearing the coat, which had the thrift store's tag hanging idly from its sleeve. Nick grabbed Freddy's hands and pulled him up to his feet as well. Nancy pulled on her coat and started slipping back into the boots she left by the door.

"Be back soon, Ben," my dad called after us.

"Yep, we will," I said, letting the door close on my words.

***

I always watched Christmas go by the same way every year: from behind my walls, safe in a blanket on the couch or at the foot of my bed, not giving the idea of stepping into the evening snow even a hair of a chance of forming. I felt and heard the crunch of light frost beneath my boot, smelled that crisp, winter air that wafts throughout the Midwest, and sighed. Yes, all of a sudden, I was overcome with just how much I'd missed the night air of Elkwood.

Despite the snow, that Christmas Eve wasn't so frigid that I felt myself go numb— not like some holidays, where the wind bites into you though it feels as gentle as a kiss. I wasn't even wearing gloves as I walked forward, Nancy by my side, slowly interlacing my bare fingers with her wool-clad ones. Justin and Bette walked much the same, Justin having to lean just a bit further than I thought looked comfortable to get a good hold on Bette's slender hand. Freddy and Nick were the same as ever: the stoic, proper stance of Freddy broken only occasionally by his need to give Nick a shove, as the latter walked with a gait and rhythm that spoke only of chaos and freedom.

We followed the streetlights along my neighborhood toward Main Street, where we passed a pack of five middle schoolers, who no doubt had snuck out of their homes to enjoy the night, not yet given the liberty of teenagerdom that our group was blessed with. The eldest of their group was Jules Baker, a tall, sarcastic girl who I had remembered being in sixth grade when I was in eighth. She acknowledged me with some recognition as we passed them by.

The conversation we had as we rolled past the post office and toward town hall was mostly disjointed, each of us paired off: I with Nancy, Bette with Justin (basically silent), Freddy with Nick. Eventually though, we met in the middle when Nick noticed town hall and brought up Freddy's dad and his hunt.

"So, how's Sarge's leg?" Nick asked.

Freddy shrugged. "He's getting better. I mean, he didn't go to the hospital or anything, just stitched it up himself, so it's probably not as it could be, but..."

"Your dad hurt himself?" Nancy asked.

"Not himself. When he was down here, he said he got bitten. One of the males snuck up on him and chomped down on his leg. They do that, bite out a tendon so you can't run. He was lucky enough not to get his ACL slit, but it still looked pretty gnarly."

"Jeez..." Bette said, shuffling uncomfortably next to Justin. Justin had his scarred hand in his pocket, but I could tell he was fidgeting a bit, rubbing it idly against his leg again.

"Yep," Freddy said. "Sarge ain't big on going to hospitals considering he knows field medicine, so he poured some whiskey on it and stitched it up after he killed the coyote."

"Badass of the highest degree," Nick said. "Maybe it was the same one that tried to snack on Justin."

"Doubt it," Freddy said. "But maybe." Justin looked a bit amused at the idea, but said nothing, and offered no nod to clarify. "Either way, he's pretty much healed up. He's stopped saying 'fuck' every time he gets out of his chair for a beer."

I pulled my coat closer against the cold and shook my head, imagining the scrawny man in sunglasses rolling over to see the coyote gnawing on him like a chew toy, taking a quick drag from his cig, and then casually, but intently, placing the barrel of the rifle against the coyote's head and firing. It was badass, I supposed. *A bit insane,* I corrected, silently.

"So that's it, huh?" I said. "No more Elkwood kids going missing."

"You say that like there's been a lot," Freddy said.

"Yeah, no, there hasn't been that many. At least, not in our lifetimes. When it was still a hunting town, wolves would run off with people all the time, apparently." I swallowed.

Bette nodded, "I read that, back in seventh grade, that we hunted all the wolves in the area until there were only a couple left, and after that, everyone thought they just died off."

"Never existed," Nick said, prompting a chuckle from everyone.

"Either way, there's been enough," Nancy said, squeezing my hand. "It's sad that that all had to happen, but... at least we're safe now."

"Yeah," I said, squeezing back. I looked past where Main Street overlapped with the side streets, through rows of little shops and houses, leading down the hill into the forest, downhill from my home. "I haven't been out at night in so long."

Nick threw himself onto the same bench outside town hall where we'd talked a few weeks prior. "And you love it, Ben, I told you at least a hundred times, huh?"

I let go of Nancy's hand and went to a streetlamp. The metal of it, stretching up mightily from the brick sidewalk, was frosted over in the winter air. I stroked it lightly with my fingertips, breathing in the snowy scent once again. "I do," I said. "I used to play outside a lot."

"We used to play hide and seek by the warehouse," Justin said, finally noticing the tag on his sleeve. He started to fumble with it, attempting to get it loose. "We stopped after Mike Loomes fell in the creek and broke his ankle."

"It was so gross," Nancy said. "His foot was twisted like, all the way to the side."

"Yeah," I said, pushing the image of Mike Loomes— a large, pimpled kid with a limited concept of deodorant —'s foot out of my mind. "Me and Lucy used to play hide and seek with Tommy Barnes and a couple other kids. We were playing the night she..." Went missing wasn't the truth anymore, was it? "...the night the coyotes got her."

"Who's Lucy?" Freddy asked cautiously.

"She was like, my best friend when I was younger. But she disappeared in fifth grade, they never found her."

"Shit," Freddy said.

"I remember that," Bette said. "My mom was freaked for like a year about me even walking to the bus stop."

"It was uh... It was rough," I sighed. "But whatever happened to her, I feel like it's not as heavy anymore. It was probably coyotes, but even if it wasn't, I think I just feel better it isn't going to happen again." I looked over to Freddy. "Thank your dad for me, I really don't think I'd have ever gone out at night again if it wasn't for him."

Freddy nodded. "Yeah, sure."

Nick rose from the bench, stretching his arms and legs. "You okay, Ben?" he said. The look on his face was genuine concern, though it seemed a bit goofy with the way the pom beanie was threatening to sink over his eyes.

"I'm good," I said. "I just felt like I needed to say that."

"Awesome," Nick said, and his hand whipped up from the bench, sending a snowball whizzing from behind him and past my face.

I waited for a moment, shocked, then looked hard at Nick. "Nice shot."

"Not my best, no."

I started walking toward him, scanning the ground in my path for ample piles of snow. He was already on the move, leaping over the bench and beelining for the walkway behind town hall. Freddy had taken several steps backward, seemingly out of the fight, but I saw him eyeing Justin as I gathered a fistful of snow and chased after Nick.

The snowball fight went on for a while, all of us drawn in one way or another. I don't think anyone wanted to force the girls into it, but Bette had other plans and caught Nick with a thick one as he wound back to the front of town hall, dodging my three initial throws. His freckled skin went pink as the snowball hit his cheek and sent him sliding down the grass hill. Impressively, he regained his footing on the sidewalk at the bottom. He was holding his cheek when he stood back up, faking a shocked look at Bette as his free hand formed the first snowball that would strike her that night.

Nancy involved herself similarly, by stepping in my way as Nick and Bette began pelting each other while Justin and Freddy circled a tree. I was confused for a moment, but then was struck by the cold reality of her mashing a hearty palmful of snow into my hair and sprinting off.

We were in a free-for-all from that point on, no teams, no mercy, just an arsenal of snowballs and a chorus of wicked adolescent laugher that lit up Main Street more than the lamps and wreathes of colored lights ever could. Personally, I still think Freddy had an unfair advantage. He was quick and had a steady aim from his ROTC training. He only missed me one time, and it was because I slipped on a patch of ice and barely stopped myself before I slid face-first into a tree. Bette and Justin eventually called for a truce and sat down on the bench where the war had started, while the remaining four of us continued on for some time.

Eventually, Nancy, Nick, and I all slowed down and had to give up as well, leaving Freddy the sole survivor of the game. "I would have taken you down if Ben hadn't chased me at the start," Nick said, panting.

"Cute, but not a chance in Hell," Freddy said, barely winded. He snatched Nick's hat off his head and ruffled his hair.

Nancy and I sat on the steps up to town hall, her head on my shoulder as we caught our breath, and Freddy wore Nick's out even more by refusing to return the beanie. I heard a little snore, and looked over to the bench to see Justin asleep, with Bette leaning against him, watching and giggling to herself at the Fairweather boys.

I turned toward Nancy and kissed the top of her head. She felt like she might be on the verge of sleep herself, her breaths slow, relaxed. "We should probably get home soon," I said, glancing at that nearly-full moon, peeking from the snowy clouds.

"Mmhmm..." Nancy said, forcing herself to sit up, stretching, and turning to look at Justin. "Who's gonna wake him up?"

"I will," Bette said. She began lightly shaking Justin, whose snores had started to grow louder against Nick and Freddy's background noise.

Watching Nick make another swipe for his hat, I sighed, letting the cold air wash over me again. My breath rolled in a thick cloud from my mouth, and when it passed by, I saw that Nick had gotten a hold on the beanie, but Freddy had gotten a hold on him, and had his lips on his as they stood just below the streetlamp in the middle of town square.

"Are you seeing what I'm seeing?" I asked Nancy.

"Yeah," she said, not seeming all that surprised as she brushed the debris of the snowball fight off of her coat.

Justin was waking as Freddy pulled away from the kiss, letting Nick take the hat as he went. Nick had still been pink from the snow, but he was now as red as the string of lights that spiraled up the streetlamp beside him. Freddy looked satisfied, victory in his eyes.

We didn't talk much on the way back to my parents' home, but what little chatter there was was pleasant, the wind-down after an energetic night. My mom wasn't mad at how long we'd been gone, but she did tell me to get back sooner next time as we came through the door. The idea of a "next time" kicked butterflies of excitement into a mad swarm in my stomach.

Nancy's parents took her out the door, allowing us a goodbye kiss and an "I love you" before they went, followed by Bette and Justin's families who I watched say goodbye out the window before they hopped in their respective vehicles to make their (short) drives home. That left Freddy and Nick, who stayed a bit longer as midnight approached, before returning to Freddy's truck and beginning the long, snowy trek back to Fairweather.

I looked over the books Nick had bought me as the exhaustion settled in over me; it was a good feeling, that adrenaline afterglow. When I finally forced myself back off the couch and into my bedroom— partially at the prompting of my father to "get the hell out of Santa's way" as he dragged a trash bag full of the next day's presents toward the tree —I was all-too-ready to sink into sleep the moment my body hit the bed.

Quickly, slumber came for me, swaddling me in what would be the most restful sleep I'd had in years, and I dreamed only of my friends, a bit younger, still playing in the dark, while soft, distant howling scored the woods behind us.

Chapter Eight
Flu Season

Christmas break faded, melting away with the snow. There'd be other snowfalls, in early February, and one defiantly near the back end of March. January, however, was clear of frost, and instead came with other clouds. In the first week of school, Nick brought up the old soda factory in Fairweather. He'd passed it on a night walk and gotten curious, but didn't have the guts to check it out alone.

"You gave me all that shit for not going out and you can't even look inside a warehouse?" I said.

Nick threw his hands up. "Look, I get it, but you fail to remember just how many meth heads roll through Fairweather."

"So, you'll walk around town at night, but you won't look through a broken window?"

Nick considered it for a moment. "Fuck you, Ben, are you gonna come or not?"

I tapped my fingers on the lunch table, chewing a handful of pretzels. "I don't know," I said after swallowing. "I know my way around here, Fairweather's not really familiar."

"Yeah, but you'll have us," Nick said, squeezing Freddy's arm. After Christmas Eve, they'd gotten comfortable being touchy in front of the rest of us, though they'd apparently been an item about as long as Nancy and I had. "Thatcher can bring one of his pop's guns, we'll be fine."

"Being near you and a loaded gun in the dark isn't exactly what I think of as fine," Bette said. Justin nodded.

"I," Nick said with a point, "get what you mean, but... Consider, for a moment," he put his hand across his chest, "the thrill, of climbing this old rusty, ladder, up above the pipes where they used to pump root beer into glass bottles. Glass, Elizabeth—"

"Not my name."

"But it could be! Just like we could find a bunch of old soda, or even better, money. They didn't have paychecks back then."

"I don't think that's true," Freddy said.

"But..." Nick said, raising his eyebrows leadingly.

"But it could be, I guess."

I mulled it over, while I looked over at Nancy. "My parents are never gonna let me go to Fairweather in the middle of the night," she said. "Like Ben said, it's one thing being somewhere we know, it's another to be somewhere we don't, especially if we're not close to home."

"Ughh," Nick sighed, leaning back in his chair. "Y'all are lame. Justin, come on, you've gotta have something to say. I am physically incapable of being a compelling arguer."

We all looked at Justin, expecting a calm, but swift dismissal. Justin was pale, his eyes swallowed by dark circles. Had he looked that way earlier that morning? I couldn't remember. He shook his head, void of a "Hm."

"Justin," I said carefully. "You feeling alright, dude?" He looked at me, and opened his mouth like he might say something, but then shut it. "Okay, you gotta go to the nurse or something."

"Babe," Bette said, "do you need some water or something?" She stood up, getting ready to lead him away to the nurse.

"He looks like he's gonna puke," Freddy said.

"I really hope not," Bette said.

Justin was still looking in my direction, although I don't think he was seeing me. He was in that state someone enters just before they fall asleep sitting up: red-rimmed eyes, heavy lids, head tipping backward. I thought about moving, but I didn't. I didn't think he was going to throw up.

I was right, too. Justin didn't throw up, he sneezed. I felt it hit my left eye, and went grabbing for it.

"Fuck man, what the hell?" I said, aggressively wiping at my face.

This seemed to shock Justin awake. "Jesus, Ben, I'm sorry, I didn't even realize I was going to—"

"It's fine," I growled, half-meaning it despite my frustration. I was grossed out, but I could tell that even lucid, Justin was barely doing more than sleepwalking. "We should all go to the nurse, like now," I said.

With our girlfriends, Justin and I left Nick and Freddy in the cafeteria. Nick was snickering a bit as I left, which became full blown cackling as I flipped him the bird on the way out. Freddy punched Nick in the shoulder, but he cracked a smile himself. I'll admit, even though I was mad, it was a bit funny at the time, and I was smirking behind the cover of the arm clamped over my eye.

Justin and I were both sent home, Justin for the fever of 102 he'd been running, and I due to the possibility that I might become sick before the day was over and spread the sickness further. Justin was still sneezing from that point on, but when a reprieve from the fits came, the nurse checked his throat, finding that inside he had scarring all along the sides, similar to strep throat. While the sneezing was abnormal, to say the least, the possibility of a strep outbreak seemed to exhaust more than worry the nurse, and she dialed our parents all the while pinching her brow and putting on her best chipper school staff voice.

I was allowed to walk home, and I meandered on the way, disturbed by the pathway home in the early afternoon. Hardly any vehicle traffic to speak of, no Nancy by my side or our classmates ahead or behind us. In the work-hours daylight, Elkwood seemed as petrified as it was in the nighttime, void of movement save my staggered stroll through the hilly roads.

My face was a bit raw where I'd rubbed at it with an alcohol wipe the nurse had given me, and I could feel, despite flushing it out with cold water, the edges of my eye screaming their irritation. I was in a daze, barely paying attention. I was startled by the deep bellow of Mr. Trellis's bloodhound as it howled at me from beyond the fence. The dog was wagging its tail, drooling openly, as its owner trodded over, bent-backed with a rake in hand.

"Shouldn't you be in school?" came Mr. Trellis's gravelly voice.

"They sent me home sick," I said. "You should probably stay back, Mr. Trellis."

"Ain't been sick in years, Benny," Mr. Trellis said. He ran hooked fingers through the dog's fur. "You're looking real pekid, though."

"Cross came down with a flu. He sneezed right in my face."

Mr. Trellis considered this for a long time before saying, "Ought to keep your window shut tight." I must have given him a look, because he quickly added, "On account of the cold."

I nodded. "Yes, sir." I looked over at the bloodhound. The big dog barked deeply.

"Alright now. You go on and rest, Benny." Mr. Trellis gave me a smile that was almost sad. I opened my mouth to say something. A question about something, that was about something else, but I wound up casting my eyes down to glance at the dog instead. My head grew hot. My skin ran cold. Another time, maybe.

"Thank you, sir," was all I left him with.

***

When I finally got home, I would find the entire eye pink, swollen, trying in vain to stay open against the constant twitching.

I spent the rest of the afternoon with my sketchbook in my lap, the book of anatomy from Nick at my side on the couch. I followed the directions to the best of my ability, the guiding circles and ovals that made up the head and muscles of the androgynous monstrosity that I was trying to make presentable. There was no clear idea in my brain I was working toward, which would always be my downfall in drawing people. No goals, no images. I was so accustomed to following the freeform path I always had.

Eventually, I gave up on it all and went to my room. As I stood, I felt an ache in my bones, the kind of creaking discomfort that latches onto you in the midst of a flu. "Damn," I said, looking at my bed. I really hoped I wasn't going to be sick, I thought. I considered the bed for a while, and as my eye twitched shut again and flared up with pain, I felt my nose begin to tickle with the hint of a sneeze. All of a sudden, I was exhausted, and shivering despite a light sweat that was forming on my forehead.

At that point, I didn't have much of a choice but to go to sleep. I crashed into the bed and wrapped myself in my blanket, desperate to quit feeling so cold. The first sneeze was violent, and I felt it shred at my throat. It was not long before I became hazy, unable to fight the sneezing fit, but too weak to continue it all the same. I faded into the dark, as my body shivered against the fever.

***

All of Elkwood can be seen from the top floor of town hall. Standing on that hill, overlooking the town, it all seems so small. It doesn't seem like so many people could live in this little place, nestled in the woods. And true enough, many of my classmates were Fairweather or Robertsville, but the amount that were locals dwarfed them. I leaned against the windowsill and stared out, pinpointing my home, just a quick sprint from the edge of the wood.

"Do you think it's going to be easy?" Nancy asked me. I looked to my right at her. She was at once looking at me and out into the town, shifting back and forth quickly, nervously.

"Probably not," I said. I was cold, I realized, and pulled Nancy to me. She wrapped her arms around me, and I felt her lips graze my neck.

Nancy's body was heavy and warm, and helped with the goosebumps that were spreading across my back and arms like weeds. I held her close and sighed as the town outside was met with thunder— a lightning bolt raked across the graying skies and found purchase on a streetlamp, turning it a bright, shimmering blue, and in destroying it, snuffing out the light of the town. No, this would not be easy, I told myself.

Against my desires I pushed Nancy off me. "I love you," she said. "I'll always love you, Ben."

I considered it with a cock of the head. I was already walking away, but I eventually found it in me to say, "I love you too."

Outside, it was snowing, and I was without a jacket or shoes. Just me in a shirt and sweatpants, walking along the ice of Elkwood, breathing in the frosty air. Out here, I matched the cold, and it ceased to bother me so much. It became warm, even. I sighed against a wind that tickled my nose, the scent of winter sinking its teeth into the hairs of my nose.

"Are you ready?" I called out into the town. The snow was blanketing my vision, veiling me from making out more than a subtle shadow, running from me. "I'm going to keep counting!" I yelled.

And I did. "Six… Seven… Eight…" I counted, but my eyes were not shut. I was actively searching in the fog. "Nine… Ten… Eleven…"

A snowball struck me, and I heard Nick laughing. He was somewhere close, but I spun and lost track of where the snowball came from. Justin was shouting somewhere nearby as well. "It's not my fault, Bette! He went off on his own, now he isn't coming back! Just come with me!" I knew in my heart that he was lying to her, that Freddy wasn't coming back because of something Justin had done. I couldn't tell her, though. That was against the rules. You have to follow the rules, or you have to start over.

"Eighteen… Nineteen… Twenty!"

Finishing the count, I saw the woods, finally, in the summer sun now. I saw Freddy leaning against a tree, a deep cut across his forehead where something had clawed or bitten him. He raised a hand up to me. "'Sup Ben? You coming?"

"Found you," I said.

Freddy looked at me in terror. "Fuck," he said. He was having a seizure, I knew in an instant, as he fell to the ground, tremors vibrating him from head to toe.

"Babe, get up," I heard Nick say. Nick wasn't there, though. He was still hiding. I needed to find him, but next round, Freddy was it.

There was only one place that anyone could be hiding. Elkwood was too open, too small for there to be anywhere decent to hide. I stepped over Freddy, whose mouth was leaking blood as quickly as the cuts across his face. I left him behind and entered the woods.

"You can't find me," I heard Nick taunt from somewhere beyond my vision. There were so many trees overlapping, and they were alive, aware of the game, in league with the hiders waiting to jump out at me. The trees shuffled when they thought I couldn't see them, making oaken walls that obscured both the way forward and the way home. It didn't matter. I was seeking, I'd find what I needed to here.

All around, I began to hear them, the shrieking howls of the coyote pack. I knew that if I saw them, they would kill me, so I shut my left eye, which was twitching, aching, and focused with my right. If I encountered the undead, it was over. I'd be skinned, my head mounted on a wall, my meat chopped up and donated to a shelter, where it would cause the worst salmonella outbreak in the last century.

This did not mean I was not allowed to use the howling to my advantage. Where the howling went, the dead children followed, and if no one had found Nick by now, then surely he was dead, and I'd be able to point at him, say, "Found you!" and move on to finding Justin before something terrible happened to him. He had more time than Nick, that was a rule somebody had made, I was positive of that much.

Through the traitorous trees I continued my march forward, calling out, "Come out, I'm going to find you sooner or later!" My throat was growing raw from the yelling, so soon I was whispering it, and my whispers were drowned out by the coyotes, who were nipping at my heels, urging me deeper into the shadow. Their pack leader, the hungry, lumbering beast, waited further behind, urging their howls with ones of its own. Thatcher could mimic them with the best, he knew wildlife better than anyone.

When the coyotes grew tired of their song, they retreated, repelled by the light that I had found. For a moment I thought it was Nancy, walking forward from the forest fire, her eyes matching the backdrop eerily as the moon glowered down. But then, the fire went from red to blue, to just barely white-yellow, the color of moonlight on a lake. I decided this was Nick I was looking at.

"You're too far away from home," Lucy said, and shook her head at me in disapproval. "Your parents will be looking for you."

"That's okay," I said. "I just want to play one more time. I'll go home before it gets dark."

Lucy walked over to me, near-blinding in her luminance. I squinted as she touched my face. She was smaller than I remembered. "Ben, you're going to get lost if you stay out here. You need to go back home."

I shook my head now. "No, I found you, it's your turn to seek."

She wrapped her arms around me, and I felt the cold strike me from head to toe. The grave breathed toxic fumes over me, and Lucy pulled me from the ground to my feet, urging me to get up before I got lost.

"Lucy," I said, stumbling as I held her hand. The street was nowhere in sight. This was a shortcut home. "I'm sorry, I'm really sorry, Lucy."

"Stop," she said. "It's time to go home."

"I lied, Lucy, I counted faster so I could beat you home," I said through tears. My head was pounding. The howling was different now.

From the fever dream I awoke in my bed, shaking, sweating, tears soaking my face and pillow. It was night outside my window, which had been left open a crack, letting in the rolling, frost-tinged air of winter. I was alone, but I could hear my parents talking outside my room. A glass of water was left on my bedside table.

I sat up, continuing to shake as I waddled from my bed to the window, wrapped in my blanket. Outside, I could see the edge of the woods, and beyond the treeline, only an endless expanse of darkness. I shut the window, and against my fears of dreaming something like that again, I collapsed into bed once more.

***

The dreams caused me to backpedal my quick forgiveness of Justin a bit. While none shook me as badly as the first— I was expecting them now —they did not quit plaguing my sleep during the illness. There was no rest in sleep, and yet I couldn't do anything else as my body and mind were exhausted. I was trapped in a cycle of bizarre nightmares punctuated by sweaty disorientation.

My mother did take time off work to take me to a doctor, at least. Of course, when you're showing symptoms of five different illnesses and yet test negative for each one, doctors usually give you the blanket diagnosis of "virus" and send you home with only a bill and an urging to take ibuprofen to stave off the fever. We followed these instructions as best we could, but with how ragged my throat had become, it had become difficult to even swallow plain, cool water. Taking pills with it was a daunting task.

Even as I cursed him for sneezing on me, why did it have to be me? I sympathized with the fact that Justin looked, even on that first day, worse than I felt, and did find it in me to forgive him again, though not without a day of silent, bitchy brooding over how utterly pissed I was to be in this situation.

Of the group, Justin, Bette, and I were the only ones to come down with the mystery illness. The night after the sneezing incident, Bette had been taken by the same fever and dreams I had. Obvious, how she might've become infected, but then there was an outlier who no one could determine how he wound up sick, too. While some kids at school also picked up milder forms of the disease, Freddy's dad coming down with it was a head-scratcher. No one could figure it out. Freddy himself didn't get sick, and Fairweather wasn't hit nearly as hard as Elkwood was by what had been so cutely named, "the weird flu."

Justin was stricken for the longest and hardest, the curse of being patient zero, I guessed. Bette called me when we were both in the gentle, uncomfortable recovery period, clawing our way back up the pile of tissues and sweat-stained pillows. She told me Justin's parents were worried out of their minds, as he barely woke up, and when he did, all he could manage was shallow, pained breathing as he sipped at the water and soup they tried to sate him on. Apparently, he did a lot of gibbering in his sleep, but his voice was so weak and strained his parents couldn't tell what, if anything, he was saying. I imagined what Justin might be dreaming: what horrific abomination of a coyote would be chasing him through the woods, what shrieks of Tommy Barnes might be overlaid into the howling of the beast who just wanted one more taste of Justin's blood.

Returning to school seemed impossible. My head had started pounding away, brought on when I was able to stay awake for more than six or seven hours in the day, a result of the dehydration and excess sleep my body had gone through. Even as I forced water to slip past my scar-swollen throat, I felt little rejuvenation, only the continued bone ache of the "virus" dragging me down.

Eventually, I did have to return to school, though. The pile of excess work I'd accumulated in my illness was too frustrating for me to manage, so I took that six days' worth of assignments and half-assed them to the best of my ability, deciding any score would be just a little better than a zero, but unable to force myself to catch up. My head was killing me. The words were swimming before my eyes.

Bette and I had come back, but Justin was still sick. Everyone was watching Bette with expectant eyes, wondering if she might give us an update, good or bad, but she never brought up the subject. It was, of course, Nick who did that, as he slid into his chair and patted the one beside him for Freddy to sit down as well.

"So, Ben, how's the eye? You see everything green now?"

"Will you shut the fuck up?" Freddy said, popping his carton of milk open.

I was only half-there, still sore in my neck and brain. I glared at Nick, and made a jerking motion with my head, like I was about to sneeze. He shoved himself backward, sliding at least five feet from the table, and prompting the staff supervisor to shout, "Mr. Lauer!" at him.

Nick apologized to them and scooted back into the table, giving me as good of a glare as he was getting. "That's not funny at all," he said.

Raspy, groggily, I said, "I think it's hilarious."

"That's your problem, Ben," he said, "you never take anything seriously. I know when something is over the line."

"Oh, shut up," I said, chuckling. I was leaned over the table, staring down at my food, too solid to consider eating at anything resembling a normal pace. Nancy rubbed my back, and I felt some of the tension in me release under her touch.

Freddy took a sip of his milk before saying, "My dad's got it pretty bad, too. I've never seen him sleep past six in the morning before. He's been in bed until I get home from school pretty much everyday."

"Jesus," Nancy said. "Is he getting better at all?"

Freddy shrugged. "I guess. I don't know, he's been moving around a bit more the last day or two, but I think he'd be getting better faster if he would quit drinking for a bit."

"God damn," Nick said. "Sarge is still chugging beers when he's that fucking sick?"

"No wonder he's in bed so much," I croaked. "Water barely even goes down for me."

"You should probably be at home," Nancy said.

"No fever," I said, though I agreed with her. "Means I get to be here. I'm probably not contagious."

"Probably?" Nick said. "Don't you ever joke about a sneeze again."

I gestured the same as before, and this time Nick did not scoot away. He only stared at me, pretending he wasn't amused with a defiant glower. I kept staring at him, lightly sniffling, until he cracked a smile. "Yeah, whatever," he said.

Bette sighed and poked at her food. She looked better off than me, oddly enough. She said her fever never quite hit the heights mine did, but she did have the same sore throat that was keeping me hungry. She took a bite of the meager mound of chocolate pudding in the little styrofoam bowl on her tray, which seemed to go down easy enough.

I reached out and touched Bette's arm. "We all miss him," I croaked.

She set her hand down on top of mine for a moment. "I know. I'm just worried. He's never been this sick before."

I nodded, not having a response to that. "He'll be okay," Nancy said next to me. "I'm sure he'll be back by next week."

Chapter Nine
The Edge of Spring

Justin was, in fact, back next week, to my surprise. The way he had been described to me made it seem like he could be out a month, or more. Some kids had gotten mono freshman year and were out of school for a month. Though, this wasn't mono, of course, because then Bette and I would have had it, too.

Looking at Justin, he could have fooled me. He was even thinner than usual, with deep, dark circles around his eyes. His skin was about the color of old wallpaper in a smoker's house, which I presumed was because, like me, he'd been drinking about a tablespoon of water a day for the last two weeks. His eyes were bloodshot as well, and I wondered if that was from the dehydration, or if he'd been having trouble sleeping. The dreams weighed on the back of my mind. It wouldn't surprise me if he had.

Of course, Justin always said very little, so his silence throughout the first few days would be no indicator of his health, but looking at him, wordlessly staring into his notebook in class, neither writing or reading words on the page, I felt a mix of discomfort and pity. Whatever had gotten him had gotten him bad. Maybe it was mono. Maybe Bette and I were just lucky.

The lunch table conversations were always made while side-eyeing Justin, who neither nodded approval or "Hm"'d disdain. It was an eerie sort of feeling, looking at him, wondering sometimes if he could even hear us. Of course, he did, because if we spoke directly to him, he'd answer, in a voice that very closely resembled his despite the hints of pain laced through it. Each answer he gave was slow, and his eyes were dreamy and distant, as if he was talking in his sleep.

One day, leaving Algebra II, which I took with Freddy, I said, finally with my throat nearly clear of the gravel it had been coated with, "Is your dad doing okay?"

Freddy tilted his head side to side, miming so-so. "Sarge is tough, but he's also a bit of a stubborn dick when he wants to be," Freddy said. He glanced around, looking to see who was around to hear. "I don't think he was nearly as bad as Cross, though. He looks like a fucking zombie, man."

I nodded. "I mean shit, I want to help, but I honestly think the only way he could get better is if his parents let him stay home."

"Or the school," Freddy agreed. "But they get in trouble with truancy shit."

"He's sick, though," I said. "But I get why he'd wanna be here too. I'm still kinda lost on the shit I missed."

We reached Freddy's locker, where he began unloading his textbooks from the first two periods of the day. "Cross is probably the smartest person in our group, but I wouldn't wanna be that behind, either. I don't know if it's all his choice though. You know how his parents are, right?"

I didn't know exactly, but I had an idea. "Bette's told me a bit. Nancy's told me whatever she knows."

"They're pricks, man. They barely look out for him." Freddy pulled out his third period textbook, US History, which he had with Justin and Nancy. He closed his locker, a bit harder than I expected. "My dad isn't y'know, lovey-dovey or shit like that, but he's paying attention, even though he's still stuck in bed half the day. I mean he notices everything, if I'd gotten..."

"Yeah," I said, thinking about the bite. Would the Crosses have realized Justin was hurt at all if we hadn't prompted him to tell them? I began following Freddy toward the junction in the hall, where he'd go left and I'd go right, like we did everyday.

Freddy grunted. "If we could make them keep him home, it'd be great, but otherwise, I don't know what's gonna happen to Cross, because he genuinely looks like he could drop dead any second."

I considered this, as the junction grew closer. "Fuck," I conceded.

"Yeah, fuck."

We reached the junction and Freddy turned to me. "Whatever happens, we gotta look out for him, because we're all he's got." Freddy clapped me on the shoulder. "He'll probably be fine."

"I don't love probably," I said.

"Probably's what we've got. Catch you at lunch." And with that, he marched off, up the stairs to the third floor. I looked to my right, down my hall, where the stairs led down to the ground floor.

"Fuck," I repeated, and descended.

***

Justin's recovery was a long struggle that stretched into February, his body too-slowly regaining his normal pale complexion rather than the haggard yellow one brought upon by the virus. He eventually regained his mannerisms, his old nods and head shakes and "Hm"s. We found ourselves set at ease somewhere in the process, but everyone maintained a small sense of discomfort and anticipation all the way to the end.

I remained a week behind throughout the recovery period, only just catching up with my classes by the back end of January. When Valentine's Day came around, finally both my schoolwork and Justin's condition had been improved to an acceptable level, though Justin's eyes still had dark, exhaustive circles surrounding them. Without a cough or fever to warn of contagion, Justin had started hanging out with the full group outside school again.

We decided a triple date to the diner in Fairweather, a red-neon-signed place called Abe's with a generally miserable looking staff, was as good (and affordable) as a dual celebration of Justin's health and the holiday could get. Thankfully, we did not all have to squeeze into Freddy's truck as we would be doing a month later, as Bette was newly licensed and drove herself and Justin while Nancy and I rode with the Fairweather boys.

I was sucking down a soda and watching Nick and Freddy see who could tie the stem of the cherry from their milkshake in their mouth faster. Nancy had her hand on my thigh, her head on my shoulder, and Justin and Bette were silently, calmly eating their cheeseburgers.

Freddy plucked the stem from his mouth, tied into a neat, tidy knot, and showed it to Nick. "Easy," he said.

Nick shook his head and spat his out stem into his hand. It was chewed and ugly, but in something that may have nearly been a knot. "Whatever, you've got Boy Scout training," Nick said.

"You've got nothing to prove to me," Freddy said.

"Oh shut the fuck up," Nick said, flicking the stem like a booger at Freddy. Freddy quickly slapped it away.

"Don't make a mess for the waiter to clean up," Bette said, glancing over at the lone waiter. We were just about the only ones in the whole diner, save an older woman in the corner in a thick scarf.

The waiter was maybe only a little older than us, seventeen or eighteen. He looked tired and greasy, like maybe he had this full shift right after a P.E. period at his school, if he went to school at all. I didn't recognize him. The nametag on his red-and-black striped button-down read "Cameron." He regarded us with a bit of distance, like because we were not kids he recognized, he could not be a kid either, he was just a worker. It was perfectly normal, and yet it gave me a bit of the creeps. Still, he was a pleasant enough server, and filled our drinks regularly throughout the evening. I gave him a decent tip when we left.

Nick shrugged and snatched up the stem from the floor where Freddy had batted it to. This seemed neither to please or bother Cameron, but Bette nodded in approval, followed shortly after by Justin. When Nick returned to his seat, he put his arm around Freddy and leaned into the table, speaking to the whole group.

"Alright so," Nick said, raising his eyebrows to call attention, "Thatcher's got something to ask everyone while we're all here."

We all looked at Freddy, who had been forced forward into an uncomfortable position by Nick's arm. He straightened himself, bringing Nick with him, and said, "So Sarge is better, for the most part. And Cross is looking a lot better, too. And Sarge said to kinda celebrate everything being safe back in your town and he and Justin feeling alright, he wants to take us camping over spring break."

Nick looked thrilled at the idea. Justin gave a nod, albeit a slower one— he was still complaining when he did speak about some lingering stiffness in his neck. Bette and Nancy didn't seem as stoked about the idea, though Nancy didn't look unhappy. Bette was the first one to say anything.

"I don't know," she said, her glasses slipping down her nose as she did, causing her eyes to shrink suddenly. She pushed them back up and continued. "I feel like me and Ben just got better and Justin's still pretty sick."

"Oh, come on," Nick said. "Spring break's over a month away, Justin will be fine by then."

"He said we could also push it to summer, but Nick is starting a job at his dad's store in the summer, so... y'know," Freddy added.

"I mean, I could skip a week," Nick said. "But come on, we'll all be doing shit in the summer, but we'll be doing fuck all in spring."

Justin nodded again. "I'm sure I'll be good by spring break," he agreed. "And in summer, who knows who will be working or busy then. I might be going to stay with my grandparents for like a month, too."

Freddy leaned back, as he spoke, prompting Nick to withdraw his arm. "I don't have a strong opinion either way. I like camping. Don't know if y'all do. Or if you've ever been." The last comment seemed particularly addressed to me.

"I think once, when I was like four," I said. "But after... y'know. There was never a situation where I would've gone."

"I haven't," Nancy agreed. "But I wouldn't mind it if Ben's going." I couldn't tell by her tone if she thought I would be saying yes or not. I thought about it. It sounded kind of fun.

Nick looked at me. "Ben, you're a night owl like me now, you know you wanna. Look outside, the sun's down, you freaking out?"

I smirked. "No, I'm good. It sounds fun, but I don't know. It's still kinda weird. It's not the same as being here or in Elkwood."

"Hence why it's awesome." He leaned in again, and loudly whispered, "Sarge might let us shoot his gun."

"Christ, Nick," Nancy said.

"I'm just saying it would be fun!"

"Not a chance in Hell do I want to shoot Sarge's gun," I said. "But... maybe it would be nice. Plug that last little crack in the whole nighttime anxiety."

"Attaboy!" Nick said, turning to Nancy. He cocked his head expectantly.

"I did say if Ben was going I would," she conceded. This pleased Nick. "Will me and Bette get our own tent though?"

"I will do you one better," Nick said. "All the couples will get their own tents, and Sarge will get one of his own."

"Seriously?" Bette asked. "Freddy's— Sarge —is just fine with that?"

Nick mocked disappointment in his face. "Bette, would a guy nicknamed 'Sarge' really be so behind the times?" Bette stared at Nick, indulging him no humor. "Nah, Sarge doesn't give a shit. He knows about me and Freddy, too, and was cool enough not to say anything to my dad."

Bette nodded. "I— Well... If you really wanna go?" She looked up at Justin.

"Honestly," Justin said slowly, putting one hand out, a point being made, "I still feel awful. I do think I'll feel better in the spring though. Why not? It'll be something different than what we all normally do." He looked at Bette. "And we'll get our own tent," he added, smirking a bit. Bette blushed a little and shook her head.

"Okay," Bette said. "We'll come."

"Fuck yes!" Nick said, loudly enough that the old woman in the diner actually shot us a look for once rather than ignoring us. "See, Thatcher, I told you they'd do it."

Freddy shook his head. "Yeah, whatever. I didn't think Ben would want to."

"I don't blame you," I said, though I was a little hurt that it was me who was the point of contention. I really couldn't blame him, though.

"Either way," Nick said. "Get pumped. We might even get to do a little target practice if we're lucky."

***

The weeks went on by in a slow wave, one that all blurred together into a slushy, gray color as we all anticipated— for better or worse —the coming trip out beyond the trees. School was an oppressive overlord that held time hostage; those final few weeks, as we waited, seemed to last twice, and sometimes, quadruple, as long as they had before.

There was but one notable event in that pregnant period after Valentine's Day. See, bullies have an odd code of honor they follow. It's not often they'll strike you at your weakest. They're a bit more insidious than that. They like to let you build yourself back up just enough, to that half-built tower of blocks that teeters this way and that, easy to crash into and break back apart again. Once you're back down, they won't keep kicking over blocks, they'll give you time to regroup, reconsider, convince yourself that you might be able to build just a little higher next time.

It would seem Tommy and Isaac had been eyeing Justin's tower for a while. Tommy never forgot Freddy's warning: he avoided Freddy's purposeful marches through the halls, dropped his gaze when Freddy turned his eyes quickly upon him. And yet, he still didn't ever seem to get his fix on tormenting Justin. He hung around, always looking like a snide comment or easy insult would spring like a frog from his mouth, but always slinked away before they could escape.

Justin's illness had repelled Tommy for a time, as nobody wanted to come down with the weird flu, and once I even heard Tommy say to Isaac that he felt bad for him. It had also hobbled Justin, and even as his strength came back he was still a bit like a wounded deer, limping silently around, oblivious to the traffic coming his way. Once he was in the interstitial stage between fully recovered and just-surviving, on March 2nd of that year, Tommy saw his moment to send Justin's tower scattering across the table.

I was tailing behind Justin that day, not yet caught up to him from rummaging for the next period's textbook in my locker. With a bit of effort and a slight spur in my step I would catch up soon. Then I saw them, closing in like sharks from either side of the hallway. Freddy was in a class on the ground floor; we were on the third. They'd planned the moment well. Of course they knew there would be retribution, but they knew that the rush they'd get was well worth any consequence that may come.

Justin, with his books cradled comfortably on his left forearm, was nearly tall enough that he could be out of Tommy's reach— Tommy had always been the shortest of the boys, even when he ran with me and Nate and Emma in elementary school. The only boy who was just a hair shorter was Isaac. Still, Tommy had learned to spring up and grab and pinch and smack easily, playing basketball throughout middle school and freshman year despite his lack of optimization for the sport. Using his right foot to pop himself off the ground, he came with a shot-blocking swipe that sent every book Justin held thundering onto the ground with a loud slapping sound.

Isaac and Tommy began their laughing, as I started to close the distance between myself and the three of them. Others in the hall had stopped or briskly circumvented the scene. Justin was frozen in place, looking down at his books. I couldn't see his face. "What the fuck, Barnes?" I said as I got closer.

"Oh shut up, dude," Tommy said.

Isaac was about to say something as well, when Justin's hand grabbed the collar of his shirt. "What's your deal?" I heard Justin say in a soft, crackling voice. Something about it sent the hairs on my arms standing up. Justin was still looking at his books.

"Get your fucking hands—" Isaac managed, before Justin jerked his arm, sending Isaac to the ground and sliding along the tile floor. Tommy looked at his friend, and then at Justin, a bit perplexed, but then stepped up as well. Justin was looking at him now, not at the books. Tommy was just quick enough to get off a hearty shove that sent Justin stumbling, just a bit, before gaining his balance again.

Isaac remained on the ground, and I remained just out of the conflict as Justin grabbed Tommy around his neck, rather than the collar. "Hey, Justin, hold on," I said, seeing a bit of fear hit the edges of Tommy's pupils.

As Justin held onto Tommy's throat with one hand, he let his other come swinging, a thin branch in heavy wind, and struck Tommy in the side of the head. He then leaned forward and spoke again in the soft voice, "You deserve everything that's gonna come to you, Barnes. Everything." Tommy was choking. "Leave me alone, and it'll come later. But it's going to happen one way or another." Justin let Tommy go.

"Jesus, dude," Isaac said, on his feet. He came and grabbed Tommy by the shoulder. Tommy was catching his breath in short little wheezes, looking up at Justin as he backed away. "You're a fucking freak, Cross."

Justin said nothing more to them, and began to gather his books as Tommy and Isaac left. Those who had looked on at the encounter were slowly dispersing as well. I carefully walked to Justin's side. "Hey, you good?"

Justin looked up at me, quickly, startling me. Then he nodded, looking very much himself, and the jolt went away. "Just wanted to scare him off," he said, leaving it at that. He continued to gather his books, and we walked together in silence toward the next period.

The fight, if it could be called that, pleased Nick and Freddy to their cores. Freddy was regarding Justin as he and I settled into our chairs with the distant, gleeful gaze of a proud but inexpressive father. Nick was the one who spoke, as was expected.

"Cross, you scared the fuck out of Barnes!" he said, loud enough that the cautious among us (Nancy, Bette, and I) looked around to make sure the staff supervisor didn't hear. Mrs. Litzinger, the senior algebra teacher, was not the most observant. Even us sophomores had heard how easy it was to cheat in her classes. She took no notice of Nick's profanity, and perhaps he was feeling extra bold because he knew her reputation as well.

Justin gave a shrug and poked at the plastic-wrapped cookie on his tray. He had been quiet as ever throughout class, and had hardly acknowledged Bette as he sat down at the table. I wondered if he was more shaken by the situation than he'd let on— back in autumn it had all gotten to him very quickly.

"It was quick," I said. "I barely got there before he chucked Anderson across the room."

"Learned that trick from Thatcher, huh?" Nick said, looking eagerly at Justin. Justin bobbed his head side to side: maybe. "You gotta have something to say, man. Tell us you're going to Disneyland or something."

"It doesn't matter," Justin said. "They were fucking with me. I made them quit." He looked up coldly at Nick, but then softened his gaze as he turned it to Freddy. "I learned a little from Thatcher."

"Attaboy," Nick said, apparently satisfied with this answer. "You two could go into business, chucking around annoying hobbits."

"We could start with you," Freddy said, ruffling Nick's hair. "You're only taller than Bette by an inch or two."

Nick shoved Freddy's arm off. "Watch it, or I'll get Cross to chuck you. You've got competition."

"That so?" Freddy said, flicking Nick's cheek.

Justin gave a, "Hm," and picked up the burger on his tray. He ate it silently as Nick and Freddy's bickering slowly but surely roped Nancy and I in. Even Bette got off a few quips Nick's way. From that point on, the wait for the camping trip was all there was; a bumpy, downhill roll into the valley ahead.

Chapter Ten
Into the Forest

The night before departure, my sleep was neither dreamless nor restful. I was shivering against the cold that was, unbeknownst to me, threatening that late-March snowfall, which would turn the town white one last time before spring truly arrived. In my dreams, too, I was cold. The details remain hazy, no matter how long I spend unpacking the events of the dream. I can only, clearly, remember the end, as I laid just a few yards from Mr. Trellis's home, staring up at the stars.

In the dream, the cold was represented by the soft, but frigid hands of Lucy on my neck. She was stroking along each side, whispering to me that I needed to wake up before it got too dark. It was, in the dream, midnight, and the moon was full and high, so I disregarded her warnings with a relaxed sigh and nestled into the grass.

"Ben, it's time to go," she said. I looked at her, feeding her a concoction of frustration and sadness.

"I don't want to leave," I told her. Her eyes were absent of pupil or iris, just glowing orbs of moonlight, brighter than the thing itself above her. She smiled, but her eyebrows betrayed her disappointment.

"We're okay. You found where we are, you don't have to stay. You can go wherever you want."

I sat up and turned to her. "No. I want to be with you. I'm happy here with you."

Lucy looked up at me. She was still ten, still a small girl. What once might have been a crush, superficial adolescent romance, had become a soft adoration when I looked at her. She was a cute kid, and always would be. I felt in my heart that I needed to protect her. I was bigger now, so this time, I could.

"It's too late," Lucy said. "You have to protect yourself." She considered her next words with a cartoonish, thoughtful look of a child, her fist against her chin, her brow so furrowed that I would believe, were she not see-through and made of light, that the wrinkling of it was hurting her. Finally, she found what she needed to say.

"You know you can only see me because you're sick, Ben. I know you know."

I shook my head. "We were playing hide and seek."

Lucy's eyes became angry, her mouth pouted. She wasn't sure how to get through to me, and I knew that nothing she said would change my mind. We were here together because this was where I needed to be. Coyotes were howling in the woods. I grabbed a stick and readied myself for the fight.

"Stop, Ben," Lucy said.

"I can protect you," I said.

"Ben, look at me." I didn't. I didn't want to see whatever she had to show me. She could show me later, we had all the time in the world. "Ben!"

Against my wishes, I turned my head to Lucy, and saw the horrible thing she wanted me to see. There was no skin on her face. No flesh. Just bones, cracked and scarred in some places. "Stop," I said.

The skeleton spoke, "You have to leave me here, Ben. Run before they find you."

I heard the howling, and turned to face the pack. The lone coyote watched me from the trees, and cackled its hellish barks. I held the stick in my hand, knowing that if it charged me, I could not kill it. It was larger than what Nick had told me. It looked even bigger than Mr. Trellis's bloodhound. It was crowned: what appeared to be grasping branches sat atop its head like antlers.

Laughing as it bounded, the Coyote ran at me, and I swung.

***

I woke from the dream with a gasp that scratched the walls of my throat. I found, again, the window was opened just a crack— I must have forgotten to close it while I was trying to draw by moonlight, stupid of me. The fear of the dream still coursed through me with each nervous tap of my heart. The sun was just barely rising, and I decided it was best to force myself to wake up.

I made my way to the restroom and leaned over the sink, splashing my face with frigid water. My hair was disheveled and knotted in some places. Clear sign I'd been writhing in my slumber, which did not come as a shock. I attempted to wet it and pluck it into order with my fingers to little avail.

A knock on the open restroom door startled me. I snapped my head toward the doorway to find my dad standing there, holding a mug of coffee. "Hey, bud," he said. "Didn't mean to scare you. You doing alright?"

I sighed and shrugged. "Yeah, I think so. I just... I had a dream about Lucy."

Dad nodded, looking down at his mug. He took a sip and said, "I've been thinking about her a lot the last couple weeks, too. Fifth anniversary and all."

Was it really the fifth anniversary? No... the fifth anniversary had passed. Over a week ago. I hadn't even realized. "Wow," was all I could say.

"Come get some coffee and eggs," Dad said. "You're heading off in a few hours."

After more furious wetting and finger-combing, my hair became acceptable and I followed my dad to the kitchen. He was standing at the stove finishing off a pan of scrambled eggs with a generous shake of pepper. A new mug of coffee with just a little splash of milk was letting off light curls of steam in my usual place at the table. I slid into the chair and put three fingers through the mug's handle as my dad plated the eggs.

"You had a lot of nightmares right after it happened," Dad said, sliding a blue plate with half the eggs and a fork upon it to me.

I took a drink of my coffee. "I don't remember them," I said. At the time, it was only a half-truth. Now, I can't remember them at all, but I know I had them. Any kid would, wouldn't they?

"You remember the one you just had?" Dad asked.

"Sort of," I said. "I remember the very end of it."

Dad nodded at this, and looked down at his plate. He took a forkful of eggs and began to chew them thoughtfully. Once he'd swallowed them, he spoke again. "You think you're feeling nervous about this week?"

I thought about it. "Maybe. I don't know." I thought a bit more. "Yeah... I think so."

"I could always call Freddy's dad, tell him you aren't feeling well."

I shook my head. "No... I think I should go. I mean, I want to go."

"Yeah?"

"Yeah. I mean, it's... scary. I still get a little nervous about the dark, and the woods, but having them around makes it better."

"Aunt Katie was a lot like that," Dad said. I looked up at him. He continued, "I had a cat that ran away when I was, oh, eight, nine? I found it about a month later, it had gotten grabbed by a bobcat or something. It messed me up pretty bad, so bad I didn't like going out by the woods because it would make me sick."

"Oh... I'm sorry," was all I could think to say.

"No, it's okay. It's been a long time. But Katie, she used to force me to come with her when she'd go looking for fruit and things that were growing in the bushes. She probably could have gotten us poisoned, honestly... but she was always talking, making jokes, making it easier to handle everything. A little like Nick." I smiled at that. "She helped make all the fear go away." Dad sighed. He looked like he might say something else, but then took a drink of his coffee, a long one this time.

I considered what I might say carefully. We'd never spoken quite like this. The moment felt like it may be snuffed out like a candle if I didn't respond just right.

"Have you talked to Aunt Katie?" was what came of that consideration.

Dad sighed. "Here and there, but not much. She's doing alright, her and Derek. At least, I think so."

I tapped my fingers on the table. "Why... why not more?"

With another sip of the coffee, Dad looked at me, contemplation clear by the slight squint that made the wrinkles I'd been trying not to notice cracking through the corners of his eyes. "Well..." he began, speaking as carefully as I had been. "I think sometimes, good friends, you meet them in times you really need them. I'd known her before then, but I also got closer with her throughout the time after my cat died. And we got closer for a long time after that. You make connections that see you through dark spots, and get even more important as you walk through the light ones.

"Sometimes, though, you have these great connections. And then something happens that affects you both. Neither one of you is ready to feel the pain, and it might hit one harder than the other, but you go through something so horrible that... That just looking at the other person's face reminds you. Until... you don't really recognize them like you did before it all happened."

He took another sip and then set the mug down on the table purposefully. "I think, while I love Kate with *my* whole heart, she lost her heart with Lucy, and she can't bear the sight of anyone or anything in this town anymore. She had to go somewhere far away, and never deal with it again. She'll tolerate me calling, maybe even coming over for a drink around a holiday someday, but she can't bear the sight of me like she could before. I tried to pull her out of there, like she pulled me out when we were kids, but I was too late, I think. The damage was done before the police even told us what happened."

I looked at him, digesting his words, wondering. Something flashed in my mind, looks from the porch or the window, the Luntzes looking... oddly. But instead of thinking on that too long, I changed my train of thought. "Things weren't the same for me, either," I said.

"No, they weren't," Dad agreed. "Nate moved away, and you never seemed to want to be around Tommy or Emma again for too long."

"Yeah," I said. "Tommy's a bit of an asshole now."

"Language," he said, half-earnest, but then smirked. "Yeah, Justin's mom said something about it on Christmas Eve. Shame Tommy turned out like that. But he'll grow up. Everyone does, in one way or another."

I liked that thought. I thought about Nick's loud mouth mellowing with age. It was sort of sad, but I could see him, older, maybe sitting in a booth somewhere, talking on the radio or in a newsroom. He would be waiting for Freddy to come back from his final tour overseas so they could finally talk about adopting a kid, maybe even two. I could see Nancy with her hair professionally styled, writing notes for a magazine article in a small notebook she kept in her jacket. Bette was sitting in a studio apartment in California, the sun setting outside, as she sketched concept art for a show on a large canvas. Justin brought her a cup of tea, in his other hand a file for the court case in which he was the defending attorney; he was good, always to the point. They all were so proper, and I felt proud of them, though their futures were so far away.

"Your friends are good kids," Dad said, patting me on the hand. "I'm glad you found your people."

This seemed to end the conversation. I didn't mind that anymore. Something had been set at ease, the dream now forgotten. I took a drink of my coffee and continued to eat my eggs.

"You all packed up?" Dad asked as I put my now-clean plate in the sink.

"Yep," I said, "I packed last night."

Dad nodded. "Good. Make sure you've got warm clothes when you head over to Justin's to meet them. It's probably going to be cold all week."

***

I walked past the house that the Luntzes once lived in with my duffel strapped dutifully around my torso, bearing the weight of a week's worth of clothes and my drawing materials. The house did not loom as I passed today, it instead watched as every other house did: vacantly.

Dad had been right. Even though I was wearing a jacket and jeans, I felt the cold air swirling around me, nibbling at my ankles like a hungry kitten. I sucked in the crisp scent— slightly staler than it'd been back on Christmas Eve —and marched along, wondering if I was keeping the others long. We had said 10:30 to head out, putting us at the campsite at noon, and it was just barely 9:45 when I'd walked out the front door, but Freddy, ever-disciplined, was an early riser, and thus Nick would be forced to follow, baggy eyes and all. Nancy liked to show up to things early, and had had breakfast plans with her mother and Sandra, hence why she did not accompany me on the journey to the Cross home.

I arrived to find my fears half-realized. I was the last to arrive, but nobody was in any rush to leave just yet. Freddy's truck wasn't loaded with any bags other than his, Nick's, and Justin's.

Justin answered the door for me, seemingly wide awake and in an agreeably chipper (though reserved as ever) mood. He was wearing an Elkwood Antlers hoodie from school, a blood red garment with painted white letters and a deer's antlers splayed symmetrically and powerfully on either side of the text. Inside, Nick was laying half-asleep with his head resting on Freddy's lap. Freddy was stroking Nick's arm politely, slowly, as Nick mumbled to himself. Both had camouflage jackets on, Nick's clearly a bit too big, though not so big it could be Freddy's— it must have been one of Sarge's. Bette was curled into an awkward position on the loveseat, an indicator she had sunken in when Justin got up to answer my knocking. Her hair was tied back in a ponytail and she had a wool headband wrapped around her ears and upper forehead; it was tan and matched the sweater she was wearing. Nancy was in a chair when I walked in but already rising to meet me, wearing a puffy green vest, as well as dark jeans that looked a bit too high end and tight to serve for camping, but I found the view too pleasant to comment on that.

Nancy leaned in and kissed me, blessing my frigid nose and lips with her warmth. She sighed contentedly as she pulled away. "You're freezing. How long did it take you to walk? About the usual amount? Feels like you've been out for an hour."

I smiled. "About the usual," I said. "My window was open when I woke up, though. Let in a lot of cold."

"I told you you need to double check before you go to sleep," she said, pinching my nose with warm fingers.

Playfully I batted the pinch away and caught her in a light squeeze. "I thought I did."

"So, we wanna load up now or you want something to eat?" Freddy asked. Nick was stirring in his lap, starting to notice my entrance.

"I ate before I left," I said. "Are you all ready?"

"Just been waiting on youuu," Nick grumbled, rubbing his eyes.

"Someone could have called. I was up a lot earlier than this. Thought I was a little early, honestly."

"Technically, you are," Nancy said. "I guess we were all just eager to get going. I ate really fast, and you know Mom never finishes her meal, so Sandra got her food to go and dropped me off."

"Sarge likes to get places ASAP," Freddy said, helping Nick to sit upright. "Couldn't help myself."

"Fuck," Nick said in what seemed to be agreement.

"By the time we got here, Cross and Bette were already ready to go."

"I was Justin's wakeup call," Bette said. "His parents are out of town." Justin nodded.

"So, now the question is how we're gonna do it," Freddy said. "Truck's got five seats, so Ben, you might need to have Nancy ride in your lap."

"No complaints," I said.

"I'm fine with that," Nancy said. "How cramped will I be though?"

"Like, pretty," Nick said. "Backseat's not so bad but it's definitely small height-wise."

"That's why I didn't tell Bette to sit on Cross," Freddy agreed.

"If I'm in the middle you can put your legs on me," Bette said.

"Works for me," Nancy said.

We loaded our bags into the bed of the truck, which had the roof put on to keep them from falling out ("No way am I dealing with bungee cables without Sarge," Freddy said). Nancy was using a duffel bag her father had given her: a large, dark, cumbersome thing that was bigger than my bag. Bette had a gray suitcase that looked like a matching piece of a set to a smaller case Justin was using. Freddy and Nick both had big, army green bags that together took up almost as much space as the rest of us combined.

The drive began at 10:17 AM by Justin's truck clock. Thirteen minutes early isn't so bad at all for a group of high schoolers, but that was weeks of anticipation and Freddy's regimented genetics for you. With Nancy settled (a bit slouched) in my lap, her legs serving as Bette's second seat belt, we rounded the road that led to the interstate, and left Elkwood behind for Fairweather.

***

That is, not quite to Fairweather. The camping grounds that Sarge favored were in the woods that spanned between the two towns, past an exit to a state park named for neither. Tall Stag State Park was not particularly well known or interesting on its own. It was that run-of-the-mill type of wooded hiking spot, with park rangers who insisted the homeless could not park their vehicles after 8 PM, but often did not stay at the park past 8:30 to enforce said rule. The exit itself only took twenty-five minutes to get to, just shy of reaching the exit to Fairweather, but once we were off the highway, the long drag of the journey began.

Out here, the woods were dense and tall; as I looked out, seeing what I could around Nancy, I could have believed the trees were ten feet thick and hundreds tall. Oak and birch and pine and spruce all rolled along the hills, over cliffs, hiding sheer drops that would take at least a leg if not a life if you fell down them. It's hard to believe even now that those woods are the very same that spanned all the way to Elkwood. It's all one forest, even if the one I thought I knew seemed so small in comparison.

It was a slow ride up the bumpy road to the campground. We'd make our way to the main area where Sarge was waiting for us, Freddy had told us, then follow him up the road to his preferred spot. Sarge had scoped it out before he came down with the weird flu, and had said it seemed like a good place, but once we got close we'd have to abandon the cars and hike our way to the clearing he wanted to break ground at.

Justin had his head against the window and was peering out, his face obscured from me. He might've been sleeping. It was hard to tell with him, silent as he was. Bette was obviously asleep however, hugging Nancy's legs like a blanket as she snoozed against Justin's shoulder. Nick had been asleep for the first leg of the journey, but was now rattling on about the possibility that we'd be hunting something.

"Really depends on if it's deer season or not, honestly. I didn't really have a calendar to check if it was or not. Do you know?" His question was directed at Freddy, who was silently staring through the windshield as he drove, focused on making the drive as smooth as possible.

"Hm?" he asked, swerving slightly around the remains of a raccoon.

"When's deer season? We gonna hunt?" Nick asked again.

"Season for firearms is in November," he said.

"What? Bullshit."

"Yeah, honestly it was probably illegal when Sarge went down to hunt the coyotes. I don't know when it's actually fine to shoot them. Deer with antlers are late November though."

Nick, dejected, slammed his head against the seat. "That's lame."

"Anything to keep you away from a gun," Nancy said sleepily. She tried and failed to stretch. I caught her before she could sink down between my legs and the driver's seat.

"I think you'd like it," Nick said. "It's exciting, you know it is."

"Absolutely not," Freddy muttered. The truck rumbled as it met gravel. The parking area was not far.

"Thank you," Nancy said over the driver's seat. She looked down at Bette, who was still squeezing her legs. "They're out," she commented, nodding at Bette and Justin.

Quietly, Justin spoke up. "I'm awake."

"Shit," I said. "I thought you were asleep a while ago."

"I haven't slept at all."

"Gonna be tired as fuck once the tents are up," Nick said, reaching to roll down his window.

"It's too cold to have that open right now," Freddy said without looking.

"Come on, man, we're almost there anyway."

"Exactly. So keep the heat in before we're all hiking in the cold."

Nick put his head back again. "Booo," he groaned. "Boooo, Freddy."

I was warm enough beneath Nancy that I felt inclined to agree with Nick for a moment. "Booo," I said.

"I'll turn the car around," Freddy said.

"Booo," Nick and I said again. Freddy began turning the wheel left slowly and dramatically until we stopped, then righted his course and continued forward.

When we crested the hill that opened into the parking lot— which was really a large area that had been cleared and laid with gravel, not exactly a lot in the traditional sense —I was struck with how little cars I could see. Other than Sarge's jeep, there were two trucks of similar era and make to Freddy's, as well as a couple smaller vehicles that were brought by single, lightly-packed campers. On the far end of the parking lot there was a road marked with caution signs, open but advised against, I quickly assumed. It led further into the woods, where the canopy obscured it from the cloudy midmorning sunlight.

We pulled into the parking spot left of Sarge's jeep. I continued to look down the dark road, catching slight flickers of light, what I assumed were beams of light piercing the ever-so-slightly shifting branches. Nick's door came open first, and he fell to his knees in the gravel, dramatically sucking in the flow of crisp air.

"Sweet, fresh air," Nick sighed. The rest of us pulled ourselves from the vehicle, Nancy and I fumbling around to get her out of the car without falling. Eventually she scooted forward, following Bette and Justin out the right door while I went left.

Sarge stepped around his jeep, his boots kicking up dust like a desperado. Smoke rolled from the cigarette below his mustache. "Hard trip, Lauer?" he said. His voice was low, stony from decades of smoking, but oddly tender as well. He reminded me, in some ways, of my dad.

I took him in with the distant curiosity of a child seeing a fireman for the first time. He was dressed in forest-camo fatigues, more intricate and brown-shaded than the ones worn by Nick and Freddy. His coat was a thick, canvas-like, black cloak of a thing, which was zipped up to his scruffy neck. Atop his head was a fisherman's beanie; the small, wooly sort that made my scalp itch to look at. Missing from his face were the sunglasses he'd worn the day he came to town, revealing beneath two baby blue eyes with red rims and thin, branching crow's feet. I absentmindedly glanced down at his legs, wondering what his scars looked like now, then glanced at Justin's hand. He was flexing it slowly, subconsciously.

"No, sir," Nick said, popping up to his feet, stepping into the worst salute any of us had ever seen.

"At ease," Sarge said. He ruffled Nick's hair and then turned to the rest of us. "Drive up alright, kids?"

"Wasn't so bad," Nancy said. She was still straightening out her vest and jeans.

"So, Cross is the tall boy here," Sarge said. His eyes came to me. "You must be Ben, then."

"Yes, sir," I instinctively said.

Sarge offered me his right hand. He was missing the tip of his pinky. "No sir necessary, except from Freddy and Nick." I shook the hand and felt my knucklebones rub against each other beneath his grip. Sarge pulled away and offered the hand to Justin as well. Justin was guarded with the scarred hand, but returned the shake. "Let me see that," Sarge said.

Justin turned his hand over. "I got bit a while back," he said. The scar on his hand was pink and lightning-esque. Sarge inspected it, reading his palm.

"Nasty fuckers, aren't they?" Sarge said. I swallowed a fit of nervous laughter at the concept of a full adult— one of our parents, even more so —cursing. Nancy's hand had flitted up to her mouth, and Bette was holding her mouth shut tight with puffy cheeks, staring wide-eyed at Justin. I met Nick's eyes. He smiled and nodded with palpable enthusiasm.

"Yeah," Justin said as his hand was relinquished back to him."It was scary. I thought it was going to kill me."

"Probably would have," Sarge said, matter-of-factly. Something about that coaxed a laugh out of me, prompting Nancy (giggling silently herself) to elbow me in the ribs. Sarge looked up at me over his cigarette and smirked. "Either way, glad you made it out. Would have been a much sadder trip if it was in memoriam of you."

"Alright, sir, what's the plan?" Nick said. He was shiftily eyeing a large, black case in the back of Sarge's jeep, the type of case that could only mean one thing. I felt a scurry of fear through my chest, followed close after by a bit of something else. Wonder? Excitement? A gun to a teenager is a bit like a magic wand. Even though I'd had no desire to shoot before, when it seemed like it was Nick's ill-thought pipe dream, seeing that case instantly warmed me to the idea.

"Well," Sarge said, taking no notice of Nick's current object of affection, "Figure I'll just lead you all up the road to the spot we can leave the cars." He was referring to the dark road, where the motes of sunlight from before were no longer visible. "Then we'll unload and hike up further into the woods to the little spot I've got picked out. It's a little out of the way, but it's private, so there won't be much outside interference. About as close to being really out in the sticks as you can get."

"Right," Freddy said. "Let's load back up."

"Any of y'all wanna ride with me?" Sarge asked. "Must've been pretty tight all in Fred's truck there."

"Oh yeah," Nick said, already climbing into the jeep.

"God help me," Sarge said. "Well, guess that's good enough. We'll take it slow getting up there."

"Sure thing," Freddy said. He was standing very stiffly, until Sarge's back was turned. Once it was, he purposefully climbed back into the truck, urging us to follow.

The jeep started first, with a strong, powerful stutter of the engine. The large tires had dug divots into the gravel where the vehicle had been parked, and sent clouds of dust just like its master's boots up as it rolled along. With Justin in the passenger seat and I fit snugly between Nancy and Bette, the truck sputtered to life and began to follow the jeep. The taillights of the jeep were crimson, glowing in the shadows of the road ahead. I shifted with a bit of anxiety and put my arm around Nancy as we went in after it, taken over by the darkness.

***

We were led for the first leg of the drive up the road only by the tail lights, cast totally in red as we pushed through the woods. When light finally broke the canopy again, I could no longer see where the road began. We were in deep, and were going deeper. I expected to be a bit more afraid, but once I'd gotten used to the dark, the idea of being far from the exit was no longer quite as frightening. It was even a little exciting.

Finally, we reached a clearing— dirt in its entirety, no gravel in sight. Sarge pulled his jeep into the clearing, giving space for Freddy to park beside him cramped as it was. Both turned their vehicles off, snuffing the lights out, and leaving only the meager slivers of sun that were lighting the forest floor to illuminate our way.

It was still out here, I decided, as we unloaded the luggage from either vehicle. Still in the same way I found the creek behind the old warehouse back home. Peace in the quiet breaths nature was taking, the little chirps of birds and the ruffle of the newly budding leaves caressing each other in the wind. It smelled of pine, and grass, and springtime, even though without direct sunlight the cold was biting at my neck.

The luggage that Sarge brought was split between him and Freddy. Sarge wore a large canvas backpack with a sleeping bag rolled and bungeed to the top, and a metal canteen dangling from a clip at its side. Nick was, to his dismay, not allowed to carry the case in which Sarge's firearms were contained. I saw, with a mixture of relief and disappointment, the case was padlocked, and would surely only be opened by one of the many keys on the intimidating keychain Sarge carried.

All of us strapped with our bags, Sarge gathered us up before him. "So, it'll be about twenty, maybe thirty minutes through the woods before we get to the spot. Then we can take a rest, have something to eat, and then set up the tents. Sound good?" Everyone showed their approval with silent nods.

We followed Sarge into the forest, Freddy behind us to keep us moving and make sure no one fell and got separated from the group. Hiking through the woods was a far cry from walking around Elkwood, hilly as home may have been. It was constricting my legs, making my muscles burn as we crossed the fifteen-minute mark. The ordeal made me feel a shame in being out of shape that had never occurred to me before— I wasn't overly fat or skinny, just average if not a touch pudgy, but I figured so long of limiting my time outside had done a number on my abilities. Not to mention, we seemed to be climbing uphill much steeper than I expected.

When we broke the treeline into the clearing, my chest was burning and I was ready to strip off my jacket. Nick tore into the clearing behind Sarge panting and heaving, though less than I or the girls were. Justin seemed pretty comfortable, though I could see a sheen of sweat above his brow. Only Freddy and Sarge seemed to be particularly unaffected by the trek.

"Pretty good walk, huh?" Sarge said. He had also been dragging a cooler up the way with him. It burned my arms looking at it as he opened it. Inside was packed full with ice, bottles of water, and sandwiches in plastic bags. He started handing out the sandwiches to us as we sat in a semi-circle in the dirt.

Nick, mouth full of ham and swiss, turned to Sarge. "How oog find dis spoh? It's like—" he swallowed, unmuffling himself "—really far out."

Sarge ashed his cigarette onto the ground and took a sip of his canteen. "I like to hike up in this park. It's an old forest, makes me feel connected with it, being so far away from everything. This seemed like a decent area for camping, and well, I wanted to do something for y'all, considering you've all been such good friends for Fred." Freddy looked down, hiding his embarrassment behind his sandwich. I couldn't imagine it— Freddy goddamn Thatcher sentimentally rambling to his father about his odd little group of friends. But then, maybe Nick had been the one who shared everything, always unaware of how much he should really be saying unless it was truly dire he kept his mouth shut.

"It's nice," Nancy agreed. She was taking small, polite bites of her sandwich, listening and honing into the sounds of birds beyond the treeline. "I haven't been very far into the woods back home. I took a walk with my parents once but we could still kinda hear town from where we went."

"There's nothing like the quiet in the woods. Nothing like it at all." Sarge took a long, dreamy drag from his smoke and sighed a hearty cloud into the air.

Justin let out a small hum of agreement. He'd eaten quickly, and now was taking in the forest through sleepy eyes. There were frogs croaking somewhere nearby, more birds fluttering across the branches above. He looked at peace absorbing it all.

"So…" Nick said, glancing over at the case. "We gonna get to do some shooting?"

Sarge chuckled. "Yeah, I think we will. I brought some targets up with me."

"Fuck yeah!" Nick said. He happily began stuffing his face again.

"You sure?" Freddy asked. "Won't the rangers be mad if they hear the shots?"

Sarge shook his head. "Nah. I don't think the rangers care much about what people do up here, long as we're not hunting any live game. Long as we let the wildlife do what it does they ain't gonna bother us any."

"If you say so," Freddy said, seemingly unconvinced.

After lunch, we set up the tents. Four in all, with Sarge's being the smallest (not much bigger than a child's tent) and on the far side of camp from the other three. The three for each of the couples could each have fit another person inside, so they were roomy and comfortable, even for Justin. They were organized in a wide semi-circle around the pit Sarge had dug for the fire we would light in the evenings.

"Pretty good, huh?" Nick said, standing just outside the middle tent, he and Freddy's.

"Not bad," I agreed. Nancy was laying on the ground inside our tent, left of Nick and Freddy's. She had rolled out her sleeping bag, and looked like she could fall asleep at any moment.

Sarge was smoking as he rolled a log into the pit in the middle of camp. He rubbed his eye hard. He looked tired himself, maybe as tired as Nancy. It seemed strange, as I thought of him as this unstoppable machine because of Freddy's stories. Then again, he had been sick for a long time, almost as long as Justin, who was leaning shut-eyed against a tree.

Sarge had also changed into a pair of shorts while he was in his own tent. I could now see the scars on his calf— winding pink streaks and pockmarks. It wasn't just on the back of his leg, either. It was on his shin, ankle, and leading up to his knee. He hadn't just been bitten. He'd been mauled. I imagined how determined he would have had to have been to stay in the woods and patch himself up with how wounded he was and shuddered.

Catching me looking, Sarge smirked. "Yep. Nasty as hell, isn't it?"

"Yeah," I said. I couldn't think of anything else. I saw a flash of teeth in my mind. The barks of coyotes played over in my head.

"A tough bastard, that one," Sarge said. "But I'm alive, that's all that matters."

I nodded, unable to summon any words. Sarge continued about his camp work, and I stared at the log in the fire pit, nervously rubbing at my arm.

"Hey," Nick said, startling me out of my trance. "We're gonna go walk around while it's still light out, you want to come?"

"Yeah," I said. I shook away the thoughts of the coyotes and regained my bearings. That was all done now. "Yeah, that sounds good."

ELKWOOD KIDS

Our walk wasn't too eventful— most of it was careful, shifty stumbling down steep, downhill slopes, the six of us realizing quickly that the only really traversable part of this stretch of woods was the pathway back to where the cars were parked. Freddy was a bit annoyed that his father had picked a spot where they couldn't move around much, but didn't care enough to push the issue once we got back to camp.

Afternoon became evening, and we all settled around the fire Sarge had built as the chill air became biting. Nancy sat close to me as Sarge began to cook dinner. It was a standard camp affair, hotdogs on sticks, but he said he'd be doing a bit more complex cooking over the fire later in the week. We all ate enthusiastically, hungry from the long day even in spite of our earlier lunch, and evening became a dark and moonless night. The entire group decided that we'd be going to bed early tonight, us all being exhausted. Tomorrow we'd get up early to really dig into this trip (and to Nick's elation, the gun case).

This would be the first night that Nancy and I would sleep together. We had nodded off together before, but this was an entirely different feeling. As I laid myself down and she nestled in beside me, wrapped in the sleeping bags we'd carefully zipped together, a sudden and mind-wiping peace overtook me. I felt warm and loved as she buried her face in my chest. I sighed, squeezing her tight, and the sounds of crickets just beyond the walls of our tent lulled me to sleep in just moments.

This would be my last dreamless sleep for many years after.

Chapter Eleven
Targets

The morning that came carried no sunlight. It was before dawn, and I awoke to Nancy's face close to mine. There was an immediate understanding in the stillness of the forest. I pulled her to me.

We made love in the quiet darkness, keeping equally quiet ourselves, and when it was done we laid together basking in the moment, stroking each other's shoulders as the sun began its slow rise. There wasn't any of the panic of normal teenage relations, the need to quickly clothe and scramble to appear innocent. We felt, stupidly, like adults in that moment. Mature. Comfortable.

Once dressed, we pulled ourselves from the tent at around six in the morning. By then, the sun had peaked defiantly over the shade-casting trees. We were the first to gather around the fire pit, and we sat and spoke in hushed tones while we waited for the others to wake up. The early morning was colder than the evening had been, and I shuddered a bit as I waited for Sarge or Freddy to rise and make the fire for us.

It was Justin and Bette who arose first, in fact. Bette's hair told a similar story to Nancy's, but I made no comment about it. Nancy was in the throes of brushing her mess back out, and Bette began the moment she found a log to sit on. Justin's hair was in shambles as well, but he made no move to fix it. He just took a deep breath, and stared silently at the charcoal in the fire pit. He was wearing the jacket Nancy got him for Christmas, but in losing weight (and he didn't have much to lose to begin with) from his illness, it no longer fit him quite as well.

Freddy followed not long after. He was bare-chested at first, but pulled on a tank top as he marched past us and to Sarge's tent. He tapped on the zipped flap and then came to the pit to begin building the morning fire.

"Long night?" Bette asked.

Freddy nodded. "Seems like you all had one too."

"Long morning, really," I said.

"Mm. How long have you all been up?"

"We've been for a while," Nancy said. "Bette and Justin came out fifteen minutes ago or so."

"Not so bad then. I wish I'd woken up sooner. Lauer's gonna be out another hour at least if I don't go throw some water on him."

"Incorrect!" Nick shouted, startling us. He'd emerged from the tent, fully dressed, including his pom beanie. "If I overslept, y'all would've shot every bullet before I got a chance."

"Ugh," Freddy groaned, as he poked at the steadily growing flickers in the pit with a stick.

Nick stomped over to Freddy and gave him a dramatic, Bugs Bunny kiss on the top of his head. Freddy swatted at him as the rest of us giggled to ourselves. "Get excited," he said, plopping down on the ground.

Sarge came out not long after the fire had kicked into a comfortable crackling. He looked more tired than any of us, except maybe Justin, who was still rubbing away at his eyes. The breakfast he handed out was nothing special, I can't remember now what it was. Maybe a granola bar, some fruit snacks? I remember being hungry not long after the meal was finished.

When breakfast was over with, Sarge stood up and sighed. "Alright, who's ready for some target practice?"

The targets Sarge had brought were the kind you see in a shooting range— white backgrounds, with a dark silhouette figure overlaid with white rings to mark the vital points to shoot. Sarge set up five of them, against trees at varying distances. We were standing around the case, looking out at the targets in silence as Sarge kneeled down with the keys to the padlock. My heart fluttered as I heard the lock turn.

Inside the crate, atop foam padding, the dark steel of a bolt-action rifle and a six-cylinder revolver faintly caught the sun. Around the firearms were seven pairs of heavy earmuffs. Sarge began handing them out, warning, "Don't put 'em on until I tell you to. And make sure you listen closely to everything I tell you."

He explained that he'd be raising his hand when he wanted us to take our earmuffs off, and that he wanted all of us to stay behind the crate. Nobody was to take a single step forward while the person with the gun was aiming. (I looked at Nick: he was trembling, unable to look directly at Sarge as he was gushing over the rifle. I assumed he was listening, but that didn't inspire much courage.) Sarge said everyone would get to take three shots with each gun— that would be plenty at least for today.

Sarge demonstrated for us first. He said, before instructing us to muff up, "I'm still a little out of practice. Since that flu hit me I haven't gotten much time in at the range." Once everyone was firmly behind the line and their muffs donned, Sarge aimed at the middle target. I watched his body language— sturdy, calm. He pulled the bolt back, cocking the gun, then, with a deep exhale, he pulled the trigger.

Even through the muffs I could hear the crack of the bullet as it exploded from the gun. The target burst just left of center on its chest: a clean, large hole torn through it. Sarge flicked the safety on the rifle and lowered it. He followed the same procedure for the revolver, aiming it with both hands, producing both a quieter noise and a smaller hole in the target, as thin curls of smoke wafted off the barrel and disappeared into the late morning air.

The demonstration out of the way, we began to take turns. Nick was of course the first to volunteer. He took the rifle into his hands gleefully. As we all returned our earmuffs to our heads, I heard Nick say, "God this is so fucking cool." Then the shot rang out, and he fell backward from the recoil.

Sarge put his hand up and we all removed our muffs. He took the gun from Nick as Nick sat wide-eyed in the dirt, laughing hysterically. "What do you think?" Sarge asked him.

"It's exactly what I wanted it to be."

Freddy and Justin both took their turns, managing to keep their feet planted better than Nick had and having varying but respectable accuracies on their marks. When it came to me, I looked the rifle up and down, and a wave of discomfort struck my stomach. "I think I'd rather just shoot the little one," I said.

Sarge nodded. "That's alright."

The girls both declined a turn with the rifle as well, and when the revolver came through, Bette declined her turn with it. Nancy fired her shots shockingly well with it, landing a headshot on both of the leftmost targets and a chest shot on the one in the middle. I let the other boys take their turns before me. Nick struggled to hit any meaningful point on his targets, but at least all three bullets hit the paper. Freddy was a crackshot, hitting three separate targets right in the heart. Justin declined to shoot this time.

I stepped up with the freshly loaded revolver now, and waited for Sarge to give me the go ahead. I chose the middle-right target, one that hadn't seen much action save for a hole in its bottom-left corner from Nick's turn. Following Sarge's example, I took a breath with planted feet, and squeezed the trigger as I calmly exhaled.

Recoil vibrated my arms down to the bone, and the gun kicked up in my hands. I'd been aiming for the chest, and as I caught my bearings, I saw that that had been a good call. There was a clean hole directly between where the target's eyes would have been.

I lowered the gun, trembling. It wasn't a bad feeling— just an overwhelming one. My finger retreated from the trigger slowly, flattening against the side of the cylinder as I let vibrating air escape through my gritted teeth. I could just feel the warmth of the barrel, not hot enough to burn, but obvious against my skin.

"Nice fucking shot, Ben," Freddy said.

"No shit," Nick agreed. "You fucking killed him."

The culmination of emotion began to retreat, and I regained my bearings with a shaky chuckle. "I don't think I'll ever hit a shot like that again."

"One in a million," Sarge said. He was smiling, nodding, but I couldn't see his eyes behind his sunglasses. "You gonna take a couple more, then?"

I did, neither of which were as impressive as the first one had been. One in the shoulder, the other in the gut. It was a little unfortunate that I didn't end on the high of my first pull, but Nick and Freddy were still gushing about it, quelling my disappointment quickly. By then, there had been a slow roll of clouds crept stealthily over the afternoon sun, and the area around us was cast with a peaceful gloom.

Sarge packed the gun case back up and led us back to the campsite, mentioning he wanted to get a tarp over the fire so the pit wouldn't get too wet. He muttered something about "damn weatherman," as he hadn't been counting on rain. That was the curse of eastern Missouri, of course. Predicting the weather was always just an educated guess.

***

When evening came, there was still no rain. Sarge had set to work on making a meal on the cast iron pan he'd brought— a large, intimidating cooking implement that he mounted over the fire and repeatedly warned us not to touch under any circumstances. Stirring together sausage that had been kept cold in the cooler and a can of beans, what Sarge described to us was something he called "cowboy stew." It was supposed to be warm and filling, which sounded pretty damn good as the lack of sunlight sent tremors of cold through us.

"Anyone want a beer?" Sarge asked. I looked around, seeing Nancy, Bette, and Justin as confused as I was.

"Yep," Freddy said, and walked to the cooler.

"We can drink?" Justin asked.

"Fuck yeah you can," Nick said. "Toss me one, Thatcher."

Freddy threw a brown bottle underhand at Nick, who caught it and then opened it with his teeth, a sight that sent a shiver of sympathetic pain down my jaws and back. "You want one?" Freddy asked me, pointing.

I shrugged. "Sure, why not." Freddy threw me a beer, followed by the bottle opener he knew I would need (once he'd cracked his own bottle). Justin declined but both the girls asked for one. I passed the bottle opener around as dinner was served by Sarge.

The food was warm, and I found myself sitting comfortably in spite of the cold. Nick and Freddy were doing their usual half-earnest bickering, Freddy intermittently squeezing Nick in a tight hug, prompting a strained squealing from Nick before he continued his verbal barrage. I had my arm around Nancy and was talking with her about her plans for the summer. She was going on a vacation and her mom had asked if I wanted to come. It was exciting, but scary, and I didn't know what to say. Where we were right now was the furthest I'd been out of Elkwood without returning later the same day.

Before I could answer, Sarge exclaimed, "Ah, shit!"

"What's up?" Freddy said, as we all quieted down and zeroed in on Sarge. Sarge was looking through the cooler, shaking his head.

"Ah, I left one of the bags with the food for the rest of the week at home. Shit."

"Damn, do we need to pack up?" Nick asked.

Sarge tapped his foot. "No. I don't know. That'd sure suck, wouldn't it?"

Freddy said, "Like yeah. But we need food. If we have to go we have to go."

Sarge looked around. I felt a pang of disappointment in my stomach. I was actually having fun. The dark wasn't bothering me at all, even being so far into the woods. I wasn't ready to go home, not so soon. And then, Sarge said, "Would y'all be comfortable staying up here?"

"What do you mean?" Nancy asked.

"I know my way around here. I could head down to a convenience store and pick some stuff up if y'all are okay staying up here while I'm gone. Since it's dark and steep I probably wouldn't be back until after midnight."

Freddy looked skeptical. "You wanna hike up that trail in the dark? Alone?"

"I'll be fine, Fred. It's up to you all if you'll be fine, though."

Justin spoke up first. "I think we'll be okay."

I didn't like it. But I also didn't disagree. It might be a little scary being out here without an adult, but the idea was also kind of fun. "Yeah, we'll be alright," I said.

Steadily, everyone but Freddy offered an agreement. He looked at his dad with a hard, flat-mouthed stare, the kind he gave us when he first sat down at our lunch table almost two years ago: uncertain. Finally, however, he sighed. "Just be careful, Dad."

"I will," Sarge said.

Sarge began preparing for the trek back to the cars. He loaded up his bag with his canteen and some clothes, but didn't appear to be taking much more with him other than a flashlight. Once he was packed up and his boots were laced tight, he began fiddling with his keyring, and from it he unfastened the key to the gun safe. "Just in case," he said.

Freddy took it from him. "Alright."

We all waved as Sarge set off into the night. The six of us were now alone in the dark as the fire flickered. Freddy chugged his beer and started on another. There didn't seem to be a shortage of those.

Alone, we began chatting and drinking like we had on many days back in Elkwood, Nancy telling us all about the things she'd heard about people in school, particularly the ones we didn't get along with. Justin had put the fear of God into Tommy, and apparently he and Isaac had been getting picked on themselves by a few of their old victims: squirrelly, nerdy kids who no longer felt like they had to be afraid of the big bad wolves. Justin was reluctant to revel in it, but smirked a bit and nodded as we all toasted to him. Nick was four beers in, and as he had been drinking less, his tolerance was down, and he was getting very tipsy— and loud.

"I love you, man, I don't think you understand that," he said, clapping down on Freddy's shoulder.

"I think I do," Freddy replied.

"No, no, like you're like, fucking—" he burped "—hot, Thatch-cher."

"Thank you," Freddy said, shaking his head and smiling uncomfortably.

"And you're like nice as shit, or whatever, you know. You take care of me. You take care of all of us. You fucking—" burp "—threw Barnes over the table… you make sure we all feel safe. That's why you're so good."

Freddy shook his head. "Nah. We should have gone with my dad."

"No, no, no," Bette said. She was drunk too, her cheeks flushed beneath her big glasses. "We're okay, we've got the big gun."

"We've got it!" Nick agreed.

"And, you're fucking strong, and Ben and Justin are pretty strong too."

"Hey!" Nick said, looking at her with fluttering eyes. "I am strong too."

"Pfff—" Bette spat. "You're fine."

Nick flexed his muscles. "I can beat Thatcher's ass no p-roblem."

Freddy lightly pushed Nick, sending him into the dirt. "We'll be fine. I'm worried about my dad, too though."

I was only on my second beer, but I was feeling a bit of the fuzziness creep in. "He's like a badass, though, right?"

"I guess," Freddy said. Then, reconsidering, he admitted, "Yeah, he is. It's still scary to be out in an area like this alone at night. It's a sharp drop if he trips, and there's no daylight."

"Or phones…" Nancy said in a quiet voice.

"Or phones."

"Still, it's not like he isn't ready for anything," I said. "Even if something were to happen, we'd know if we woke up tomorrow and he wasn't here, you know? We know which way he would have gone, where to look for him."

Freddy nodded, but he seemed unconvinced. Nick sat up beside him and gripped his head. "Hey," he said, looking up at Freddy. "Fucking quit it."

"Quit what?" Freddy said, shooting his eyes down at Nick.

"Being so… mopey. You're being a little—" this time a hiccup came "—bitch."

"Bitch," Bette agreed, lolling her head to the side, resting it on Justin's shoulder. "Quit being a bitch."

"Whatever," Freddy said, but he was chuckling.

"Biiiiitch," Bette repeated, and she snuggled deeper into Justin's arm.

"It's probably time to turn in, huh?" I said.

"Probably," Nancy said. She put her hand on my leg.

"Nooo…" Bette said. "We should just hang out and party all night."

"You're falling asleep, B," Nancy giggled.

"Nuh uh."

"Open your eyes."

Bette was quiet for too long, her mouth hanging open for many seconds, before she said simply, "Nope."

"Exactly," Nick said. He pulled himself to his feet, using Freddy's arm for support. He teetered the entire way up. "We all gotta drink more beer."

"We need to save some for the rest of the trip," I said.

"Fucking, no," Nick said. He stumbled to the cooler and retrieved a new bottle, once again opening it with his teeth. "We need to get wasted and have fun before we run out of shit to do out here. Once it gets boring on the fourth day or so we can go into town and get more beer and get really drunk."

"No," Freddy said. Nick chugged the beer, getting it two thirds of the way down before he had to stop, letting out an awful belch that elicited a disgusted laugh from me and the others. Freddy took the bottle from him with ease, and when Nick swiped for it back, he missed and fell into Freddy's arms. "Bed."

Nick took a deep, whining breath and then agreed, "Bed."

"Boo," Bette said. Her voice was nearly inaudible. "Boo, Freddy."

"Go to bed, Bette," Freddy said, setting the beer on the ground and beginning to drag Nick back to their tent. "I'll come put the fire out once he's down and out."

"I'll put you down," Nick grumbled into Freddy's chest.

Justin sighed. "Come on, babe, let's go."

"Noo..." she whined, but stood up with his help anyway. As they headed for their tent, she called to us, "I love you two, goodnight."

"Love you too, Bette," Nancy said as she disappeared into the tent with Justin. Nancy then turned to me. "I love you," she said to me, in a lower voice. Her hand creeped further up my leg. I understood.

"I love you too," I said, and we went for our tent, passing Freddy and telling him goodnight on the way as well.

When Nancy and I finished what we were doing, we half-dressed in shirts and underwear and snuggled into the sleeping bag, listening to the sound of the fire being kicked over with dirt. I had a moment of worry that Freddy had heard us while he was out by the fire alone, but I honestly think he would have said something. I'll never know for sure.

Once again, I told Nancy I loved her, as she pressed her face into my neck and squeezed me.

That would be the last time we slept together.

Chapter Twelve
First Blood

It was in the dead of night when I awoke needing to use the restroom. Nancy's head on my shoulder, her leg wrapped loosely around both of mine, were warm, and my tired eyes screamed against the urge to wake up. Eventually, I could hold no longer, and I lightly shook Nancy awake. She groaned. "Babe, I gotta go to the bathroom," I whispered, and she groaned again while turning over.

I pulled on pants and shoes and stepped out into the night. My t-shirt blew in the breeze. The only sound in the woods as I passed by the other tents was the rustle of branches bowing in the wind. I scanned my flashlight (the same I'd used when I broke into the Huntz home nearly two years prior) along the ground, watching out for snakes or any sharp rocks that could pierce my needing-replacement tennis shoes.

I found a tree a short stint from camp that seemed agreeable to being desecrated and did what I needed to do, all the while blinking against the crust of sleep in my vision. What time was it now? Two? Three? I wasn't sure. I only knew that the stars were bright against the blackened sky, and the moon was a full, hazy eye, looking me over.

The short yelp came like a firework against the silence. It was a higher voice, definitely human, not a coyote or fox or something of the like. I shined my flashlight in the direction it came from as I pulled my pants back up. The crust in my eyes was quickly vacating. My heart began to beat quickly.

Seeing nothing, I followed my light, keeping a mental note of the direction camp was before I set forward. I was worried someone had wandered off and gotten hurt. However, there was a thought in my mind as I crunched (trying not to) through the leaves along the forest floor. What if it wasn't one of the others? What if someone else was trying to lure me out here? But, it was like Sarge said. This was such a secluded spot nobody else would be out here anyway. That set my fear to rest.

I could hear it now. A bit of a struggle in the leaves ahead, beyond another smattering of trees. I slowed my pace even more, but was certain now that someone had come out here and fallen. I considered running back and waking Freddy up, but I had to be sure before I caused a commotion. I continued forward, rounding the last tree to see what was ahead.

Instantly, I was embarrassed. What I saw was Bette, flat on the ground with her glasses on, and Justin straddling her back, one arm around the front of her face. They must have snuck off in the night. "Jesus, guys, you have a tent for a reason."

Justin looked up at me quickly, startling me. His eyes were wide. I heard a crack, and looked down, to see that Bette was biting down on Justin's hand (the one that was not scarred). He shouted and yanked it away from her face. When she looked up, the left lens of her glasses was severely cracked, like a spiderweb.

"Ben, help!" she shrieked, louder than I expected. I began to process things. I realized they were both fully dressed, and Justin was too high on Bette's back to be doing what I thought they'd been. He was bleeding from the hand she'd bitten, but as I looked at his scarred hand, I saw it too was bleeding: a dark, viscous torrent of something blacker than blood.

"What the fuck are you doing?" I asked. It came out dry, small, as my heart and Adam's apple became one in my throat. I thought I might throw up.

Justin's eyes were still wide, and with an animalistic grunt, the very same he'd made when throwing Tommy Barnes across the hallway, he put his bitten hand on Bette's head and shoved her face into the dirt below. She let out a loud sob. She was pleading with me to get him off of her.

Justin's voice came out similar to his own, but it was wrong. The syllables flowed at odd intervals, the pitch warbled. It was like his own speech was pieced together by old recordings of him speaking. "You want to know what grabbed me in the woods, Ben?" My spine turned glacial, as the whispered wind caused my shirt to billow. Justin was smiling, drooling and sputtering as he spoke. "It wasn't a coyote, that's for sure. It wasn't a bear or a wolf either."

"Justin, get off of her," I said. My voice was weak and hoarse. I was about to start crying, I could feel it.

"Do you want to know what did this to me?" Justin's voice wasn't matching his lips, I realized. They were just off, by a millisecond or two. He was panting like a dog. "You'll find out soon. He's almost out of the valley now. For the last hunt."

The moonlight shifted, and became a spotlight over Justin and Bette. I remembered the way the light passed over them at homecoming, and my stomach heaved. I looked down at Bette, who was still sobbing as Justin held her in the dirt. Then, I looked back up at Justin.

"You can feel it, can't you, Ben? You've got him in you, too. You'll feel the call."

Justin had always been a scrawny guy, even before the flu. The moon cast his lankier-still shadow against the ground behind him. He looked like a young tree that would never bear fruit: gnarled, thin, crooked. I made a decision.

When my shoulder hit Justin's chest, I felt something crack beneath the impact point. Justin was not screaming as I rammed him. He was howling. He fell, rolling off Bette as he clamped his scarred hand to his chest, all the while making that awful noise.

Bette was crying as I pulled her to her feet and began pulling her away. I had to get Freddy up. He had the key to the gun safe. If Justin tried to attack her, or any of us again, we'd need protection. Maybe even Sarge was back by now.

"He took me out into the woods— because he said he was s-scared to go alone," Bette sobbed. I was crying too, I realized, the beam of my flashlight hazy as I followed it to where I knew camp should be. "Then he— he hit me really hard."

"It's okay," I said, trembling through my tears. "You're gonna be okay."

"Wh-why did he do that?"

"I don't know, Bette, I don't know."

I couldn't hear Justin howling anymore. I didn't like that at all. The woods were still and quiet again. Was I going the right way, or was I leading us further into the forest?

There were twigs snapping, off far aways from us. My heart was beating so hard I could feel it in my teeth. Bette choked out, "Where'd he go?"

"Shh," I said, and turned my flashlight out.

We were in the dark, and I pulled Bette behind a large tree and squeezed her, trying to calm her down. "It's going to be okay," I whispered. "We need to be quiet." I felt her nod in understanding against my shoulder. Tears were soaking through my shirt, and the night breeze chilled them uncomfortably.

We listened for more snapping of twigs, but I could only hear the trees brushing against each other overhead. "What are we going to do?" Bette whispered. She had gotten her voice under control. I pulled away from her and sighed under my breath.

"I... I don't know. We need to get to camp and wake everyone up in case he tries to hurt someone else. Freddy has the keys to the gun."

"Fuck, Ben, don't shoot him." Her voice wavered.

"I'm not going to. And Freddy wouldn't. But maybe if we had the gun he'd be too scared to try anything."

That was when we heard the gunshot, loud and nearby, that echoed out through the night. It sent my blood running cold all over again. "We need to get back there right now," I said, and turned my flashlight on. Bette was ready to go, and followed closely behind me, no longer needing to be dragged.

We were running back to camp, but I realized that we'd gone much farther downhill than I thought, and getting back was a drag. My ankles were already beginning to protest the incline. When I'd set out earlier, I must not have noticed the slope. Still, I pushed forward, trying not to play over what I thought was happening in my mind. There was a certainty in my head nonetheless that we were about to return to camp to see Freddy standing over Justin's body with a smoking gun. We'd tell him he had to do it, that he would have killed him like he had tried to kill Bette. It'd take years to heal those wounds, and never fully. But at least we'd all be together.

Before we reached camp, we crashed into Nick. He was shirtless, wearing only his pants and shoes and breathing heavily through tears streaming down his face. I whipped the flashlight around and saw Nancy was with him. She was dressed but was carrying her shoes in her hand.

"Holy shit," I said. "What's going on? We heard the shot."

"Where's Justin?" Nick asked.

"Fuck Justin," I said. "Are you okay? Where's Freddy?"

Nick looked at me with his mouth agape and then began to stammer through tears. "He shot him, Ben. He shot him right in front of me."

My mouth went dry. I looked at Nancy. She was crying, too. "What are you talking about?" I asked. "Who shot him?"

"Sarge, Ben. He came back and he came into our tent. He shot Freddy. He shot his own fucking son, right in front of me."

I opened my mouth, a million questions wanting to flood out. All I could manage was, "Oh God."

Then, the scream shredded through the woods.

Oh, looking back, I can see how Justin was willing to concede it was coyotes, but it wasn't. It was something guttural, feral, neither canine or feline. It was something like anger, but more like pain. More like something was starving and just couldn't bear not shrieking. It wasn't like any animal I'd ever heard, but something in me at that moment told me it was human.

All I said was, "Run."

Chapter Thirteen
Ghosts

The trees were coming at us like linemen, attempting to tackle us as we tore forward into the night. I was using my flashlight in bursts, deciding that whatever we'd heard was more likely to find us if we were constantly showing light. Not that we were very discreet anyway.

Nancy had pulled on her shoes as she was running and had started to fall behind Nick and I, the fastest of the bunch. Bette was dragging Nancy by the wrist, trying to give her a boost by yanking her along and letting go as she passed her. It seemed to do the trick, and soon enough we were barreling downhill, somewhere out in the thick of the forest.

I could hear more of that anguished, guttural wailing, but it remained far behind. Perhaps it had gotten distracted, drawn to the gunshot rather than our footfalls. I hoped beyond hope this was the case, that it would put all its attention on Sarge and Justin. Still, I could hear

Justin in my mind, between each of my gasps of air as I sprinted. *"Do you want to know what did this to me? You'll find out soon enough."*

My leg caught a root sticking up from the dirt, and I fell forward, narrowly catching myself with my arms and pushing into a roll, as I began to tumble down the slope. I heard Nancy yell my name, already far behind me.

Nick was chanting, "Fuck, fuck, fuck," as I continued to roll, twigs and rocks nipping at my limbs as the distance between myself and my remaining friends widened. I could feel the sting of open cuts on my body, the burn of dirt rubbing into the wounds. In the dark, without my flashlight on, I was so disoriented I couldn't get my bearings to catch myself on anything, and continued to fall.

Finally, the ground plateaued for a moment, and I came crashing into a heap in a small clearing. My head was swimming, and my lip was freely bleeding. I tried to pull myself up, and immediately had to tuck myself to my left as my dinner came spilling out of my stomach into the dirt. "Shit," I said hoarsely, as my throat burned against the bile.

I could hear the others coming, and no longer could I make out the roaring from our campsite. With some effort, I managed to stagger to my feet, and was shocked to find that in one of my clamped fists I still had the flashlight. I scanned my surroundings.

Trees. Just trees as far as the eye could see. The slope continued even further down— if I'd had just a bit more momentum, I might've continued to tumble until I hit something that would have stopped me harder than the flat ground. All there was around us was sprawling forest, and I had no idea which way I'd fallen. Were we near the cars? If we were, would it matter, if the keys were still with Sarge and Freddy?

It hit me then. Freddy. My mind dramatized what Nick had said. *"He came into our tent. He shot Freddy, Ben. He shot his own fucking son, right in front of me."* In my mind, Sarge was a silhouette, opening the tent slowly and silently. The shadow of Freddy's father stood over him, the only part of him visible being those eyes: vacant, crazed, like Justin's had been. He aimed his pistol and shot Freddy in the heart, just as Freddy understood what was happening.

I began to sob and held my hand over my mouth so as not to be too loud. What was happening? Why? My body trembled, trying to let out a cry of pain that I wouldn't allow. I could see, with my arms up close to my face, that I was, in fact, bleeding freely from several soil-smeared wounds. There wasn't anything I could do about them, so I just left them alone as the crunching footsteps of the others continued down the hill.

When they finally reached me, Nancy immediately crashed into me with a hug. I squeezed her tightly and found the shape of Nick and Bette over her shoulder, blurred by the tears in my eyes. Nick was gripping his hair and panting, and Bette was silent, watching while hugging herself as tight as I held Nancy.

"What are we going to do?" Nick asked. "What the fuck was that back there?"

"I don't know," I said. "Justin said... he said whatever it was was the thing that bit him."

"What the fuck? Did you hear that fucking scream? That thing had to be massive! No way that tackled him and he got away!"

"He told me, Nick. He told me." I released Nancy and looked into her eyes. They were full of tears, but she was blinking them away as she looked back at me. "Are you okay?" I asked her.

"N-no, but… It's fine. We have to figure something out."

"I don't even know where we are, man," Nick said. He was stomping around the clearing.

"Be careful," I called to him. "There's another drop over there."

"This is so fucked up," he muttered. "He just… He just shot him like it was nothing." Nick crashed down onto the ground on his knees. "Maybe he did get bit by whatever that thing was, but why would he shoot his own kid? What the fuck kind of animal is that?"

I opened my mouth, but then I heard the soft sound of a whisper. I couldn't make out what it said, but I clearly felt a voice say something just by my ear. I whipped around. "Did you guys hear that?"

"Yes," Bette said without hesitation.

The moon was not bright tonight. The light that did pierce the forest was faint and ill-defined. But, with my flashlight pointed at the ground, I could make out the beams of the moon rough-sketching the shapes of the trees.

And yet, the light did not stay still. The tree silhouettes seemed to sway and churn, like the moonlight in the clearing was swirling all around us. "What the fuck is happening?" Nick asked, backing away from the treeline and toward the rest of us.

The whisper repeated, followed too-soon by another. And another. I heard, I was sure of it, in the nigh inaudible speech, "Ben."

"Stay close together," I said dryly. I recognized, though, how hard that was. Everything in my body was shrieking to take off running, damn the direction, damn the creature at the camp, just get me the hell away from these voices.

"Did they just say my name?" Bette asked.

"Who?" Nick said.

"You don't hear that?" I asked him. He shook his head. I could make out two, maybe three distinct voices in the whispers. Clearly Bette heard them as well. I looked at Nancy. "Do you hear them?"

"No. I just see that." She pointed to the treeline, where a trail of what appeared to be moonlight streaked between two thick trees and then vanished. It was followed by another. I glanced over my shoulder, to the trees opposite where Nancy was looking. The same streaks went by. Something was circling us.

The whispers came again, and this time their message was clear. "Come out and play in the woods, Ben." It was a young girl's voice, unfamiliar. I looked to Bette. She was trembling. "You can be like us if you wanted."

"Who is that?" Bette asked. Her voice was small.

"I don't know," I said. "Stay close."

"What do you hear?" Nick asked.

"They're... they're telling me to come out there."

"Who?"

"Man, I don't know. I don't know what's going on."

I looked back at the trees. The streaks of light had quit their circling, and instead, I could see the occasional wisp of moonlight peak from behind a trunk and then vanish. It was strange, almost like they were playing peek-a-boo or something. Childlike.

"Ben, come back!" I heard, far behind me. It was Nancy's voice. Quickly I turned around, looking around for where she'd gone. She was just right next to me. None of them were near me, actually. Where did they all go?

I scanned with my flashlight, and realized with a drop in my heart that I was no longer in the clearing. I was surrounded by trees, tight corridors of forest. The ground beneath my feet sloped further down into the wood. How long had I been out?

I took an inventory of myself. I was stinging all along my arms. As the cruel, revealing beam of the flashlight showed, I was streaked with mud and blood, shining with sweat. I must have taken off running. But why? What was happening to me?

My left eye flared up with pain and my vision went dark on that side. I felt my nose drip, like it was bleeding. "Fuck," I exhaled, wiping at my eye with my shirt to try and avoid worsening it with the dirt on my hand, as if my shirt was not dirty itself from my downhill tumble. Eventually, I touched my fingers to my nose and checked to see if it was in fact bleeding.

Beneath the light in my other hand, I saw that the fluid on my fingers was not red, but a deep, sticky black. I felt my stomach churn. What was it? And then, with a tremble, I remembered. I remembered Justin's scarred hand weeping black blood as he held Bette down.

What the fuck was happening?

Again, Nancy called for me to come back. I froze. I wasn't sure what to do. I was separated, in the thick of the woods alone, and something would certainly hear me if I shouted back at them. Then again, the thing that was hunting us would hear Nancy anyway. I didn't know if I could get back. The slope was so steep my calves were burning.

"Where are you going?" I heard. The voices from before.

Without hesitation, I spat my words. My vitriol surprised me. "Get the hell away from me."

"That's not very nice." Shards of light began streaking between trees. "We just want to play with you." I tried to follow them with my eyes, keep watching them, but my left eye was still clamped shut, and I was struggling to rotate on the incline. "We just want you to meet our friend."

"Like Justin did," a different voice added.

"Like Sarge did," another said.

I shook my head and started marching back up the slope. "I'm coming!" I shouted, and tried to increase my pace.

"No fair," one of the voices said, and one of the lights whooshed past my face, blinding me for a moment.

"Ben!" I heard Nancy shout.

Then, shortly after, Nick shouting, "You're not going anywhere, stay right there!" Was he talking to me? I wasn't going to stay here, not with whatever these voices were.

"She wants to play with us, too," one of the voices, different from the one that blinded me, said. "She's got our friend in her."

"Fuck off," I said, and pushed forward.

With my flashlight, I could just see where the slope curved over and became flat. "Guys!" I shouted. "I'm here!"

Nancy's face appeared over the slope, and she offered me a hand to pull me the rest of the way. I took it and allowed her to yank me into the clearing, where Nick was wrestling with Bette. Bette was vacant in her eyes, expressionless as she fought against Nick. "Where the fuck did you go?" Nick yelled. "You can't just run off like that."

"I don't know what's happening to me, but I think it's happening to her, too," I said.

When I blinked, I was once again gone from the clearing. I was laying flat on the ground at the bottom of a hill, but my flashlight was not in my hand. I looked around and found it, pointing turned on at the shape of Bette and Nancy, who seem to have fallen down the same hill. "Fuck," I muttered, before shouting, "Nick!"

I got no response.

The woods were deathly quiet. I felt every cut on my body singing little tunes of agony. I definitely had new ones from the fall, and my eye and nose were still gushing the black fluid. I called for Nick again, and again got no response.

Somewhere, far out there, I heard the shrieking of the creature. Silently, as my heart began to pound, I hoped Nick was safe, and I scrambled over to Nancy and Bette to shut off my flashlight. In the pitch darkness, I laid down between them, and listened.

"I tried to get you to stay home," a familiar voice said, and I was suddenly bathed in moonlight, brighter than any of the others that had lured me away before.

It was impossible, but as I raised myself up and met the glowing figure face to face, my eyes welled up with tears, and the dark fluid began to wash away.

"Lucy?" I asked, and she smiled.

The dazzling glow of pale light aside… she looked exactly the same as she had that day. I pulled myself up and stared at her, my vision blurring through the tears.

"Hi, Ben," she said softly. "You need to get moving."

I blinked. "I thought if we hid here, then maybe—"

"Hiding won't help," she said. "He can smell you."

"What… what is he?"

Lucy shrugged. "He's something bad."

I heard the shriek again, and with it, Lucy was gone. "Wait!" I yelled. There was no reply. I must have hit my head coming down the hill. Even if I did though, it didn't matter. I started shaking Nancy and Bette.

Chapter Fourteen
The Coyote

Bette awoke, blinking slowly and uncomfortably against my light. I saw she had black fluid coming from her mouth. For a moment I shied away from her, but upon seeing how scared she looked, I dropped my guard and continued trying to wake Nancy.

"Where are we?" Bette asked hazily.

"I don't know, but I think... I think *we* brought us here."

Bette put a hand to her forehead and wrinkled her brow. "But... why would we..."

"I don't know," I repeated. Nancy was starting to wake up, and I saw now her forehead had a deep cut on it. She was even hazier than Bette.

"B-Ben..." she said.

I helped her sit upright. "I think you've got a concussion, Nancy."

"Fuck," she said. She touched the cut and winced.

"I don't know how much time we have, but we need to move."

Nancy's eyes were slow as she looked up at me. "I don't know if I can."

"You can," I said. "I'll help you."

I hoisted Nancy up with one of her arms slung over my shoulder, and we began to limp along, with Bette just behind us. I tried to keep us moving quickly, but there were so many trees I had to keep correcting the course in awkward ways.

I couldn't stop thinking about her. The way she smiled at me, her voice... it was all the same. Like being ten again, looking up at the stars with her. I was still crying, softly, as I trudged along. Nancy noticed.

"It's... it's gonna be okay," she said, patting my chest with her free hand.

"I know," was all I gave her.

We were walking aimlessly, of course. Stumbling through the darkness with not even the slightest idea where we even were in relation to the campsite, let alone the cars, let alone God damn civilization. As we walked along, the only thought that gave me even an inkling of hope was this: Lucy wouldn't lead me wrong, and she told me to get moving. At least I could trust her.

I don't know how long we walked. It could have been only a few minutes, but it felt like hours as I heard the shrieks die down into nothing. We kept moving, and eventually Nancy woke up enough to walk on her own, so we picked up the pace and continued to march through the forest.

"Guys, where are you?!" I was floored to hear Nick's voice. It was near, but I couldn't tell where. I was scared to yell for fear of it hearing us.

"Nick!" Nancy yelled, soon followed by Bette. Realizing it wouldn't matter now, I started to yell for him too.

Nick continued to shout for us until we finally all met in the middle. He was panting, covered in dirt and bleeding from his lip. "Are you you again?" he asked me.

"Yes," I replied. "I don't know what I did, but something is wrong with me and Bette."

"No shit. I don't even know where we are."

"Me either," I said. "Do any of you remember which way we fell?"

"No idea," Nick said.

"Just down, so not toward camp," Nancy said. I knew Bette, like me, would remember nothing.

"Fuck," I said, and dropped to one knee to take a break. "We have to keep moving, but let's all catch our breath."

"We need to find somewhere to hide," Nick said. "Those fucking lights are gonna find us again."

I couldn't tell them all what I'd seen. Somehow it seemed crazier than everything else that had happened. "I really think we have to keep on our feet if we don't wanna get found."

"For all we know, we could just be walking deeper into the woods," Bette said.

"That's right where that thing wants us," Nick said. "What the hell is it?"

"Something bad," was all I could say. My guts lurched, but I held back what little remained of my cowboy stew.

Bette rubbed her arms. "Justin—" her voice caught when she said his name "—said it was something old, that it had been here for a really long time." She was staring blankly between Nick and I, not exactly looking at either one of us. "He said, 'Between the first dead leaf and the last snowfall, it hunts.' He said it's always hungry and it keeps growing."

"What the fuck happened to him?" Nick said. "What happened to Sarge?"

I looked at Bette, and saw that both of us were having the same thought. "I think it was the bite," I said. "And I think me and Bette can hear the voices because…"

"Because we got sick, too," Bette said.

Nick looked at us, his mouth a black pit as it hung open in the dark. "So are you both just trying to trap us, too?"

"No," I said. "I think we're spacing out because of the sickness, but it doesn't work the same as the bite."

"How do you know?" Nick asked.

I shook my head. "I don't, really. But I need you to trust me so we can get out of here."

Nick gave a sudden, violent shudder as he rubbed his elbow cautiously. He was still shirtless. While the night was warm enough, he was covered in goosebumps. He looked to Nancy, who nodded, then to Bette, who did not look back at him. She was staring out into the woods in silence. "Okay," Nick finally said.

With a sigh, I started moving again, followed by the others. It was coming back now, in a vengeful snarl, that fear of the night, of the woods, that had haunted me since I was ten. My heart was racing in my chest, yanking on my ribs like a prisoner. I hadn't realized until this moment just how terrified I was of being out here. My body began to shiver as I walked.

Where had she gone?

In the midst of my fear, I kept returning to Lucy, out here, speaking to me. I told myself that I'd hit my head, and maybe I had a concussion like Nancy. But then, why was I trusting her? Why shouldn't I just lie down out here, in the woods?

That thought spurred me. Something in my mind was prodding at me, like I could almost hear a voice between my ears, *"Just give up, you don't even know where you are. The soil is cool, Ben. Rest, Ben."* It was a deep, fatherly voice. One of comfort. I was drifting. The world seemed to spin, and I lost sight of Nick. Yes, I could just lie down, and the others wouldn't be slowed down. I could wait right here…

Nancy grabbed my shoulder, bringing me back from the daze. She was in front of me. "You're not running off again," she said, and grabbed my hand. I squeezed hers back tightly, then offered my other hand to Bette. Bette took it, and we followed Nick, who had marched to the front of the group, leading us now. My breath came out in gasps as I tried to shake the panic of disorientation off of me.

"Of course," the voice in my head whispered, *"Nick's the one that brought you all out here. It could have just been him and Freddy, but now it's all of you. Maybe he's willing to trust you, but can you trust him?"*

"Stop it," I muttered.

"What?" Nancy asked, looking at me startled.

I shook my head and rolled my neck, trying to shrug the voice out of my body. "Not you. They're back. Maybe. I don't know."

We looked at Bette. She nodded a confirmation quickly and pressed on, pulling Nancy and I behind her.

It was then that we heard it, closer than it had been even when we were beside the campsite. The roar that echoed through the woods was shrill and feral, and sent all of us careening forward from the very force of the sound. It was behind us.

"Go!" I yelled, and we took off.

This was different than it was before, when the shrieking was in the distance, abstract. Now I could hear the tearing at the leaves, the ragged breathing of something that stood much taller, much wider, than any of us. I heard the sound of wood snapping and breaking, a crash. Had it broken a tree down, simply by running through it? Was it that big? I didn't look back to find out.

In the midst of its haggard breaths, it was letting out other noises. They were strange, bouncing, unlike any growling or barking I'd ever heard. Each noise was distinct, and yet some repeated. Strung together, with quick spaces between. It was funny, it was almost like...

No, it couldn't be.

Yet... I could have sworn for a second, it sounded like it was talking.

The train of thought was cut short by the thing letting out another shrill howl, and this time, I felt my left eardrum shiver and pop. My ears began to ring loudly, and I couldn't make out what Nick was saying ahead, but he was definitely shouting something, probably expletives. I didn't reply, only continued to run, keeping my eyes on the ginger head in front of me as he weaved clumsily through the trees.

I could feel it now, slamming limbs into the dirt. Was it running on two legs or four? Two seemed worse, somehow. Two legs seemed too human. Especially if it was— *It wasn't,* isn't *talking, quit thinking that,* I scolded myself. It took my mind back to Justin, and I wondered if he was hunting us too, running at its heels like a faithful hound, yapping at the prey just within reach. Would Justin be running on two legs or four now? And where was Sarge? Where was that gun in the dark, waiting to shoot us in the leg or gut and leave us for the creature to devour?

My legs were burning, but I could not stop. What little adrenaline was left to pump through my veins was pushing me forward, just a bit further, we'd have to find safety somewhere, somehow.

The scream that came next, as I was thrown forward onto my face, was beside me, and undeniably human.

I rolled with the pain of my now-bleeding face, and turned to finally, defeatedly, face the thing behind us. The scream was Nancy. I was already breathing quickly, panicked, as I watched her be raised ten, then twelve, and perhaps more, feet off the ground. My flashlight, laying in the dirt beside me, perfectly spotlighted what was about to happen.

The creature that held her was on two legs. For something so tall, it was disgustingly thin, near-skeletal, save the distended belly that was smattered with coarse, black hair, as were its legs and shoulders. Beneath the hair it was so pale it almost looked blue. The skin was tight over the elongated bones of the creature, and I could see midnight veins streaking webs across its body. On each of its sapling legs it had massive, dirty feet, each with five toes that ended in long, broken, nails. On each hand, one of which was holding Nancy above its head, it had fingers that stretched out at least a foot, and each finger had a long, pointed claw twisting out impossibly in knots from the fingertip. It was naked, and more human than I could have anticipated. A towering, horrific mockery of what a person should look like.

And then, I looked at its face.

The head might have resembled a human from far away, but this close, I could see it was oddly elongated, the mouth stretching forward and smashing the still-human nose up against the rest of its face like a pug. Teeth slipped over its cracked, dry lips at odd angles, each of them broken or sharpened in inconsistent ways, as if cataloging all the types of predators that may stalk these woods. Its ears, they were human, but they'd been forced downward, onto the straining neck of the creature. I wondered if it could still hear. The eyes sat in dark, sunken holes in the face, giving the pale head a skeletal appearance.

It was crowned with two growths on its head: what appeared to be antlers, like that of a stag, each three feet long, maybe more, but asymmetrical, twisting in different directions. But, as I looked, I realized the antlers were moving, each point actually was five points, each of the five points had five more angled points, and all of them were flexing and moving, groping at the air.

The antlers were made of hands.

I could see now, every once in a while, the tight skin bulging where something beneath tried to push through. Fingers all across the thing's body, clawing from within, trying to burst through. The creature, the Coyote, its entire body was some kind of prison.

Nancy was screaming. Nick was screaming. Bette was backing up in the dirt, trying to stand and falling as she made meager, hollow distance between her and the goliath in front of us. I was only able to look on. A tail, not unlike a dog's, but also covered in that same coarse fur, flicked out from behind the creature's back.

It looked down at me, then Bette, then Nick. The cracked lips peeled back further, revealing the black gums that held the shattered fangs in the creature's mouth. It was smiling. I heard, through the ringing of my ears, a roll of three shrill exhales from its mouth. A laugh.

"Ben!" Nancy yelled.

With a new shriek, the Coyote bit down on her torso, and began to eat.

I wish that I could tell you she died instantly. I wish I could say, "She didn't suffer, it was quick." I told her parents that, but I don't want to lie again. The truth is, Nancy was screaming the whole time.

She was screaming even as I got to my feet and turned away and began to sprint faster than I had even before, tears streaming down my face. Nick and Bette were running too, but I did not pay them any mind now. I didn't, at that moment, even care if it caught me. I just couldn't bear to see it. I was hoping if I ran fast enough, I wouldn't have to hear it either. I was wrong. It began with her screaming for me, then she screamed for her mother. In the end, she was just screaming.

The last sound she made was a yelp not unlike a dog whose tail has been stepped on, and then she died with a wet cracking sound.

We ran from it, all the while my sobbing prevented me from seeing where I was going. I was whispering to myself, over and over, "I'm sorry, I'm sorry, Nancy." I could feel wetness on my nose where her blood had splattered in the initial chomp. I clipped a thick tree with my shoulder and felt a flare of pain shoot over me, but continued on the same as I stumbled along the forest floor. I couldn't tell if I was running with or against the slope, or if the ground was flat.

I could hear Nick and Bette nearby, both of them letting out their own sounds of fear and anguish. Nick was cursing and sputtering as he weaved through trees, while Bette was simply crying. It wasn't the same guttural wailing that was choking out of my throat, just a distant sadness, all she had left after all she'd lost thus far.

My mind was swimming with the flashes of horror I'd seen before my body had taken things into its own hands and run away. The way on that first bite she twisted. The screaming that lost its humanity with each chew. I felt lightheaded. If I left my mind to its own devices too long, I might faint, but I couldn't get it out of my head. I thought for a moment that I was relieved Freddy hadn't had to feel what she had, that he'd died before the attack truly began. Then, grief for Freddy seeped in, too, and I wept harder.

A root treacherously snagged my foot once again, and I went tumbling. All the little cuts on my body began to flare up with pain I hadn't noticed in the now-drained flood of adrenaline. I did not try to stop myself, I only let myself fall as I continued to weep. This time the tumble did not last long. I crashed chest-first into a thick tree and the last of the air in my lungs was expelled in a choking gasp.

Nick was shouting my name, but the ringing in my ears had returned, and he sounded far away. I felt hands on my shoulders and sides: the both of my remaining friends pulling me up to my feet, screaming for me to get moving. I couldn't see. It was so dark, my flashlight left behind where Nancy had died. With some effort, I was up, but my ribs had to be broken, as my whole chest began to sing with agony.

A wind swept through us, and I heard Nick scream.

"No," I choked out, still catching my breath. The force of the Coyote passing and grabbing Nick had sent me backward, and I was leaning against the tree, grasping at my side.

Bette was grabbing at my hand, pulling me up. "Other way, other way," she was saying. I didn't quite understand what she meant. My eye was filling up with darker darkness than that of the woods. I couldn't see her. I turned to where Nick was screaming, and saw only the large shape of the terror.

"Get the fuck off of me!" I heard Nick scream. He was fighting against it. It was letting out those chortling little laughs at him, letting him know it didn't care how much he struggled. Nick was caught in a net of curling fingers. The antler that held him was pulling at his clothes, twisting his arms, trying to force him into submission. A clawed hand reached up, and the Coyote pulled Nick to its face.

There was a cracking sound, and Nick began to scream again, this time not in defiance. Bette was trying to pull me away, but I couldn't. I knew it was going to catch us. Why spend the last moments I had running?

Light filled the woods, and I saw the creature even clearer now, gnawing on Nick's shoulder as he continued to fight weakly against it. I was blinking against the light rapidly, only getting flashes through my unobscured eye, as I watched three shapes drift into the clearing and grab onto the creature.

She was back. Lucy's arms were wrapped around the creature's neck; despite how small she was, she seemed to be strong enough to make a difference. With a snarl, the Coyote's jaws released Nick, who was now dripping blood down his bare torso. On Lucy's left, standing atop the creature's back, was Margaret Diermann. Margaret was pulling on the creature's bicep, trying to shake Nick free from its grasp. On Lucy's right was Jules Baker, who had left a note for her family on Christmas Eve that she was running away (none of us had known this when we saw her that night). I guess she didn't make it far. Jules was on the ground, holding onto the creature's leg, thrashing with it and trying to topple it.

The creature began to speak again, in that language so removed from me I couldn't even begin to understand what was being said, and its fingers slipped away, allowing Nick to fall to the ground. There was nothing else to do. I ran to Nick.

"Fuck," was all Nick could say, repeated in hazy breaths as I hoisted him by one arm onto his feet.

"Run!" Lucy screamed, and she pointed to her left. Nick and I obeyed, though I still wasn't sure whether or not Nick could see her. Bette was following us. The creature was shrieking and fighting against them as the light faded behind us.

Bette caught up and was beside me now. "Ben, was that—"

"Yeah," I said, unable to form any other words through the searing in my chest.

We went as far as we could, but Nick was slowing down, his breath getting slow. I was holding him up again after a while. With every step, I was certain it would appear again, crashing down on us and taking all of us one by one. Even now, the shrieks had died down, and there was no sound at all in the woods but us, raggedly panting in the dark.

Then, I saw it. Through the thick of the forest, a clearing, lit up by moonlight. "Come on," I said, and pressed forward.

We broke the treeline, and entered a clearing that seemed impossible, massive in the middle of these woods. There was one tree that was thicker than all the rest standing in the center of the clearing, stretching its branches high into the night sky, where the moon itself was competing with the faint glow of little orbs that flitted around the tree. At the far right of the clearing, there was a cliff-face, and high into it a small waterfall broke through, trickling into a running, clear creek that surrounded the tree.

It would have all been very beautiful, if the great roots of the tree were not littered with bones.

"What the hell..." Nick murmured, then collapsed to one knee, dragging me with him.

"Get up," I said, pulling on him.

Bette was scanning the tree cautiously. "This is horrible..." she whispered. "Who are these people?"

I wasn't sure. There were human skulls of various sizes, all around, stuffed into hollows in the trunk and shattered against the roots. There were also animal bones, dog collars, antlers and sharp teeth, all strewn around haphazardly.

"Victims," I said.

One of the skulls, one that was attached to a spine and ribcage, began to shudder. Bette let out a yelp and Nick groaned as the eyeholes of the skull lit up with the same moonlight glow of the orbs all around the tree.

The lights in the skull bled outward and grew, until they formed into a human shape, and once again, Lucy was standing before us.

"Come across the water," she said. "You'll be safe here for now."

Chapter Fifteen
The Pack

We dragged Nick over the narrow creek and into the boneyard at the base of the tree. Margaret and Jules were here now, too. Margaret had appeared from a shattered chunk of ambiguous bone, and Jules had come from a fractured skull nestled between two roots. I looked at them, unsure what to say. Bette's mouth was hanging open.

"It won't be able to get you guys here," Margaret said.

"Why?" Bette asked. She looked all around, expecting, like I was, to see the Coyote come crashing into the clearing at any moment.

"It can't cross running water," Jules said. "The creek will keep it out."

"So we're safe?" I asked.

Lucy shook her head. "Not exactly. They're still out there."

"Who?"

"Justin and Sarge," Bette said. I nodded, feeling my spine turn to ice.

"For now, they can cross," Lucy said. "It'll send them here to drag you over the creek. Then, it'll eat."

Bette kneeled down next to Nick. He was looking dumbly up at the trio of ghosts, his eyes misty and distant. "He's going to die," Bette said.

I looked at Lucy and the other two. "Can you help him?"

"I don't think so," Lucy said. "Even if we could, he's bitten. He'll be like them someday, if he survives."

"Does he have to be?" I asked. "Is there a way to help him?"

I heard a bark that startled me. A dog— Mr. Trellis's missing shepherd —came bounding over to Lucy's side. It was just like the others, made of pale light. Lucy spoke as she scratched the dog's ears. "He's going to feel it everyday that it's active. When the first leaf turns brown to when the last snowflake falls down, he'll yearn to feed, to come back to the woods."

"To become one of them, someday," Margaret added.

I looked down at Nick. He looked over to me, and let out a wincing chuckle. "Fuck, man," he said, hoarse.

"What do you mean, 'one of them?'" I asked.

"It used to be human," Jules said.

I sat down beside Nick. "How the fuck do you all know all this?" Lucy looked a little shocked to hear me curse. She had that nervous smirk children get when a friend does something Not Allowed.

Lucy collected herself and spoke. "It tells us things. It tells us stories when it isn't hunting."

Margaret looked up at the tree, to where lights were flitting. "They hurt," she said. "You spend all your time hearing these stories, and it's like pieces of you are disappearing. Turning you into something else."

"We can't leave as long as our remains are here," Jules said, kicking a skull against the tree. "The others, the ones that lure you away, using the sickness to trick you—they're the ones that have lost their minds. They're just puppets now."

I didn't know what to say. "Why?" came out.

Lucy sat down beside Nick and I. She took my hand into hers. She was so warm I felt my whole body tingle. "It's hungry. Always. It has to keep eating, but it grows around its food. Years and years ago, it was only about as tall as you are now. But the more it eats, the faster it can hunt, the further it can travel in a night. And the more bones it can add to the pile."

"Bones feed the tree, the tree grows taller," Margaret agreed.

"Once the tree is big enough, it'll be satisfied. It won't be hungry anymore," Lucy said. "At least, that's what it thinks."

"So Justin's going to turn into one of those… things?" Bette asked. She'd pulled her knees to her chest and was sitting close to me. I instinctively put an arm around her, drawing her gently to me to console her.

Lucy nodded solemnly. "Him and the old guy will, if they survive."

"But they won't know where to find us," I said.

Lucy gave me a sad look. "They know exactly where you are," Margaret said. My heart dropped. "But, they're slow. It'll be finishing its last kill off before it comes here, and even then, it won't be patient enough to wait for them to get you across the creek. It'll go looking for a deer or wolf to feed on before it checks in with them."

"We can't just wait here," Bette said.

"So go," Nick coughed. "Just go while you two can move."

Lucy put her hand on him. "You'll be trapped here like us if you die here."

"It only comes out in the fall and winter, right?" Nick said. "Just come back for me and all the other bodies in the summer. I can wait until then."

"It doesn't work like that," Jules said. "When it stops hunting, the tree won't be here. Not until the next cycle."

Nick put his head down in the dirt. "Well, fuck," he sighed.

"We're not gonna leave you," Bette said. "We'll find a way to get you out of the woods. And to a hospital."

Nick laughed, and blood wept from his wound. "I'll be fucking rabid for next Christmas."

"Shut up," I said. "We'll figure this out."

"What about us?" Bette asked. "We got sick, too." Lucy looked away.

"Lucy?" I asked her, leaning forward. She gripped my hand a little tighter.

Her words came slowly, carefully. "We don't think you'll change if you didn't get bit, but..."

"We don't know," Margaret said. "It won't tell us. All it said is that it was spreading, like—"

"Roots," Jules said.

There was a shriek out in the darkness, and Bette flinched into my shoulder. Nick was forcing himself to sit up. "Alright," he groaned. "We have to get to the cars." He looked over at Lucy. "Nice to meet you, by the way. Do you know which way we need to go?"

Lucy nodded, but before she could say anything, I said, "What if they're waiting for us?"

"What do you mean?"

"At the cars. What if they're waiting for us there, so we can't get away?"

"They only have until sunrise," Margaret said. "They'll be searching. They won't let you sit here and wait it out."

"So what then?" Bette said. "Are we just fucked?"

Lucy considered this, and for a moment, I thought that she might not quite know what "fucked" means. She sighed. "We can lead you to the cars, but you'll need to time your run. When the others are here, it means that it's off hunting. You'll have to outrun them."

"Outrun G.I. fucking Joe and Justin while I can barely stand," Nick coughed. "Great."

Lucy looked over at me, then over at the other ghosts. Mr. Trellis's dog bristled up, and began to growl. "Here they come…" Lucy said, quietly.

"Bette!" came Justin's voice, from beyond the trees where we could see. "I'm sorry, please help me!" I looked at Bette. She was gritting her teeth, eyes twitching behind her cracked lenses.

"Nick!" came Freddy's voice, and all our eyes widened.

"Freddy?!" Nick yelled.

"Nick?!" Freddy yelled back.

I looked at Nick and shook my head. "Dude, wait—"

"He could be hurt!" Nick shouted at me, and began to limp across the creek. "Freddy, we're here!"

"Nick, Justin's out there, too, don't!"

We heard the shot, but did not see the muzzle flash. A bullet struck the tree behind us, and the orbs of light began to lap around the branches frantically, a hive disturbed. Nick leapt back across the water backwards, and tripped over a skull. Bette and I jumped to the ground and laid flat.

"Come out, kids," Sarge said, just loud enough for us to hear. "Come out and play." As he hit the word "play," something in his voice changed. Became a little higher. Sounded like Freddy.

"We're hurt," Freddy's voice said, lacking emotion.

"What the fuck," Nick whispered.

"Please, come out," Freddy said. "We need help, Cross isn't thinking straight." Another shot rang out. The dirt and bone fragments beside me kicked up into a cloud. I began to crawl for the tree trunk, trying to get to the other side.

"I'm sorry, Bette, I didn't mean to hurt you," Justin said. "Please don't hide from me, I'm sorry!" Bette was crawling near enough to me that I could see her, but not so close we could both be shot at once. Nick was slower. Still so grievously wounded. There wasn't much I could do to help him.

Lucy, Margaret, Jules, and the dog were gone. Or, they seemed gone. There were four orbs flitting around, the lowest on the tree, avoiding us but close enough to keep an eye. I silently thanked Lucy for moving, not drawing attention to us. If you stick together, the seeker finds you, I thought.

"What's wrong, kids?" Sarge called. "You're being so ungrateful. We planned this trip for you and you're hiding away."

"HELP ME!" Justin's voice broke in. I felt my spine tremble, my skin give way to chilled sweat. The cuts along my arms burned. "I'M SORRY BEN, BETTE, PLEASE HELP!"

We were rounding the tree when I heard the sound of something large landing in the pile of bones. *Don't look, don't fucking look,* I thought as I looked behind me.

Freddy's body was recognizable only by its size and the blond hair atop the mangled skull. Even missing his legs he was still tall, and where his musculature was not shredded to bits, he was still thick and sturdy looking. Truthfully, he was mostly just a torso now. On what was left of one of his arms, however, I could see bite marks smaller than those on Nick. Crescent-shaped. Human.

Nick wailed, and another shot rang out, hitting the bark of the tree. Nick picked up the pace, no tears on his face, but red with fury, panting, catching up with Bette and I quickly as we took cover behind the behemoth oak.

From a knot on the trunk, Lucy's face reemerged, and she glanced around, as if she was worried who might hear. "You need to go fast, it's coming."

I said through my teeth, "I thought it was hunting."

She shook her head quickly, panicked. "It should be, but it's fighting it. I don't know when it'll go away. But the one with the gun is going to catch you anyway if you don't go."

"Why does he have his voice?" Nick asked. "Why is he talking like—" Nick sniffed, and the tears finally came. He glanced around the tree, and more bark tore away from the trunk as another bullet came whizzing across the creek.

Nick laid down beside me, shaky breaths escaping his mouth. Bette and I each gripped one of his hands. "We have to go, Nick," I said.

"Freddy's here," he said. "We can't let him get trapped here."

I looked at Lucy. She looked down at the ground. "We can distract them, but you're not going to make it carrying them both." Three orbs of light drifted down next to us. "Margaret and Jules can show you where the cars are."

Bette nodded at me. "Do it," I told Lucy, and she and one of the orbs were gone. The other two began to flit across the stream and back into the woods.

Shots began to ring out, but quickly stopped. I heard snarling from the shadows. I released Nick's hand and stood, Bette doing the same. "Try to get a head start," I told Nick. "We'll catch up to you." Nick was struggling to stand up, but once on his feet, he took off after Margaret and Jules's lights. "Fast," I said to Bette, and we ran back around the tree.

In the time we'd been on the other side, he'd already begun to change. All of Freddy's hair was gone, and he'd gotten thin. More of his skin was missing. Feeding the tree. We ran to him, and I grabbed his blood-soaked waist, Bette hooking her hands under the remainder of his mangled arm. We set to carrying him the way Nick had run.

I was struck by the four-legged shape of something tall and thin, coming bare-chested from the darkness. It was screaming as it hit me, pure rage that had lost what humanity it had left. As I lost my grip on Freddy, I went to the ground, and Justin began to beat me.

The first three blows made contact with my face and tore skin open. My nose hurt, but it wasn't broken. My eye surged with pain. Later it would blacken and close. For now, it simply welled back up with the dark fluid of the sickness, as more blows came down on my chest and arms.

I felt something in my body surge. A fire that caused all the blood to overheat. My face was feverish. I screamed and felt my vocal chords tearing as I swung back at the face of my once friend. I struck his gnashing teeth, and felt the flesh on the back of my hand tear. He screamed and hit me back, sending stars swirling through my vision.

"You could have just let yourself change—" he hit me, "You could have been like us—" he hit me, "You could have been so—" hit, "much—" hit, "more—" hit.

My vision was black and red. Justin was a tinted blur behind it. I could barely see him sneering down at me. "You're gonna die, and be trapped out here." His teeth, the sole visible part of his face, were mismatched from the words, even as the voice behind them became higher and feminine.

"You're gonna be trapped just like me," Justin said in Lucy's voice, and he raised his fists.

I put my hands over my face, knowing they wouldn't last long against the coming onslaught.

The shrill shrieking that came was not Justin, nor was it the creature in the woods. Justin was pulled from me, and I heard growls become choking coughs, become near-silent wheezes. I shuffled away on my back and began using the inside of my shirt to wipe at the blood in my eyes as quickly as I could. My touch stung. Through my blinks, I still couldn't see, as the bones near where I was laying were kicked around and the strained breaths beyond my sight turned to silence.

Footsteps were coming closer to me, and I continued to shuffle backward. A hand took mine, but I ripped it away.

"Ben!" Bette yelled at me. Her voice was a snarl. I looked at approximately where her face should be and kept blinking. She came into view, fading from red to orange to the pale yellow of the ghost orbs drifting around the tree.

From the corners of her mouth and from her nose, Bette was leaking the black fluid, and she was panting in pain and exhaustion. Still, she was extending a hand to me, not ravenous or dazed the way Justin had been. I looked down between her legs, and saw the shape of him laying on the ground. I wasn't sure from here, but his neck looked… wrong.

"Come on," Bette said, bringing my attention back to her face. With the other arm, she wiped her nose and mouth.

I took her hand, and she pulled me to my feet.

I didn't look at Justin again. I went back to trying to pick up Freddy. Bette grabbed my arm from behind.

"Ben," she said. I kept trying to pick him up. He was even thinner, he had even less skin. Blood slicked my hands, and I couldn't get a grip. "Ben, leave him!"

"We have to take him away," I said.

"Nick will understand," she said.

"It's not about Nick," I said, and shrugged her away.

"Look at me!" she shouted. I turned to her, and the tears that entered my eyes turned her into a distant photo, out of focus. Her eyes were black as she spoke. "We can't make it out if we're lugging him around. We have to get Nick and get to the cars."

"I can't," I said.

"What can't you?"

"I can't…"

She stepped forward and put her arms around me. She squeezed me tightly, and I sighed into her shoulder, making no attempt to hug her back. "I can't let anyone else get stuck here."

"We're going to be stuck here if we don't go," she said into my neck. "We have to get out of here."

Bette stepped away and looked up at me. I wiped at my eyes, stinging them with sweat and dirt, but she became clear again, her blue eyes no longer swallowed by the blackness. She was teary as well, but unlike earlier that night, she held onto her composure. "Okay," I said, and looked down at Freddy. He was almost bones now. Most of the rest of him was on my clothes, blood that would not feed the vampiric tower of the forest.

We turned our backs on Justin and Freddy, setting off on the path Nick had followed. As we crossed the creek, I felt dread as the tree's sinister safety slipped away. As we passed the treeline, I began to jog, and, wordlessly, Bette did the same.

***

Once again, we were without light. I could hear Bette breathing next to me. It was ragged and gravelly at first, but soon became shallow, tight inhales as we trotted through the maze of trees. We tried the best we could to keep our trajectory straight, following precisely the direction Nick had run, but that quickly proved to be more difficult than I had hoped. Our jog slowed to a brisk walk, the kind you do when you're faking running in P.E.

I wondered where Lucy and Mr. Trellis's shepherd were. We hadn't heard a gunshot since before Justin had grabbed me. Now the woods were deathly silent, a bark-strewn mausoleum. There was just the panting, our breaths overlapping as our feet crunched through the soil. I was glad to not be alone. I think Bette felt the same. Silently, I wanted to grab her hand, to make sure she knew was there, but the trees were packed tightly. We couldn't have run together.

Wherever Lucy was, I hoped she was okay. I had no idea what her rebelling would mean for her. Would she, could she, be punished by the monster?

That was when we heard the shot. It was to our left, and close. I felt Bette stop short beside me. "Nick," she whispered. Another shot fired.

"Let's go," I said.

We turned toward the shots and started running as fast as we could. More shots were ringing as we went. My heart started to pound. Not him too, I thought. If he doesn't make it...

I saw two small orbs of light cut through the black veil ahead. They were moving quickly, and zoomed between Bette and I. "Margaret?" I yelled after them. One of the orbs lit up brighter, but it continued on without stopping.

"Ben!" I heard Nick yell.

Another shot fired as I yelled Nick's name back at him. I heard it ricochet off a tree nearby. "Keep it down," Bette said. "We find Nick and we go."

"Ben, you out here too, boy?" Sarge yelled. "I thought Cross would have taken care of you by now. Guess string bean's a little worn out from the cracked ribs, huh?" Sarge fired another shot into the woods, and I caught sight of the muzzle flash between the trees. He wasn't aiming our way. In fact, he appeared to be aiming toward the sky.

"He's... confused," I whispered.

"He's lost his mind," Bette said in agreement. Another shot fired into the sky, and Sarge let out a frustrated wail into the dark.

We tried to keep our footsteps silent, and found Sarge was doing the same. The woods would go as still and silent as the grave for several seconds, and we'd creep around the brush, hoping we'd bump into Nick and be able to run for it. The first couple times, I'd thought Sarge had stood in place, but he was searching. A shot would fire, in a different place than it was before. The closer we got to where the gun was firing, the more I wished I had earplugs. It felt like my brain was ringing.

"You'll never find each other out here," Sarge said, his cadence melodic. "I've got all the time in the world, but your friend is practically pissing blood. You should have waited at the tree for me. I would have made it quick for you."

Nevermind that he was just around a tree from Bette and I as he spoke. We froze there, waited like statues, as Sarge's ragged breath thundered in the quiet forest. Bette's fingers clamped tightly around my forearm as we anticipated the shadow of Sarge to round the trunk.

"I could have made it quick." Sarge's voice was flickering as he repeated himself. There were hints of Freddy, of Margaret, of others I didn't recognize, fluttering in and out of his speech. "Now I'm gonna make sure he eats you slow, like he did to Nancy." My heart began to pound. What was fear drifted off me like petals in the wind. There was fire beneath. I opened my mouth to shout, but Bette brought her palm to my lips and held tight.

"Hey!" came Nick's voice, from about thirty feet away. Sarge, hinting no hesitation, fired his gun again, in the direction the shout came from. I shook Bette from me and seized my opportunity.

It was as if I couldn't hear the noises I was making, but I could feel them— knives in my vocal chords which would leave my throat raw for weeks afterward. My arms swept around Sarge, and I threw my entire weight into him, sending us both skidding across the forest floor. There were brambles that caught at my arms, tearing the cuts I'd endured open further, but the pain seemed to only spur me on. I swung a fist and found purchase against a sweat-drenched mustache, and Sarge let out his own soundless roar of rage.

There was no world in which I could have fought Sarge myself. Even in that moment, I knew I was going to die as soon as he caught his bearings. After my initial punch, he grabbed both my wrists and rolled with me, bringing a knee into my chest as we went. The wind was shoved from my lungs like a popping balloon, and my entire body heaved. I thought I might vomit, as Sarge released himself from me and brought the outside of his fist hammering down onto my back.

Alone, I would have been killed then and there, or worse, maimed and left for the Coyote to feast upon when it returned. It was only by Nick's last shove of adrenaline, tackling Sarge as I had, that kept me alive.

There were sounds of struggle, and I could just make out the shape of Bette, coming and pulling on the silhouette that had mounted the other in the fight. As I began to push myself to my feet, my fingers recoiled from the shape of something hot in the dirt. I checked it with careful fingertips, and with a breath of calming understanding, I wrapped my hand around the grip of Sarge's pistol.

Bette let out a yelp, which was followed by the sounds of someone being beaten. I was on my feet now, and looked over the scene. Their shapes were all just shadows, obscured further by the black eye, now fully formed, that Justin had left me with. Still, I was able to make out that Bette was catching her bearings, while Nick was being savaged by the man atop him.

"Get off him!" I shouted, and my entire neck flared up with pain. Sarge froze on top of Nick, and cocked his head to the left, questioning me.

"You think you're going to shoot me, Ben, is that it?" he asked. He was standing up from Nick slowly. The colors were barely there, but I could see that red was dripping from his fists.

Sarge began to turn toward me as he spoke. "You're not going to shoot any—"

As he spoke, I exhaled, and the trigger flattened against the gun.

The noise sent another shock of pain through my ears, and I let the weapon go limp in my hand, sliding my finger off the trigger. Sarge was staring me down, standing tall, even as the blood drained from the hole where his eye had been. When he fell, he fell away from Nick, and a soft thud was the only sound other than Bette's frantic breaths.

I held the gun tight, wondering how many bullets were left inside. It was not the same revolver we'd all practiced with. It was the sort of gun a police officer or soldier might carry. Any number of bullets could be in the clip, and I had no idea if the next trigger pull would carry anything with it. Still, I held on tight, telling myself that I might need it, if only to save us from the same fate as Nancy. I walked to Nick and dropped to my knees beside him.

"Thanks," I said.

Nick was silent. Not even a breath came in response.

"Nick," I said.

"Ben, let's go," Bette said weakly. She was standing up from Sarge. I heard the jingle of keys in her hand.

I felt my whole body shake, but no tears formed. Maybe I was dehydrated, or maybe there'd just been too much pain for me to really cry then. Bette was pulling me to my feet, and I was trembling, looking down at Nick, whose face was turned away, dyed black by his own blood in the gray of darkness. Bette was setting off the way we'd been heading before, approximately.

"Nick," I said, one last time. "If you're still there, please say something."

For once, Nick Lauer had no words to say.

Chapter Sixteen
The Final Hour

That final charge forward was void of words. Even the sounds of our panting had vanished, muted by the weight of it all. Every part of me hurt.

It was just the two of us now. I didn't know how we were going to get back. Even in the light of day, the road to our campsite could scarcely be called that. Bette had her license, but could she drive Sarge's hulking vehicle out of the woods without us careening into a tree, or several? Wouldn't that be a way to go, a car crash after all this?

We found ourselves fighting with slopes the entire way. My calves and ankles were pleading with me to collapse into the dirt one last time, but I spurred myself forward with a new, solemn thought: Someone has to tell their parents what happened here. They need to know it isn't safe out here.

With that thought, my mind began to wander, and the wandering helped me keep pace, no longer focused on the pain in my legs and chest, nor the stinging around my rapidly shutting eye. I drifted back to the pack of coyotes, remembering just how many Sarge had slaughtered, adults and pups alike. How soon into his massacre had he been bitten? Was all that bloodshed just a cover for it? And Justin, he must've been in this for the long haul: pretending over months that he was traumatized by what happened when he'd been planning this all along.

It fell to us to tell the truth. How to even describe the truth? Would anyone believe us if we told them a monster had been killing the kids in Elkwood? The thought crossed my mind, that maybe they'd think Bette and I had done it, and they'd send us to an asylum somewhere for hallucinating the Coyote.

My mind drifted further, and arrived on Lieutenant Dunn. Working these missing cases all these years, surely when he found out about this new slough of death, he'd listen to me. I'd lost Lucy, my friend had been attacked, and now this? He'd listen to me.

Or maybe, he'd pin Lucy on me, and ship me off to the bin like the rest.

"Bette," I said, breaking the silence of the forest.

She did not speak, but she glanced back at me, acknowledging that she'd heard me.

I continued, "Can we... can we even tell anyone?"

"I don't know," she said, small. "Who could ever believe this?"

"I can't," I admitted softly. "But maybe... the cop from Lucy's case would listen?"

Bette considered this as we crested the slope of the hill, and found ourselves looking at the silhouettes of the jeep and truck. As we got closer, I saw that another measure had been taken: Freddy's tires were splayed out, gouged and deflated. We walked to the jeep, which was left untouched: not the stealthiest escape vehicle in the world, but I guess out here that didn't matter.

As Bette fumbled trying to unlock the door, about to answer my question, we heard the screech again. "Bette!" I screamed.

The sound of the Coyote's foreign dialect came, but I felt as though I knew exactly what it was saying in its deep, authoritative voice.

"Where are you going, children?"

The creature's body rose up from its four-legged stance as it broke the treeline, standing tall over everything. It presented itself, arms wide, nails wavering and clicking together. Its whole body was streaked with the blood of our friends.

"Bette!" I yelled again, staring into the Coyote's eyes. It was moving slowly, sure of its victory. If we ran, we were dead. We had no choice but to try and drive, and even then, we were probably dead.

I heard the jeep's lock click, and the door pop open. "Get in!" Bette yelled, and threw herself into the driver's seat. I looked up at the Coyote, who was closing the distance with ease. I tried to run around the jeep as the engine sputtered to life, and it stepped to cut me off.

"Come back home, Ben," it was trying to say. The syllables were in a bouncing cadence that struck my ears like sirens. I heard voices I'd never heard melding with Justin, Sarge, Nancy, and Freddy. The Coyote closed the distance more.

"Aren't you both so tired?"

I trembled as I saw the Coyote raise one of its gnarled hands, ready to slash or grab me. Even as I trembled, I felt my own hand raise in time with my attacker's.

As the sound of a gunshot broke the night, black blood spurted from the Coyote's hip, and a pained shriek warbled into the darkness. I fired again, and this time, the oily substance sprayed from its stomach. The Coyote lurched and stumbled, its claws tearing into the ground around it, kicking dust into the air. With a half moment's opening, I ran around the jeep.

I watched in horror as I saw what I thought was the jeep flying into the air, then understood as I flipped and hit the ground. My chest struck dirt and the wind left my body. My ankle was cut. It burned, and I screamed. The Coyote was slithering across the ground licking my blood off its claws. *"Ungrateful,"* it called me in Sarge's voice.

"Shoot it again!" Bette screamed. The car began to turn, circling me so that the door was behind me as I faced the Coyote down. It smiled through its marred face, and let out that laugh once more.

"Kill me," it said as Nancy. A great clawed hand came forward, and I flattened myself against the soil below. Bette screamed as the claws came just short of the jeep. *"Go on,"* it said as Freddy.

The first hand was above me, raking the dirt, coming for my head. The other was in the air, about to strike downward. Smells of rotting meat and sour leaves filled my nose as the giant head came closer, gnashing teeth at my feet. *"You cannot do it,"* the Coyote hissed. I looked into those eyes, a deep green that caught the jeep's light. I heard the dirt scraping behind me, the air swooping above me. Thousands of misshapen fingers grasped inward, forcing the antlers to bend.

My foot came up and caught the jaw of the monster. Its head did not flinch, but the great arms paused long enough for me to move just to the side of the closing trap. Claws struck dirt from above, claws raked dirt into the air. The Coyote was hunched as its arms came back to itself. I saw a tangle of something above the emerald eyes. Feeling the cold upon my skin, I realized half my shirt had been torn away as the grasping antlers tried to snag me. My finger squeezed the trigger of Sarge's pistol. I did not see whether the bullet made purchase, but I did hear a deep, whining screech escape the creature before me. I made a break for the car.

Hearing wheezes as the Coyote began to rise, I kicked the ground, forcing myself to my feet ungracefully. I was running full tilt, my eyes ahead but my chest nearly parallel to the ground. The dirt around me flew in clouds that danced through the jeep's headlights as I ran toward the open car door.

I pulled myself into the seat beside Bette, feeling my arms flare up in protest at the effort. Fatigue hit me with a thousand tons, and I felt my whole body flatten against the cushion below me. Every cut and scrape I incurred from rolling down through brush and bramble sang a stinging song, and I looked wildly at Bette. She revved the engine and put the car in reverse.

Bette tried desperately not to collide with the beached truck or any of the trees. In the clarity of night, this clearing was not really much of a clearing at all. It was a simple pause in the forest's flowing growth. Even with the headlights, it was so dark. I couldn't have given Bette assistance if I tried. I wasn't even sure where the road was. None of the openings in the trees looked large enough to be where we came from. I couldn't see the Coyote either. "Bette, it's getting up," I guessed, hoping to spur Bette to move faster. My voice was scratchy and burned in my throat. I felt my eye swelling shut.

A ritual chant of, "Shit, fuck, fuck," overtook Bette. Her voice was cracking, and I could see in the dim green light of the radio digits, tears had begun to stream down her face again. The scream came again, and I saw branches bending in reverent bows before the windshield. We were wedged between Freddy's truck and the trees.

In the glow of the headlights, I saw the cloying fingers. Arms sprouted from wrists and palms, and more arms sprouted from them. Bette let out a sob. It had flanked us into a trap.

"Come out of there," the Coyote said. *"Our game isn't finished yet."*

"Bette," I said. Her knuckles laced white over the steering wheel.

"Bette you need to floor it, right now," I said.

"What?" she said, snapping her gaze to me through the tears. The Coyote was bending its knees, beginning to crouch, as hot drool steamed in the chill of night dripped from its jagged jaws. I knew a pounce was coming.

I tested my seatbelt, finding it was tight. "We're about to die anyway," I choked out. I could feel the moisture draining from my throat. "But if we make it, no one's going to believe us if we don't have a body."

"Children..."

Bette's sobs ceased. Like me, she tested her belt, then looked up into the eyes of the Coyote. It was running its antlers, grasping fingers and all, along the ground. Preparing to charge. "Ben..." Bette said quietly.

"Just do it," I said.

"Come out and play, children!"

The creature's body began to shift forward. "Bette!" I yelled again. Her foot came down on the gas, and I heard the roar of the tires shredding indents in the soil. We soared forward, as the jaws of the creature came wide and ready above us.

The whole jeep shook as we made contact with the monster's midsection, and then continued to roll forth, its momentum unable to be stopped.

We saw it, holding onto the jeep, gnashing its teeth. I was unable to stop what was happening anymore than Bette could. A thick tree glided across the ground toward us at a lightning pace. I made my peace. Meeting the dark eyes of the Coyote, I smiled, and before I could say, "That's for Lucy—"

A chorus of breaking glass and groaning metal was an instant lullaby. Everything went black as the Coyote's upper body collapsed against the hood of the vehicle, and became still.

***

I cannot say how long I fainted for. As I woke, I could feel the pain of bruising along my collarbone, where my seat belt had strained and successfully kept me from flying headfirst through the barely-intact windshield. Laces of agony crept up my calf from the claw marks. My vision came back spotty at first, but I could see beneath Bette the deflated airbag from within the steering wheel, and that she was shallowly breathing with her eyes shut.

A moment of elation hit me. We were alive, and we'd killed the son of a bitch.

"Bette," I said. "Bette, wake up."

Her eyes fluttered open, and she found my face. "Did we... did we do it?" she asked.

"Yeah," I said. "I think we—" As I looked to find the corpse of the beast, I only saw the trunk of the tree before us, splattered with black.

"Where is it?" Bette asked.

I looked around. It was still too dark to see. "I don't know. I don't... I saw it pass out, I thought it was..."

With some effort, I slid out of the jeep, Sarge's gun held out in front of me like a flashlight, and scanned our immediate area. I found that with each breath I took, my lungs seemed to rattle, like a clogged vacuum. My lower chest flared up with pain and I buckled just slightly at the knees. I was sure the seat belt had broken a rib. That wasn't important, though. I used the faint headlights of the jeep to look for any signs the creature was here. Aside from the inky blood on the tree, there was nothing. No footprints to suggest it had limped away, either. It was simply... gone.

"What the fuck..." I groaned weakly against the pain, before dragging myself back into the jeep.

"I can't..." Bette said quietly.

"Wha—?" I wasn't quite there yet. I was trying to figure out where the creature was watching us from, Sarge's gun held limply in my grasp.

"Can we... can we wait until it's light out?" Bette asked. I turned to her. Her eyes were full of tears. I nodded.

She turned the key of the vehicle, and the headlights went off, leaving us in the dark. I heard Bette's seat belt click, and then felt her reach across the seat and embrace me. She began to sob into my shoulder. With a shuddering breath and mist returning to my gaze, I flicked the safety on the gun and set it on the seat between me and the door, then returned Bette's hug.

We stayed like that for a time. Her cries became shallow, and she eventually crumbled into my lap in exhaustion. Before long she was asleep, a silent but total snooze brought on by fatigue. I looked down at her, adjusted a bit to the dark, and saw now with her glasses abandoned that she had thin cuts beneath her eye where the lens had been broken, and she was bruised and bloody on one of her cheeks. I thought of Justin, and even though he'd beaten me even bloodier, I could not materialize the thought of him striking Bette. Merely entertaining it made my stomach heave.

The idea of the two of them together was more pleasant, and I found myself drifting back to homecoming. The light catching Bette's face, the look of pure adoration in her eyes, kept the nausea away for a moment. I was suddenly pining for that moment— to go back and put my foot down. Coyotes, Nick? Why did you have to try and find an easy answer? We could have gotten help, made sure Justin never got sick...

In my mind Justin and Bette spun with the music, and I drifted with the memory, to where I was looking into Nancy's eyes. My teeth clenched, and the tears came again, no longer able to hide away. Like a blanket, I squeezed Bette, and tried to think of anything else, but the creature was standing before me again, lifting her to its jaws. Screams resonated through my mind, and I let out an ugly, hoarse sob into the darkness.

Some time later, a voice broke the still of the darkness, as I was finally collecting myself. "Ben!" I heard Nick yell.

Rather than reply this time, I remained motionless and quiet.

"Ben!" came Nick's voice again.

Bette did not stir. I considered waking her as I looked around, seeing nothing in the woods around me. I couldn't even place where he was.

"Ben!"

Something about that third one made my spine prickle. Listening closely, I waited for the yell to come again, and soon enough, it did.

"Ben!"

It wasn't... different. It was Nick's voice, unmistakably, and it was getting closer, to my dismay, but it was repeating. The yell had no variance in inflection. It was like a recording. I turned the gun's safety off as more yells came.

"Ben!"

"Ben!"

"Ben!"

On the last shout, I saw what was coming from my right, a tall shape staggering through the black forms of two trees. They were human, but walking at an odd angle, limping and looking with their head turned to the side. Their walk was almost perpendicular to where their gaze was.

The neck turned loosely and violently, a sudden arc that ended with the head now facing the jeep, though it was limply dangling on slouched shoulders. And with that jerking motion, they yelled as Nick again.

"Ben!"

Though it was still a stagger, the figure was approaching faster now, and as they closed the distance between us, I began to recognize, through streaks of oil-toned blood, the face of Justin, as he beelined for the passenger side window. I hit the automatic lock instinctively, and as Justin collided with my door and began to fumble with the handle, I heard the previously unfastened locks shift into place.

Realizing that he couldn't get in through this door, Justin pressed his scarred and bloodied face against the window, and drew his chewed lips back over black-stained teeth into a grimacing smile.

"Go away, Justin," I said quietly. Bette was moaning, beginning to stir in her sleep.

Justin was pawing at the window like a dog now, his fingertips bending back in painful, ninety-degree strokes. "Ben…" he whispered, his mouth forming the word just after the sound left his lips.

"Go away, Justin," I repeated, and pointed the gun at the window. Bette was waking now.

"Ben?" she said, and then looked up, starting when she saw Justin's face pressed against the glass.

"Bette-tell-him-to-let-me-in," Justin said, pauseless, his cadence bouncing, punctuated by the asynchronicity of his lips.

"Go away!" I yelled. Bette joined me. We were both chanting at Justin to go away like a spell, while he demanded in the voices of each of our friends to be let into the car.

"Please-Ben-let-me-in," he said in Nancy's voice. When that came, my teeth clenched together, but I continued the "go away" mantra through them, tasting blood as I spoke.

Now Justin had begun to shake the car, putting his weight into rocking the jeep on its axles, trying to flip it. I knew that if he successfully overturned us, the vicious cracks in the windshield would shatter, and he'd be able to enter. He was stronger now, and there was no doubt in my mind that if he kept rocking, especially with us trapped on the slight slope against the tree, he'd be able to topple the jeep.

The words coming from him were no longer English. They were in the Coyote's unfamiliar language, but they were easy enough to understand: *Let me in—* over and over.

I held onto Bette, and said, "I'm going to have to shoot him." She looked up at me and shook her head.

"It's not going to do anything, his neck is snapped and he's still here. That thing... it got away and you shot it twice."

"I have to do something," I said.

Bette looked down, then at Justin writhing and sputtering black over the window, and then back to me. "Okay, but be careful."

I allowed Bette to shift backward so I could try for a clear shot. Justin fought with the jeep, building and building his momentum for the final shove. As I began to raise the weapon toward the window, Justin froze. The sun had begun to peak over the horizon, lighting up

Justin's face just-so. His expression in the early dawn was clear. Rage filled his eyes as he cast them down toward us.

And, with a growl, Justin tore off into the woods.

"Where's he going?" Bette asked, looking around.

I followed where Justin had run with my eyes. *Back toward the tree*, my mind told me, but I couldn't be sure. The woods seemed even wilder and more labyrinthine as the rising sun illuminated them. "With the other," I guessed. "Lucy said we had until morning."

Bette pulled herself back into the driver's seat without another word. She glanced over at me, opened her mouth, and then shut it, as the birds of the forest began to hail the morning. The sun washed over us, killing the night in a slow tide. I nodded at Bette, and she turned the key in the ignition, bringing the engine roaring to life. We'd made it.

Chapter Seventeen
Lesson Learned

The drive was silent. It was so early we only saw one other car in the parking area at the entrance. The driver was not present, and I morbidly wondered if they were camping and had fallen prey to the monster during one of its disappearances. We left the park behind and slowly found our way to the highway, zooming at a comfortable pace in the relative lack of traffic despite the air of discomfort over us.

When we reached Elkwood, the town was only just waking— most people worked 9-to-5, and most said 9-to-5s were two minute drives from their homes. We rolled through the town unrecognized by those who were out, avoiding our homes and going straight for the police station.

As Bette parked the jeep outside of the brown-brick building before us, I said lowly, "We have to tell them it was Sarge."

Bette did not look at me. She simply nodded.

The keys were left on the seat of the jeep, no longer needed. We limped into the police station, and the tired desk clerk immediately came awake with concern in her crows-feet eyes. I knew her by the name Ms. Vitter, but I'd never spoken to her before today. "Kids, are you alright?" she asked. We were covered in blood, cuts, and black who-knows-what. I nearly shouted at her, but caught my composure.

"We need to report some murders," I said. Through my broken ribs, my voice was now a shuddering whisper. "Five murders."

We both refused to speak to anyone but Lieutenant Dunn. I was adamant that I knew him and I was only comfortable speaking to him. Bette began to cry and beg. "I'm scared, and I just want to talk to someone familiar," she said.

Eventually, we were separated into two rooms, and a long wait began. I was nursing a styrofoam cup of water, sitting at a cold metal table. Checking the clock on the wall, tapping my foot, the forty minutes that passed by waiting for Dunn felt like hours, but eventually, he came through the door, looking tired but determined: red-eyed, firm-lipped, tight-jawed. He regarded me with a nod before shutting the door and sitting across from me, setting down a pile of paperwork as well as a to-go coffee cup.

"I was wondering if you were going to come at all," I said. My whole throat stung as the raspy statement slinked out of me, and I doused it with another sip of the too-warm water.

Dunn laced his fingers and rested them on the table, sighing. "Well, I was talking to Miss Hurley about the night you both had. She seems pretty shaken up."

I nodded. "I've been trying not to think about it too hard in here, but… I guess I have to now."

Dunn's turn to nod. He opened up a notepad he'd brought with him. "Tell me everything that happened, and take all the time you need, alright? I know this is very hard for you."

So, I recounted the tale as closely as I could without mentioning the Coyote or the ghosts of the dead girls. I omitted the parts that left Justin at fault, replacing it all with vague, stammering scenes of Sarge committing the violence that ensued. I told him I didn't know where any of the bodies were, that when we'd gotten a hold of the gun and shot Sarge, we left and didn't look back. I told him Bette had crashed the jeep in a panic, and we'd waited until sunrise to come back so that she'd be able to see. All the while, Dunn was taking notes, but… not as quickly as I expected. Almost as if the details I was giving didn't matter much to him. When I reached the end of the story, he scrawled a few more words, set down his pen, and closed the notepad with an approving nod.

"It's a good story," he said.

"What?" My heart started fluttering, bringing protest from my ribs. I looked Dunn up and down through my wince. His eyebrows were raised, a smirk spreading across the right side of his mouth, as if he was amused by my confusion.

"Frankly," he said, with a pat of his notepad, "I thought I was going to have to throw the book at you. You were resourceful enough to come up with something usable, though."

I leaned back in my chair. "Why?"

"I'm good at my job. Better than they think I am, even." Dunn looked up to watch the clock, letting seconds tick in the air. I looked down at his arms. The left sleeve of Dunn's shirt rolled up beneath clean, manicured nails. My throat seized as faint, but apparent scars emerged. The gnashes and streaks left little mystery. Dunn had been mauled by something large.

"I called Sarge personally about our coyote problem. We served together, did you know that?" I shook my head. "I keep tabs on you, always have since that first case. I got pretty sick last winter, like you, and your buddy Justin, and Sarge. But, then again, I get sick every winter. I've got you to thank for that." He raised his eyebrows: asking if I understood. I nodded, showing that I did. "To think of all the people who could have come back, it was you. But, hey! You made it out, so you get to live on with this. Like I do. That's enough."

"You can't—

"I can, I have, I will. You lied to me, now you get to live with that. With everything that happened, that should have happened."

Dunn shook his head. His tone suddenly changed, back to the cop from when I was ten years old. "We'll be able to put this all away pretty quickly thanks to you. You did a good thing, son."

All the parents were informed, and my mom and dad came to me shaking, in tears, gripping me tight and asking if I was okay, apologizing profusely when I wailed from the pain in my ribcage. Telling them that I was fine was all I could do. Dunn was watching me expectantly as he reunited Bette with her parents and met the rest of the families at the door. I managed to break my parents' vice grip when I saw Nancy's parents enter the lobby.

I told them it was quick. I told them I loved her and I was so sorry I couldn't help her. And like the Luntzes, they told me it wasn't my fault. They told me they forgave me as they hugged me and sobbed for their daughter.

I looked to Bette, who was with Justin's parents, and knew they were telling her the same. She met my eyes, and the tears came, blurring her, and the world around us.

***

Instead of one funeral, there were four over the next several weeks. Of course, none of the bodies were recovered, but the deaths were officially considered murders by the Elkwood Police Department, all pinned on Sarge, and that was that. I went to each funeral in the wheelchair my parents insisted on while I was in the hospital.

Justin's funeral came first. It was quiet, and uncomfortable, and I made it a point for my family to sit with Bette's so I could grip her hand through the service. She cried silently, with a dignified forward push of her jaw. I could only bring myself to look pained, but no tears left my eyes as the music swelled and ended the affair.

Freddy's funeral was arranged by his paternal grandparents, who I had never met and thus only recognized due to his grandfather's blond locks, the same as Freddy and Sarge. They were kind and reserved, Freddy's grandpa having that same military sternness that I'd come to expect from the Thatchers. Here, Bette and I could cry willingly, mournfully, without feeling sickened by the body that would have been buried in the empty casket.

Nick's father was a no-show the following day. Nick's funeral following directly after Freddy's was fitting, and as I sat beside the church pew, sneaking guilty glances at Nick's mother, the arranger of the whole affair, I wondered if they were both beneath the tree now, laughing and shoving one another even as moonlight phantoms. I sobbed, but smiled to myself at the thought. *You may have taken them from us,* I thought, feeling that maybe, somehow, the Coyote could hear me, *but now they'll drive you crazy 'til the end of time.*

When it came time for Nancy's funeral, my body felt like it was going to combust. The tears on my face were frigid against my burning skin, and Bette was a distant snowflake, her icicle fingers melting in my palm. Nancy's parents were in hysterics, to be expected, and my own parents were rife with sorrow themselves. I'd heard my father, later that night, say that Nancy had been a part of our family, and I'd only slept that night by virtue of the exhaustion that followed the sorrow.

There was no funeral for Sarge, who all of Elkwood now held as a meritless murderer. I wondered if Dunn was out there crying for his friend somewhere, just like me. I kept expecting him to show up, to change his mind about letting me go. He never did.

Bette and I were given special permission to skip the last two months of school, which both of us took, returning to the park we used to draw together in and spending entire days in silence, needing each other's company, but having very little to say. Four voices were missing from any conversation we could have. All we heard was the breeze and the spring birds chirping around us.

When summer came, I cried again, knowing there was no way back to them, at least not until the hunt started once more.

Chapter Eighteen
Leaves

It was in the middle of September when I noticed the first brown leaf.

School had begun, and Bette and I crossed into our junior year with a thousand eyes on us. Everyone knew what happened, or at least the tale that I'd helped Dunn spin for the town, and to them we were ghosts, mysterious strangers that had vanished entirely from the town with our friends. What classes we had together, we sat in the back of the room side-by-side, silently avoiding contact with our peers, pushing away the attention of our teachers to the best of our ability. The classes we were apart, I often had my head hidden behind a textbook, choking tears back into my eyes.

I saw the leaf fall during lunch as I stared out the cafeteria window. It drifted slowly and deliberately, as if it wanted me to see, and then disappeared below the windowsill into the grass.

With that, I knew the hunt was on again.

VINCENT C. RUSSO

Tommy Barnes was the first to go missing. One day, he just wasn't at school anymore. There were rumors about him running away or one thing or another, but there was no funeral, no great search party. Tommy came to school and was his usual, obnoxious self, and then, he was no more.

Others disappeared, most of whom I can no longer recall the names or faces of. In fact, there were so many in the months of autumn, just before December crested on the horizon, that they all seemed to blend together and become one amorphous thing in my mind. Sometimes the police were called to investigate, but Lieutenant Dunn always wound up reporting that they'd done all they could do.

Sometimes, I could hear them. Once they were already gone, I could hear my classmates, the old ladies that had lived alone for decades at the edges of town, of cops who were part of the search parties. They were in the woods, sure, but also the streets at night. I never caught glimpses of them, but I could hear them, passing me by, letting me know they were still there. Were they moonlight echoes, or the mimicry of the pack? I never found out.

One afternoon, I passed Mr. Trellis's house, stopping to pet the bloodhound as I walked. I could hear Mr. Trellis inside. He was crying. I wish now I'd gone to speak to him, but I walked on by. I'll always wonder if he knew the truth, or if it was all just too much and broke his heart no matter what the truth was.

Bette and I sometimes... leaked. It was never so much the black sludge that came the night of the massacre, but we'd occasionally have a dark tear come from our eyes or nose, burning and itching until it was scrubbed clean. It was never something we worried over, at least not out loud. We'd call out the streaks to each other the same way you'd tell someone there's lettuce or pepper in their teeth. Internally, I think I was scared one of us would try to kill the other, and I was never certain who it would be.

My nightmares were incomprehensible messes of antlers and blood and grabbing fingers and gunfire. I could make out Nancy's screams in them, or Justin's animal wails, or the last breath I ever heard Nick take, but there was never a clear thread through the thrumming darkness but death all around me.

Bette and I spent Christmas together, walking along the snow-laden roads of Elkwood silently. We'd gone to the bench, the site of our snowball fight the year prior, and sat upon it, holding hands tightly to make sure the other would not go sprinting off into the woods. It was a nice night. No voices through the trees interrupted our holiday. Perhaps the Coyote called a truce for Christmas, like in World War I. Bette had whispered to me how grateful she was that someone else had made it, that she was not alone. I hugged her tight, and told her I would never leave her alone.

The news came January 2nd. My parents told me that we were moving to St. Louis, away from Elkwood. I took their words in with a shallow breath, and the tears came before the words. "Why? All my friends are here."

"Ben…" my dad said. "We have to get out of here. People are still going missing, and it's getting worse, and—"

"And what?" I was spitting. "Anything, everything horrible that could have happened to me has already happened. How can it be any worse than this?"

"You could get taken!" my mom yelled. "You barely speak to us, or anyone. When it's daylight out we never know where you are. Whatever's out there—"

"Only comes at night." I shook my head. I wanted to tell them the truth, but I knew they wouldn't listen or understand. They were staring at me like I was insane already. Why confirm that suspicion? "It doesn't matter what happens, I know when I'm safe and when I'm not. If I stay home at night it doesn't matter where I am when the sun is up."

"You don't know that," Mom said.

"I do! I know it better than anyone here. Better than either of you, better than the police. The only people who know anything about this are me and Bette."

The three of us were quiet for a while. I flexed my fingers into and out of a fist, trying to regain my composure. I could feel the burn at the edges of my eyes. If I continued to cry, it would come out black. I was always able to hide it before anyone noticed, but now they were both looking right at me, expecting me to sob. I wiped at my eyes and took a deep breath as my father spoke.

"Ben. We have to get out of here. Too much has happened to you. To us. All of us."

My throat heaved as I forced the searing tears to stay buried deep beneath my eyes. "What difference will it make, anywhere else?"

"Maybe somewhere else..." my dad said, looking down at the floor. "Maybe somewhere else... we can learn to move on from all of it."

I shook my head again. "I don't want to— I don't want to just move on. I don't want to forget them."

"Ben," my mom said, "moving on doesn't have to mean you forget. But you don't have to drive yourself crazy remembering either."

"Nobody that we lost wants us to stay here and never be happy again," Dad added.

There wasn't much point in arguing any further after that.

I thought about asking Bette to go to prom. Creating one last good memory might have been what we needed. Every time I was going to say the words, however, they caught in my throat. I felt nervous, not that she'd say no, but that she'd think I was trying to replace everyone. I thought of her and Justin, swirling around each other, of me and Nancy, and my heart would beat so quickly I thought it might stop. *It's not like that,* I told myself. *We're just friends, we just deserve, need, to have anything at all.* It never helped. The guilt always outweighed my rationality.

When summer came around, I said goodbye to Bette as my parents put the last of our bags into our car. All the furniture was packed into a truck. The emptiness of the house seemed to echo outward into the town. I remembered Lucy's room, so long ago now. The feeling of stalking, expecting, followed me out of my once-home just had it had out of hers. Soon, I was standing beside the vehicle that would drag me far, far away, while my mother watched me uncertainly from inside. The morning was cool for June, and Bette, come to see me off, was rubbing her arms as we stood in that final moment.

She had taken the news quietly in January, sad and silent as I explained in vain that I didn't want to leave. There hadn't been a rift between us per se, but there was that tense understanding that things were coming to an end. Now that we were here, the tension was stiffer than ever, waiting to be broken, neither of us willing to make the snap.

"I'm really going to miss you," Bette said softly. "But... I'm glad you're going to be safe."

"I don't know—" I stopped myself. I didn't want to undercut the sentiment. We both knew that being away from Elkwood didn't necessarily mean either of us would be safe, but it was more important to swallow that down. I changed my gears, and met her eyes with blurring vision. "I'll miss you too."

Bette reached out and took my hand, interlacing her fingers with mine. "You were a really good friend."

I took Bette into my arms and held her as tight as I could. I felt her melt into me, squeezing me back, hot tears seeping into my shirt. I couldn't see anything through the haze in my own eyes. The moment lingered there in the silent June air.

As we finally broke from each other, a bird chirped in a tree, and we turned away, her back to her home, and me to the car to leave mine behind.

Chapter Nineteen
Sparks

Months went by in a haze. The passage of time sped up to a breakneck pace, and I only found my footing in small moments in the many years thereafter. Junior year of high school, making small groups of friends, including meeting Nate again after such a long time apart, was never enough to make a truly lasting impression, and that summer break was equally unimpactful.

Senior year stuck, however. It brought with it a new loss as painful as the ones from the fateful camping trip. Maybe it had been the stress of nearly losing me, or maybe it was something in his genes that came for him early. I couldn't say for sure. But, my dad's heart attack was swift and succinct, and my mom and I were left alone.

Aunt Katie came to the funeral. I hadn't seen her since she'd left Elkwood with Derek, and the signs of age in the lines on her face and the budding gray in her hair left me feeling strange. I supposed I must have looked a lot different then than she remembered, too. She had a long, tear-soaked conversation with my mom, but when she came to me, all we could do was stare at one another. I think she knew, looking me up and down, that everything that had happened to me had numbed me. There were tears on my face, just as there were on hers, but I couldn't feel them.

I just felt cold, and a burning in my eyes and nose.

After the funeral, we were gathered in my family's new home in St. Louis, which had still not become familiar to me. With Dad gone, it was even stranger. A place I felt almost an intruder in. I looked at Kate, and thought of the fence the people had put up around her home. Would she recognize it, or would the pool in the yard sicken her as it did me?

Most of the people left were friends of mine from school, the few I'd made who wanted to give me their support. Nate and I weren't so close anymore that he'd stuck around, but he did come to the funeral, having a clear air of discomfort at seeing my father, who he'd once known about as well as his own, in the casket. Mom and I didn't have much family to come pay their respects to Dad. My grandparents were long gone, and my parents were only children like myself.

My friends finally funneled out of the house as well, and my mom decided she was going to go pick up dinner, so Kate and I were left alone, sitting on the front porch in the crisp atmosphere of March. It wasn't so cold that I expected it, but I wondered if there would be another snow, or if Elkwood was safe for the summer right now. Before I could dwell on it for too long, Kate stole my attention.

"I can't believe he's gone," she said flatly.

"No one can," I said back. She was saying what she was supposed to, but I could tell there was something else. I loosened my black tie and looked up at the clouds. There were no pretty shapes in them, just jagged, shattered puffs.

Kate sighed. "I wish I'd told him about it all."

"About what?"

"About what happened to you. Well, I don't… I don't know what happened to you. But I know it was like what happened to her."

I froze up, but then took a slow breath, and turned toward her. "Freddy's dad didn't kill Lucy."

She shook her head. "And he didn't kill most of your friends."

I swallowed. "Sure he did." I looked down at my hands, which were now clenched. What did she know?

"When Derek and I would go looking for her, we'd hear strange noises. We never saw what was making them, but we did know it was…" She trailed off, trying to find the correct word for it. She never saw it. How could she describe it, even if she had?

"Something bad," I said.

"Yes, something bad." She looked at me with tears at the corners of her eyes. "I thought if we told anyone, they'd think we were crazy. Crazier than they already thought we were anyway."

"I don't think you're crazy." I moved a bit closer to her and took her hand, remembering how much bigger it was when I was a child. Years and years ago. "But you shouldn't talk about it."

Kate raised her eyebrows and frowned, suddenly shocked. "Why?"

"Because," I chose my next words carefully, "there's... more to it than just something bad. There's other things too, and they... You just have to try to forget it. It's better to accept the story than know what's out there."

"Ben, I—" I gave her a pleading look, and that made her, instantly, understand. "Okay." She seemed disappointed. I understood that. She was looking for answers, and I was telling her what everyone else did. Accept and move on.

I gave a little away. "I know what happened to her... and you don't want to know that. But, I also know that... she isn't mad, or wishing we'd found her. She doesn't blame us, because it wasn't our fault. She's the reason I survived. Before, during, and, in some ways, after."

Kate was confused, but tears were rolling down her cheeks. "How do you know?"

I shrugged. "If I told you, if I told anyone, you'd think I was crazy." There were no words left to say, but there were tears to cry. Aunt Katie hugged me as we looked at the clouds. When she'd collected herself and made to depart, we said a final goodbye. This time, it was actually final. I'd never see her again after that day. But, that was okay. I think I gave her peace, and I hope she passed some of that on to Derek.

Really, I only wished I was able to give myself that peace. Losing my dad was tearing me apart, and being reminded of what had happened two years prior, again, was even worse. It all burned me up, and what little joy I got from comforting those around me, it was swallowed by the fire.

Instead of finding peace, I'd spend the next few years pretending I didn't feel any of this at all.

Chapter Twenty
Flames

It was my third year of college when I saw her again.

A friend, Greg, had convinced me to come to a party one of the fraternities was throwing, the sort of thrumming, hazy affair I'd avoided out of disinterest, and partial discomfort at the late hour they took place at. Midterms were getting to me, I suppose, and for once I was willing to brave the dark and let off a little steam.

I drove to the house, a modest but attractive two-story home, and met Greg out front. We went inside together, and eventually, with plastic cups in hand, we were separated from each other in the midst of the pop music and clustered conversations.

My drink was warming me, as was the volume of people all around the kitchen, where I'd gravitated to due to the proximity of the alcohol and the distance from the world of night the party was spilling into from every door. I had poured my third beer from the keg, when I gazed over it and saw a familiar face, smiling sheepishly as she spoke to two other girls.

Bette had grown into herself. She'd always been plainly pretty, but she was stunning now. Her hair fell loosely and shimmering around high cheekbones and dimples, framing sparkling blue eyes that cut me, reminded me, all of a brutal sudden, of home. There were no glasses anymore, and I wondered when she'd gotten contacts, how soon after I'd moved away.

I guess we've both grown up a lot, I thought, tracing my fingers over the stubble on my face, remembering the times in ninth grade when I'd been endlessly jealous of the other boys who matured faster.

Approaching her was second nature, and I awkwardly interrupted the conversation at hand with, "Long way from home."

Bette looked at me with confusion, before her eyes widened, and a gorgeous smile broke her face. "Ben!"

"Hey," I said.

We embraced, sharing that tight, warm hug you give to someone you trust with all your heart. One of the other girls spoke with a gossiper's curiosity, "Bette, who's this?"

"This is Ben, we grew up in Elkwood together," Bette said as she pulled away from me. The other girls did not make the faces someone makes if they know a sad story about you, the silent gasps of realization, the downturned gazes. That was a relief. The faces they did make were of intrigue, though, wide-eyed and smirking not quite at me or Bette specifically. Clearly they'd heard my name in the past, disconnected from the bad memories.

The other girl spoke. "We'll let you two catch up." They left us while giggling to each other, and instantly, it was like nothing had ever changed.

Bette told me all about what she'd been up to. How her parents had bought a house in one of St. Louis's many counties, Ballwin, after senior year of high school, and how she'd applied and been readily accepted into an art school and decided to live there during her enrollment. She was going to school for graphic design, a swap which we'd both had a laugh about— she'd chosen to go to school for a more abstract, methodical form of art, where I was studying realism in my school, taking various anatomical and fundamental classes which bored me to tears. I was always chasing what Nick had told me, that I'd be great at drawing actual things. It was a total flip of who we'd been as children, something that didn't bother me at the time, but I look back on with some sadness now. I took in her whole life story from the moment we separated to now, and she took mine. I don't think I'd smiled or laughed like that in years, and I don't think I have since.

As we went on and on, while the party was passing around us, we naturally were standing closer to each other, touching each other's arms and shoulders as we spoke. When the end of the night was approaching, Bette had slipped her fingers into mine, and we were speaking softer to each other, breaking eye contact only to blink.

Bette reached the end of telling me about her roommates, Kelsie and Sarah, the girls she was with when I came over. Both were graphic design students as well, and the three had met their freshman year. As she reached the end of the story, she trailed off, and asked me, suddenly, "Do you live with anyone?"

"No," I said. "I managed to find a cheap apartment, I'm kinda living off the inheri—" Bette cut me off by kissing me: a deep, slow, purposeful sort of kiss, the kind that is as much a gift as an invitation. I kissed her back, and she melted into my arms.

We'd both been sober by that point, having been too interested in talking to drink. Bette told Kelsie and Sarah she was leaving with me, and we both shuffled into my car. I drove as quickly as I could, brimming with anticipation the entire way to my apartment building.

We were kissing as I unlocked the door, and Bette had already pulled my shirt over my head and kicked her pants aside as we reached my bedroom. She'd been wearing a top that bore her stomach, and I'd been glancing at her curves all night, but I was appreciating them even more as I ran my hands down her back, and lower.

Rest didn't come for many hours after that. Something in us had awoken, and it was ravenous. When our faces weren't pressed together, they were between each other's legs, and when we weren't tightly embracing, our hands were roaming all over, exploring and memorizing every detail of one another. I couldn't get enough of her, nor her me. Where before we'd said so much, catching up, there were little words now, but we understood each other even more.

Finally, I knew I couldn't do anymore, and I collapsed backward, while Bette collapsed forward with me still inside her. She buried her face into my chest, heaving even harder than I was. "I missed you, Ben."

"I missed you," I said, wrapping my arms around her back.

Bette eventually removed herself from me and laid beside me, tracing her fingertips over my chest. It was silent then, save our slow, exhausted breaths. We fell asleep like that, her holding me as tight as I held her, neither of us daring to let go for a second.

***

The nightmare began as it always did: in the woods.

I was shirtless, shoeless, dirty and bloody as Nick had been. No bugs or frogs chirped in the forest. It was me, and the noise I knew would come. And come it did— the shrieks of the Coyote that made my eardrums shudder in protest.

I did not run from the noises. I was frozen in place as the trees crashed from the weight of the approaching giant. Every bone in my body had been turned to cruel, trembling ice. Soon it would reach me, and it would shred through me, shattering the icicles inside me with its broken, misshapen teeth.

What broke through the trees into my view was not the monster. It was a person. A teenage girl, with beautiful, brown eyes. "Nancy," I said, choking the word through a fist-clench feeling in my throat.

"Don't," she growled, as she came toward me slowly. "You wanted this, didn't you?" Nancy's face began to break, the skin tearing in jagged patterns. She halved the distance between us, covered in her own blackening blood. "You wanted me to die, so you could go off and be with her, didn't you?"

"No," I said, and took a step back. Something crunched beneath my feet, and I glanced for only a moment to see the skull I shattered.

"You wanted her more than me, admit it. You were always close." Nancy was spitting black bile from her lips as she got closer and closer. Finally, she was a few feet away, and caught me by the chest, sinking sharpened, exposed-bone fingers into my skin, holding it like a shirt collar as I let out a yelp. "Do you love her more than you loved me?"

"I haven't seen her in years," was all I could say. I could not bring myself to fight her. Seeing her so scarred and bloody, her free hand broken and twisted from the gnawing, made me sick to my stomach.

"You didn't even try to save me," Nancy said, for a moment sounding like herself again. Through the black blood, there was a faint twinkle of moonlight. "You ran away, just like you ran away and didn't make sure Lucy made it home. We're both dead, because of you, Ben."

"No."

"Nick and Freddy and Justin, all because you lied to your parents. You lied to the police. You're lying to yourself every day."

"Nancy, that's not true." I don't know if I believed that. She was snarling, poking my chest with her free, shredded hand.

"You killed us. Just look at yourself."

I looked down, and where she held me, my skin was pale, my ribs showing under the tight, malnourished layer of it. My arms stretched long and low at my sides, each finger tipped with a long, razor claw. I could feel the weight of my antler crown: thousands of hungry, grasping hands sprouting and clawing for more, more.

I looked back up at Nancy, and she was void of any scars. No longer was she holding me in the air, instead I held her tight in my hand. On her face there were only the tears, streaking from fear-widened eyes. "Ben!" she screamed.

I jerked forward, and bit into her.

***

I woke with sweat on my brow, still naked, panting as I tried to decipher the strange room I was in. There were no trees in sight, and this disturbed me, until I remembered that I was home, in my little apartment in St. Louis. Elkwood was many, many miles away, but for a moment, I smelled the trees, the shops along Main Street, the creek. I turned my head to continue catching my bearings, finding that Bette's head was on my shoulder. She was awake as well, giving me a mournful look.

"I get them, too," Bette said. Her lips grazed my chest as she spoke. "I haven't had one in a long time, though."

"Me either," I said. Her eyes dropped sadly, as if she was hoping I'd say it was the first time, or perhaps that I'd had one every night regardless. We both knew that wasn't true, though.

I turned onto my side, Bette turning backward in time with me. She wrapped her arms around my back and buried her face in my chest. We were quiet for a little while. I could hear birds chirping outside the window, the only sound. Not even our breathing was audible.

Bette drummed her fingers on my chest and began to turn over onto me. I let her do what she was doing, and before long we were at it again, but it was different this time. The act was slow and purposeful as we went through it, a conscious attempt to make it last. Eventually we turned so I was above her, with a hand on her face, looking into her eyes and asking without speaking, *"Does it have to be this way? Can't we stay here?"*

I stayed inside her as we both finished, and stayed longer as we held each other in shuddering silence. It felt like we should be saying something, anything, but there were no words. There was only that familiar feeling hanging over us, that this was it.

We cleaned and dressed quickly. Those are the awkward parts, where everything has happened and it should be fading to black, but you're stuck caring for the mess that followed. Bette was checking her hair in my bathroom mirror, and I was watching her, feeling more than I had in years. Soon, she was satisfied, and we began the walk to the front door.

Lingering in the doorway, shifting her weight to either foot, she forced a smile. "It was... really, really good to see you again, Ben."

I returned the lie on my face, the truth in my words. "It was good to see you too." I opened my mouth to say something like, *"We should see each other again,"* but I couldn't. As I was looking at her now, I could feel my heart beating. Outside the window, there were no longer birds chirping. There were scared teenagers screaming.

Bette stepped forward and hooked her arms behind my neck. I took her lead and leaned forward. We kissed in front of the open door, and though I could still hear them, afraid and running through the trees, the screams were quieter. I hoped Bette would kick the door shut behind her and stay, just for a little while.

When the kiss broke, it was clear that wouldn't happen. Bette cleared her throat quietly. "Bye, Ben."

"Bye," I said back, and she turned and began the walk to the sidewalk. Her friends were picking her up, she'd told me, but still I wanted to follow her, offer to give her a ride. Instead, as I saw the silver car with Kelsie and Sarah inside, I shut the door.

I could feel the cry coming on, so hot it was burning my eyes. I lifted a hand to my cheek and touched the tears. My fingertips came away stained black.

Chapter Twenty-One
Wildfire

Before I knew it, college was over. With a degree in hand, I scoured for a career. Freelance work, when it came, was good, drawing the faces of clients or their chosen subjects for social media and book covers and websites. However, freelance work was inconsistent, and it did not fill the growing hole in the inheritance from my dad enough to negate it.

Eventually, I fell in with the St. Louis Police Department as a sketch artist. It was decent enough pay, consistent work, and came with benefits. I coasted with that job for a long time. The faces of would-be suspects filled pages and pages to the point they all blurred into each other, making a single, generic face that would flit through my dreams like a feather in the wind. When I lingered on it too long in a dream, it unnerved me, made me feel a turning in my gut that would stay with me into the first few hours of my waking. Often, I would wake with black tears in my eyes after these dreams.

Occasionally, I drew my friends. I forced myself to remember every detail of Justin's silent gaze, Freddy's sternness betrayed by laugh lines around his mouth. I drew Nancy's eyes, painfully unable to capture just how they made me feel. Nick's smirk and freckles were the easiest. That mischief was impossible to forget. After a while, my memories of them were in lead and ink rather than in color.

When I drew Bette, I drew her as she had been the night of our reunion. Older, more mature and outgoing. Happy, even, to be away from the past's hateful grasp. I wondered if she ever held her sketchbook the way she would at the park, smiling slightly as she drew me. I wondered if we drew each other at the same time. Maybe wishful thinking, or maybe the feeling was telling me something.

Something that I've never quite been able to accept.

Letting go of the past should have let me move on. Still, I couldn't help but linger in it. And, I think Bette is probably still lingering in it, too. I thought then we were saving each other pain by saying goodbye, but maybe we were assuring that the pain would haunt us. Forever, ghosts of our friends were out there, unable to move on, and we weren't even trying to hold on to what was left of them in each other.

The thought of it scared me, even as I let the years go by, my stomach starting to loosen, my hair just beginning to thin. When I turned thirty, I saw a stranger in the mirror and longed for the streets of Elkwood, for the potent wind of youth to sweep me along as it had in high school.

And with years continuing to go by, the inaction eats at me like termites. My foundation is being bored away by the thought that we, selfishly, are forcing ourselves to let them fade ungracefully in that place hidden from the warmth of summer. They were frozen. And they'd never thaw so long as we allowed the ice to engulf them.

I think about things Lucy and the others told me in the dark. It's hard to imagine that she's truly gone now, her mind lost to the monster. The thing that makes me scared is that it's making her do things to others that it did to us, to her. It could be doing that with all of them that it took, using them like puppets.

I decided over the summer that I couldn't stand for it. Each passing day weighed heavier and heavier and I couldn't do it anymore. There was only one thing I could do, and it was an idea I'd had for many years prior.

Last week I called my mom for the last time. She was happy to hear from me. We hadn't talked in a couple weeks, which I'll admit I was ashamed about, but I had been so busy I couldn't check in sooner.

"How are you doing, Ben?" she asked. I could tell she was doing something with her hands, the phone tucked between her jaw and shoulder.

"I'm okay," I lied. "Haven't had to do much at work recently."

"Well, I guess that's good news."

"Yeah." I heard a scrape of metal and realized she was cooking. "What are you making?"

"Just some burgers. Are you hungry? Do you want to come by?"

Yes, I wanted to say. *Talk me out of this, Mom. Hug me and tell me it's going to be okay, that I'm doing well, that I shouldn't go back there.*

"I can't tonight," I said instead. "But maybe next weekend I'll come by."

"That would be nice," she said. There was a long pause. "Is something wrong, honey?"

I had wanted her to ask this, I think. I couldn't offer that something was the matter on my own. Everything in me said I should confirm that something is deeply wrong, that I'm being crazy, but there was something further, deep down that screamed that this decision is the only one.

"No, I'm just tired… And I miss you."

"I miss you too, sweetie. Let me know if you're coming next weekend and I'll cook your favorite." I couldn't remember what she thought my favorite was, but I know whatever it was would have been delicious, good enough to concede, for an evening, as my favorite.

"Okay, Mom. I gotta go."

"Okay," she said slowly. "Well, I love you."

"Love you too, Mom," I said, and hung up the phone.

Here I'm sitting now, in a rental truck. The bed has a top on it so no one can see what's inside. A few minutes ago, the first brown leaf of autumn drifted from a treetop onto the hood of the truck. Soon, the hunt will start again, as it has for longer than living memory. Living memory, that is, save for in the mind of the Coyote.

I drove through Elkwood in the silence. There's no one left in town. I stopped by the Huntz home and saw a For Sale sign in the yard, covered in rain-streaked dirt and mildew. The pool was a sickly green, and full of leaves and scum. My childhood home was in good repair, but last I looked, no one lives there anymore. The lights were off, but I could see the living room, where we opened presents before trekking into the snow. The furniture was dusty inside, even the couch. Not even the faint sound of electricity broke the stillness.

Cross, Hurley, Kisner, empty too. Town hall, empty. There were some cars with graffiti and broken windshields on the sides of the roads, but a few seemed to have been driven recently, and I wondered. I wonder…

Mr. Trellis's house is the only one with a light on inside. I thought to walk up, knock on the door, but… Mr. Trellis has been dead, something like twelve years now. His bloodhound got taken by one of his kids from out of town, and the house stayed there, never being sold. But a light is on. And again, I wonder.

Seeing it all again gave me some pause, and I got to thinking, and questioning. There could be another way, something else I could do. But, that's fear talking, and I know it. If I don't force myself to go, I'll sit in this parking lot forever, staring at the road into the canopy. So, I'm going to start counting, and when I hit twenty, I'm putting my foot on the gas.

One… Two… Three…

I doubt I'll be able to get the truck to the tree. I'll have to leg it through the woods again. On my time off from work, I've been hiking a lot. Preparing for this day. I can carry a hefty bag on my back, which will be good considering how heavy the canisters of kerosene will be. I'll start on the trail there while it's still light, so I don't be caught unawares in the dark.

Six… Seven… Eight…

If it's the tree's roots holding them all there, planting their corpses and feeding on their bones and souls, then the tree is what will have to go to set them free. The monster and its victims are tied in the roots, never to be freed, until someone plucks them out by the stem.

Eleven... Twelve... Thirteen...

My dream is that the fire will set them all loose like a dandelion blown into the wind. Lucy, Nick, Nancy, Freddy, and even Justin and Sarge. Them, and all the others trapped in there. And, when the tree dies, I think the Coyote will too. It won't be able to cross the running water to put out the flames. It'll have to watch, like I did, as its life is taken from it. It'll be nothing but a ghost story, a shadow on the wall. I don't think I'll be leaving the woods either, but at least I'll get to drift away behind them. I only wish that I could have told Bette I was doing this. For them and for us.

Eighteen... Nineteen... Twenty.

I guess that's my time.

Ready or not, here I come.

About the Author

Vincent C. Russo is a lifelong resident of St. Louis, Missouri and lover of fantasy and horror. Having previously written four novellas in the former genre, *Elkwood Kids* is his debut plunge into the horror space. An interest in the myths of various cultures and years as a camp counselor served as the spark for this story.

When not writing, Vincent is typically thinking about how he ought to be writing, in between working as a childcare director, game development and songwriting hobbies, and placating his and his fiancée Grace's incessant cats (Loki and Harley) that distract him at every opportunity.

Vincent can be found on his website at vincentcrusso.com as well as on his social media accounts (instagram.com/vcrusso, twitter.com/vincentcrusso.)